THE
SECRET
STAIRCASE

ALSO BY SHEILA CONNOLLY

THE
SECRET
STAIRCASE

A Mystery

Sheila Connolly

MINOTAUR BOOKS
NEW YORK

First published in the United States by Minotaur Books, an imprint of St. Martin's Publishing Group

THE SECRET STAIRCASE. Copyright © 2021 by Sheila Connolly. All rights reserved. Printed in the United States of America. For information, address St. Martin's Publishing Group, 120 Broadway, New York, NY 10271.

www.minotaurbooks.com

Designed by Devan Norman

Library of Congress Cataloging-in-Publication Data

Names: Connolly, Sheila, author.
Title: The secret staircase : a Victorian village mystery / Sheila Connolly.
Description: First edition. | New York : Minotaur Books, 2021. | Series: Victorian village mysteries ; 3
Identifiers: LCCN 2021008137 | ISBN 9781250135902 (hardcover) | ISBN 9781250135919 (ebook)
Subjects: GSAFD: Mystery fiction.
Classification: LCC PS3601.T83 S43 2021 | DDC 813/.6—dc23
LC record available at https://lccn.loc.gov/2021008137

Our books may be purchased in bulk for promotional, educational, or business use. Please contact your local bookseller or the Macmillan Corporate and Premium Sales Department at 1-800-221-7945, extension 5442, or by email at MacmillanSpecialMarkets@macmillan.com.

First Edition: 2021

10 9 8 7 6 5 4 3 2 1

For Ruth Hamilton, an original

THE
SECRET
STAIRCASE

1

I looked at the faces of the people around the large oval table in the dining room of the Asheboro Bed & Breakfast—the place I was calling home, at least temporarily. I knew I should begin the meeting soon, but I was relishing the sight of my ragtag gang, assembled all in one place.

My childhood friend Lisbeth Scott sat to my immediate left, swiveling back and forth in an office chair and beaming at me, evidently very pleased to be here instead of overseeing the summer activities of her two kids, who were at home with her husband, Phil. Next to her sat Jim MacDonald—"Mac" to all who'd shopped at his family hardware store in the past thirty years—and Ted Wilson, who'd operated a lunch counter in downtown Asheboro since I was a teenager here, almost two decades ago. Mac and Ted talked somberly about business in town, which was sluggish in the wake of a storm that had damaged many storefronts and homes. Not that business in this sleepy hamlet an hour west of Baltimore had been exactly booming before the storm.

Across from Mac and Ted sat Asheboro newspaper editor Frances Carter, a prim lady on the other side of seventy, smiling wryly at the two men's woebegone business banter and chatting across the divide with Lisbeth. Ryan Hoffman—another old friend, in a manner of speaking: our ancient history included a high school courtship gone wrong—paced at the far end of the room, furiously texting about something possibly related to his work as a lawyer at a midsize firm east of here, just outside Baltimore. Mayor Skip Bentley sat in amiable silence to my right, apparently reading an article on his tablet on the table in front of him, his hands folded over his chest.

Missing from our small assembly were Carroll Peterson, my head researcher—and the youngest member of the team, a graduate student joining us as a summer project—and Josh Wainwright, a Johns Hopkins history professor who was . . . well, something slightly more than a friend to me at this point. I didn't have time to think about that right now. *Business, Kate! Get this group in order and get going!* I smoothed my hair and turned a stray button in my jacket pocket over and over between my fingers. I could hear the voice of my high school basketball coach whenever I used to hesitate at the free throw line, which was often: *It's now or never, Hamilton.*

This was the first meeting of the board members for

the Asheboro Revitalization Project—my brainchild and an ambitious endeavor I deeply hoped I could pull off, with the help of those assembled. And the whole thing now rested on Henry Barton—or his house, anyway. Henry Barton, a resident of Asheboro during the Victorian era (and a somewhat reclusive captain of local industry), had left his mansion and the vast tract of land surrounding it in the custody of the town when he died, without an heir, in 1911. He assumed that the town would find a buyer. It didn't. Henry had left enough money to pay for a resident caretaker and cover maintenance expenses on the house, and that's how things had been left for a century. Henry was the owner of the only factory in town, producing shovels and a few other tools, but it had closed decades ago. So for over a hundred years, Asheboro had been quietly fading away—no new industry, too far for most to commute, its people moving away and nobody coming in.

I grew up in Asheboro and went to high school here, but left for college and work, bigger and better things. Then this spring, my old friend Lisbeth looked me up and asked if I could help save the town from total collapse, and since I was between jobs, I foolishly said yes. I had decided to start by rehabbing the Barton mansion before moving on to the town's main street, a row of small businesses that could be a charming time-capsule attraction for tourists, with a bit of love and editing. The future of this whole "save the town" idea had been hanging in the balance until I'd been lucky enough to score a contribution from a major regional utility company. It had taken a bit of arm-twisting (or maybe I should call it *gentle blackmail*) to make it happen, but it had worked, and Mid-Atlantic Power's contribution would be enough to get things started—finally. The whole town needed an overhaul in short order, but we would begin with the Barton mansion, which I was looking forward to restoring to its original glory as the centerpiece of the town's renovation. I took a deep breath and brought my hands together in front of me.

"Thank you all for coming," I began. "Or maybe I should start by thanking you for agreeing to be part of this. I asked you all not only because I know you'll have great ideas but because you are the memory of the town of Asheboro. You remember what it was like years ago. Well, Lisbeth here is the exception—she's here because she dragged me into this, and I wouldn't let her walk away."

"Happy to be on the team," Lisbeth said with a smile, gesturing grandly with a half-empty juice box she must have pulled from her purse when I wasn't looking. The rest of the group sipped quietly at mugs of coffee and tea I had produced from the B&B's kitchen just minutes ago.

"Lisbeth grew up in this town," I continued, "so she's seen a lot of the more recent changes, and those matter too. Frances, Mac, Ted, you've been an active part of the town all your adult lives, and I'm assuming that means you care about the place. Frances, you and I know you're sitting on a treasure trove of historical information at the local paper, and we'll need that. Mac, your hardware store is almost untouched since 1900—and that's not an insult, believe me! It's a real asset to what we want to do. A blueprint, if you will. Ted, in your café, you've watched a generation or two of kids grow up here, listened to their gossip and complaints. You can tell us what they've cared about, and whether we can recreate those places and spaces." They were all nodding along so far, which let me know we had at least cleared the hurdle of establishing that they cared about the town. I didn't want any deserters, if it could be avoided. I continued speaking.

"Mayor Skip will represent the town, at least on an honorary basis. The first new addition to our group is Carroll Peterson, who has been helping sort and catalog the Henry Barton letters and files."

"Wasn't she off getting a degree somewhere else?" Frances asked.

"Yes, but I persuaded my friend Nell in Philadelphia—who Carroll's been interning for this year—to consider our project relevant to her studies, so she'll get credit for it. Besides, working with an untouched nineteenth-century collection of papers would be a treat for anyone focusing on library studies. Henry Barton kept a *lot* of records, and we're hoping that the files from his estate will shed some light on his family and the town, and maybe provide some details about the construction of the house."

"You're going to have problems with things like the wiring and plumbing," Mac pointed out, making a left turn in the conversation.

"We'll be careful to choose contractors who respect historic buildings and can make the modernization all but invisible, but still up to code." I hoped that statement would come true—I certainly had never done it before.

"How much you think you're gonna change?" Mac pressed on. "I mean, do you have standards you have to meet to be able to open the place to the public?"

"Mac, I can't say I'm an expert, but of course we'll be looking into that. That's why we're talking about these things now, so we can plan."

"What changes do you think you'll—*we'll* have to make?" Frances asked.

"I'm going to guess that any historic building like the Barton mansion will have to have basic toilet facilities for the public, and they should ideally be more than a line of portable toilets behind the building. The wiring should be up to code, so we don't burn the place down by accident. And one question we need to address up front is whether we want the kitchen to be functional."

"Why would we?" Ted asked. "You aren't thinking of putting in a restaurant, are you?" Whoops—I certainly didn't want Ted to think I'd be stepping on his business in the lunch trade.

"No, nothing like that, not a regular spot. But we may want to hold events for groups there sometimes, and while I know we could have them catered, I'd rather see the kitchen in action, with at least a working stove and running water—even if that means a hand pump. Look, I don't pretend to be an expert on 1880 kitchens and how they worked, but we can work up some research on that. I'd like this kitchen to look authentic."

"You're just making more work for yourself, you know," Ted grumbled. I could see my vision might be a tough sell for those who didn't feel the dreaminess of the Barton house the way I did. Well, nobody told me this would be easy. I pressed on.

"Of course, this won't be a simple project. And you may not necessarily see the value in restoring a century-old manor house on the edge of town—kitchen and all—when the rest of the town needs a boost. I get that. But keep in mind—this is part one! If we can pull off a revamp of this one house, make it an attraction, we might just get some more attention—and funding—which will help us fix up the rest of the town. I want this place to be special, to stand out. Otherwise, to most people, we'll just be another old house on the Civil War tour. Which is fine, but . . ." I trailed off, struggling to communicate what I felt the Barton house could be, in the right hands. "I want it to be memorable."

"Can we afford it?" Mac asked.

"Yes, or I wouldn't even be talking about it. You know from the town meeting last week that Mid-Atlantic Power is donating a sizeable sum for the development of Henry Barton's factory, but there will be enough to cover the basic improvements to the house. Much of it is in surprisingly good shape, but we might have to do an overhaul. I don't know that yet. But the wiring and plumbing are at the top of the list if we want to invite the public in safely."

"What's going to happen to the factory building?" Frances asked.

"That's still under discussion, and I'd love to hear whatever ideas you have. But we'll get to that in due time." I had insisted that the Barton house be addressed first, so that if we wanted to woo additional donors or organizations for support, they could get a glimpse of our vision. I figured we could wine and dine them there too, if the place really got in functional shape—the kitchen, in particular.

"Kate," Lisbeth spoke up for the first time, "Phil's at home with the kids, so I can't stay too long. What else do we need to know now, or think about? Do you want us to do something formal like vote on proposals, or how the money will be spent?"

"I'll lay out the basics, but we don't have to settle all of those things tonight. I just wanted to sketch out the broad plans. One, Ryan here will be our legal representative." Ryan, still pacing the far end of the room, had ceased texting to make a phone call; on hearing his name, he nodded and waved toward the assembled group. I gave up trying to engage him and decided to consider myself lucky he had showed up at all. I turned back to the group. "Ryan has already begun our application for nonprofit status. That will make contributions tax-deductible for donors. He can also oversee the management of the money—so nobody walks away with it—but that doesn't mean he makes decisions on how to spend it. That's up to us. Ryan will set up one or more bank accounts with oversight restrictions. Two, Josh Wainwright will be working on a history of the industrial development of this area, so we can call him a consultant or something. It may end up being a scholarly article or even a book, but it should get us some attention. Three, I'll be overseeing the construction and design aspects, although I welcome your input, and of course we'll need an experienced construction manager. Apart from the electric and plumbing issues, the place needs a really good cleaning, and I'm sure some of the early fabrics—upholstery, curtains, and stuff like that—will need to be replaced. And we should evaluate the state of the furniture, although I think it's all still there, but as I've said, changes like that need to be appropriate to the period."

"What's your timetable?" Mac demanded. The business guys on the committee were, well, all business.

"I'd love to see it finished by September, but that may be unrealistic. We should plan on a grand opening sometime before the end of the year, and make sure it gets on everybody's calendar."

If I were being completely honest with the group, I'd have to tell them I was totally winging this. My experience was mainly in modern institutions in the hospitality industry, in Philadelphia and Baltimore, decidedly *not* in antiquarian restoration and history tourism. But there was something about Henry Barton's house that got to me— not only its aesthetic grandeur but its mystery. Asheboro's one rich man lived on the outskirts of town in the post– Civil War years, not so much eccentric as . . . unknown. What could we learn about his life to fill in our picture of the time he lived in? I made a mental note to check in with Carroll about her research into Henry Barton. In the meantime, I could see that Mac wanted more hard facts and numbers.

"Listen, I know this is a big undertaking, with more specifics than I'm able to detail in today's meeting. My contacts in Philly and Baltimore should come in handy. And as I said, Carroll will be looking for more material in Henry's documents. That will help us get a clearer picture of him and how he lived."

"What about his wife?" Frances interrupted.

"What about her?" I replied.

"Mary Barton. We don't know very much about her. You know the house was a ways out of town, but she didn't mingle much, from what little I've read. Was she a church member? Was Henry? We know they never had children. But don't you wonder what she was like? Awfully shy? Was she sick in bed for years? Or mad as a hatter? You going to find anything like that in all those papers?"

"That's a great question, and I have no clue. I'll ask Carroll to keep her eyes open for any personal details on Mary

Barton. And I'd like to know if they had servants in the house too."

I looked around the table and saw that people were beginning to droop—it was getting late, and I'd been talking practically nonstop. "Okay, I think that's enough for one night. Go home and think about what we've discussed. I think we should meet every two weeks or so for updates, and you can certainly contact me with anything you come up with." I planned to stay in town while the project went on. That meant neglecting my poor condo in Baltimore, where I'd been living quietly for the past few years as I worked my hotel job in the city. But then again, I didn't have so much as a plant to miss me there. Strangely, sleepy little Asheboro now seemed to be where all the action was.

"And maybe," I concluded, "we can all find a time to take a tour of the Barton mansion by daylight, to give you a better idea of what we're trying to do. Sound okay?"

Everyone nodded, to my relief. Of course they might change their minds, but at least we had a start. I was looking forward to working with these people—and to learning more about Asheboro the way it once was. After I'd moved away for college, I never came back except for the occasional visit with my parents, and then they'd moved to Florida. I hadn't been very interested in the history of the place when I was growing up, so this would all be new to me. I knew I had some homework to do.

I ushered our board members out the door and locked

up behind them. Lisbeth had hung back. "So, Miss Community Liaison," I said to her, "how'd I do?"

She cracked a smile. "Well, at least they didn't run screaming into the night. How much do you expect from them?"

"Not a whole lot right now. But they're a significant part of this town, and I want them to be involved in this project. Maybe I grew up here, but right now I'm pretty much an outsider." I paused. "Speaking of how much people can offer—what about you? What do you usually do with the kids during the summer?"

"It's always been a problem. Neither of them is old enough for overnight camp yet. There are good day camps and sports programs, but that means I have to be able to deliver them and pick them up in the afternoon. I can make weekend meetings if Phil helps out, but weekdays are going to be hard."

"Okay, we can work with that. Maybe you and I can meet when the kids are in camp."

I felt my tired brain start to whir with the seed of another idea.

"Hey, how about this? We could plan a history camp at the mansion, with short sessions—say, one per week. We couldn't do it for this year, but maybe next. Kids could camp out on the lawn, and if we get the kitchen worked out, we could feed them."

Lisbeth kept the smile, but raised her eyebrows. "I like

it, but one thing at a time, please. Let's get the place ready for public viewing and see how that goes before we start planning ambitious youth programming."

"I know, I know. But keep that idea on the back burner, will you?"

"I will. Gotta run. Anything on for this week?"

"Like I said, I'd love to get the board members over to the house for a couple of hours, to really look at the place, see what its potential is and what needs to be done. And then I need to find a contractor."

"You've got a lot on your plate, then. Good night, Kate—we can talk tomorrow."

After she left, I shut the door behind her and armed the alarm system. Carroll hadn't arrived in town yet, so I was alone in the house, and I wanted to be careful. I felt simultaneously elated and exhausted. The Barton house was magnificent, no question, but it would take work to get it ready for the public, and I wasn't sure where I was going to find people to help. I supposed we were also going to need someone to manage publicity—and create a website, which was not my forte—but those could wait until we had a better handle on the time line.

As I paced in the kitchen, not quite ready to go to bed, Frances's question floated back into my mind. Who was Henry's wife? All I really knew was her name—Mary— and that she had predeceased her husband by quite a few years. Of course, books on Victorian history could fill in a lot of the details I needed to explain the mansion's building materials and decorations to a modern audience. But a more personal desire was unfolding in me—to put the people back into the great house, and make it come alive again in the public imagination. I needed to know more.

2

As I stood before the B&B's sweeping staircase, with one hand on the elaborately carved newel, I wavered between going right to bed and celebrating with a glass of wine first. The wine won. It had been a rocky couple of months since Lisbeth had begged me to come back to Asheboro and save the town. I had gotten approval to begin with Henry Barton's house, but I could already tell it would be a mammoth undertaking. Given how little attention the mansion had been afforded over the years, it was a wonder the building was still standing at all. Then the most recent bank president in town had drained the maintenance fund, which left the town with no money to do anything.

I settled myself more comfortably on the plush settee in the parlor, a glass of red wine in my hand. This bed-and-breakfast had once belonged to my high school tormenter, Cordelia, back when she was briefly married to Ryan—yes, the same Ryan who was now our group's lawyer. But she was gone now. Only a few months ago, I'd discovered Cordelia's lifeless body sprawled on the steps of the Barton house and had to report the death to the local authorities myself. It wasn't the best way to reintroduce myself to Asheboro, to say the least, but that chapter had passed. Ryan still technically owned the B&B, but I had plans for it; I imagined it could provide rooms for visiting guests eventually. There were four upstairs bedrooms, whose Victorian elements had largely been left intact—a miracle given Cordelia's very un-Victorian taste—and overall, the place wasn't in bad shape. I didn't expect to live here forever, although where I'd go after Asheboro was kind of vague. If I was successful in reviving the town, I'd have my choice of job offers; if I failed, most likely nobody would ever notice. I could always go back to Baltimore, maybe get a plant. But I didn't want to think about that yet.

My glass was empty, but I was having trouble convincing myself to stand up and go up the stairs. In the dim light of a single lamp, I studied the parlor. Was there any sign of a woman's touch in the room? Cordelia had probably hired a decorator. I doubted she had had many friends left to ask for a recommendation, and in any case, Ryan had said she'd lost interest quickly in the bed-and-breakfast, particularly when she realized she'd have to cater to other people. She had preferred to be the queen bee, not the maid and concierge.

But first on my list for the next day was finding some-one who knew—and respected—Victorian architecture, and could make sure that the mansion would be both structurally sound and authentically elegant. Upstairs, I went to sleep with visions of velvet portieres and a profu-sion of tassels dancing in my head.

※

I was already downstairs buttering my toast when the front doorbell rang. Luckily, I was decently clothed—or at least, clothed enough to see who was at the door. The peephole showed Carroll standing on the porch, looking fresh as a daisy. She was early. I turned off the alarm and unlocked the locks.

"Hey, was I expecting you today?" I asked as I waved her in.

"Nice to see you too, Kate," she said, grinning at me as she crossed the threshold. "No, I was going to come later this week, but I finished my project earlier than I ex-pected. So, surprise, here I am!" She popped her head into the kitchen, and, finding it empty, nodded toward the bedrooms upstairs. "You alone?"

She already knew about Josh and me, and whatever it was we had going on between us. But Josh wasn't spend-ing as much time in Asheboro as he had been. When I first blew into town, he'd been stationed in the Barton mansion's carriage house as the resident caretaker, the latest in a succession of responsible individuals given free lodging and a minimal stipend in exchange for their minimal labor in looking after the place, making sure the estate wasn't overrun by teenage vandals, treasure looters, or any kind of wildlife. But now that his term was over and I had more or less taken custody of the house—*gulp*—Josh had picked up a summer course back in the city, at Johns Hopkins. Come to think of it, I couldn't remember the last time I'd heard from him . . . Carroll cocked a curious eyebrow at me, and I changed the subject.

"Yes, it's just me. We had our first meeting of the Asheboro Revitalization Project last night, and I gave everyone an outline of the plans. You hungry?"

"Yes, actually. I drove down, since I thought I might need a car here. Am I staying in this place?" She craned her head up and looked pleased as she inspected the crown moldings. Carroll also had an appreciative eye for the details of houses. I knew she'd come in handy.

"Of course you're staying here. I even have clean sheets."

"Ooh, luxury! I'm sticking with you, kid." Carroll's snappy wit was a breath of fresh air amid Asheboro's staid manners, and she had already proven herself to be an asset to the town improvement project. Given her field of study—resources collections, with a dash of genealogy thrown in—I knew she was a good addition to my skeleton crew.

She dropped her satchel on a chair in the front parlor

and assumed a businesslike stance. "Now, where are Henry's collections?"

"Still at the library. It's still closed, so go ahead and work there. Nobody will bother you. My goal for the moment is to find a contractor who understands Victorian buildings, who can take a look at the mansion and tell us what really needs doing." I shuddered to imagine the estimates I'd get for this kind of job, but then again it was Mid-Atlantic Power's money, not mine.

"Good idea. Unfortunately, I don't know any contractors who fit that bill. Is that coffee hot?" Her eyes pointed hopefully at the pot on the stove top.

"It is. Help yourself."

She did, filling a mug and then examining the contents of the fridge. She emerged victorious with an English muffin, which she briefly toasted; she then added a smear of marmalade whose provenance I wouldn't have trusted, but Carroll was a braver soul than I. She chewed contentedly as she spoke. "So, what's on the calendar?"

"I'd like our board to take a critical look at the mansion, in terms of what they want to present to the public. I asked Frances at the local paper to look for more references to Henry's wife, Mary, because we know next to nothing about her. Did you find much when you were digging through the collections?"

"Not about her—but I was pretty focused on Henry's business dealings. I'm glad he saved so many of his business records, at least. They should be able to fill in some of our picture of him. Do you know where he's buried?" Carroll asked.

"I don't know, come to think of it." There were three churches in Asheboro, but only one old enough to have been an option in Henry Barton's time. I still had no idea if he was a religious man—we'd have to put that on Carroll's research list. "You would think that Henry, being such an important man in town, would have a major tombstone or monument in the big town cemetery, right? But I never noticed one way or the other. Maybe we should add that to the committee's to-do list."

Carroll took a long draw from her latest cup of coffee, staring off in contemplation. Then she snapped to attention and said, "Let's do something. I need to get my blood flowing. You want to go look at the mansion again? Maybe that will give us some fresh ideas."

"Absolutely." I went upstairs quickly and threw on some comfortable clothes while Carroll waited downstairs, and we were ready to go.

So far, I hadn't lost the excitement I'd felt when I drove up to the Barton property and first saw the house. Coming over the crest of the hill and seeing the house settled in its verdant valley got me every time. The more I learned about Henry Barton, the more I came to appreciate his home. He'd fought in the Civil War, and when the war ended, somehow Henry had scraped up enough money to buy the property in a part of the state that had seen its share of warfare. After some initial digging into Henry's records, we'd learned that the original building had been a simple farmhouse, and it was Henry who had turned it into something close to magnificent—with money he had earned, not inherited.

I wanted to guess that he had built this place for his wife, out of love, but we knew so little about her that it was hard to say. Maybe she'd been a coldhearted nag, and all Henry's efforts had been directed at trying to impress her. But their union was more or less a mystery at this point. I hadn't even found an obituary—we only knew Mary died before Henry by way of fragmentary town memory: somebody's great-grandmother, somebody's great-great-aunt, an old piece of the story passed down, incomplete.

"Inside or out?" I asked Carroll when I had pulled up in front of the mansion and parked.

"Let's stay outdoors. I need to move—I've been doing a lot of driving already today. Besides, the days are so long this time of year that there's no rush."

"Outside it is, then," I replied. "You know, I'm not sure I've actually walked the perimeter of this land. Of course, all the kids at my high school knew how to sneak in the back way, and I'm pretty sure that most of the guys, and maybe some of the girls, had learned how to pick a lock pretty young."

"Why is that?" Carroll asked.

"Because this was the favorite make-out place in town, if you were so inclined."

"Oh my!" Carroll feigned shock, and turned to me with a grin. "And were you?"

"Almost. Kind of. No, not really." In fact, Ryan and I had come here once, as lovestruck high schoolers, and almost made the proverbial home run, but then my nemesis, Cordelia, had appeared with her mean-girl posse and quashed that. I stopped seeing Ryan and never tried again, or even knew anybody I'd want to try it with. I just kept my head down and waited for my senior year to end, and then left town. Carroll and I walked through the dense grass that flanked the house in silence for a few seconds. She looked at my face and changed tack.

"Sorry—I didn't mean to pry. It's just—I keep being surprised that so few people in this town knew this place was here, or knew much about it."

"I've wondered about that too. It's far enough out of the town center that most people don't have any reason to come out this way, and I guess eventually they all . . . forgot. So, which way shall we go?"

"You mentioned a perimeter. Why don't we just head straight to the edge of the property and then walk around. Is there a fence?"

"There was, probably still is, but I'd guess it wouldn't keep a rabbit out these days. Worth a try anyway." We headed in a straight line away from the house until we reached what little was left of an old chain-link fence. I was glad I wasn't audibly panting by the time we reached it—I hadn't been getting a lot of exercise lately.

We walked along the path of the old fence to the back end of the mansion and beyond it. Out in the open, the Barton property suddenly felt enormous. A row of gnarled old hedges came into view, and then another, and some patches of ground of a slightly different color among the weedy grass. It all looked . . . intentional.

"Huh," said Carroll. "It looks like something used to be here. Formal gardens? That would be in keeping with the lavish scale of this place. Would you want to think about bringing those back?"

"I didn't know they existed. Maybe there's a garden club in town that would like to take on the task. Or maybe we could create a new garden club! Involve more people from the town. That'd be Lisbeth's purview as community li-aison. But gardening probably won't happen until next spring, given the scope of all the other stuff that needs do-ing. How about this: next time you're feeling energetic like you were today, I'll give you a rake and you can have at it."

"Ha! Thanks, Kate. And then you can wipe the pud-ding from my face and put me down for my nap. I'll see what I have time for. Huh, what's that—ooh, there's a ga-zebo? That would be fun to spruce up, and maybe you could serve formal teas on the lawn. What's that over there?" Carroll pointed at a cluster of trees and dense foli-age fifty feet beyond the gazebo.

"I don't know. Looks like it was deliberately planted—it's not just weeds."

We walked toward it, admiring the views as we went.

There was still a lot of open land this far out from the town, and I couldn't see a single other house. Henry had chosen well—assuming he wanted privacy and some peace.

Carroll reached the stand of trees first and disappeared into the middle of it. She stood looking at something for a long moment. I remained outside, looking at the violets and buttercups speckling the grass outside this strange clump of vegetation. The circle of vines and small trees stood like a minor fortress in the quiet landscape. Carroll carefully stepped back through the stalks she had parted, and called out to me.

"Kate? I think you need to see this."

"What is it?"

"I believe we've found Henry."

3

I shoved my way into the center of what might once have been a large ring of shrubs and small trees of varying sizes. I took another few steps toward the center and stopped, realizing what Carroll had seen. A single stone stood upright in the tall grass, roughly cut except for a smooth rectangle in the center. Within the rectangle was a simple inscription: at the top, it said *Barton* in capital letters, and beneath it, in a smaller font, *Mary—Henry*. That was all. No dates. No places of birth and death. No flowery poems or Bible verses, winged skulls or religious symbols. This was their final resting place. But, after all, who had been left to bury Henry, the loner millionaire who died long after his wife, and with no heir? Had he appointed someone in his will? That piece of the story seemed to have dropped from Asheboro's collective memory.

But that wasn't all. When I stepped closer, I saw that

there were three small rectangular stones embedded in the earth, flush with the dirt. Each appeared to be inscribed with a single name—but I couldn't read them. I'd have to scrape away decades of moss to make out those names. But I thought I understood who they were.

"So they did have children," I said softly. "And nobody knew. They must have died young, or even at birth. Poor Mary." I realized I was near tears. Carroll nodded, and she too seemed moved by the sight of the stones. She took a crumpled tissue from her pocket and dabbed at her eyes.

The copse was nestled in its own dip in the land, and I turned to look in the direction from which we'd come. "You can't even see the house from here," I said, "or maybe I mean, see this from the house. Too much of a reminder, I suppose."

"I want to know more about Mary," Carroll said, nodding as she gazed at the stones set into the grass. "I hope she loved Henry, and he loved her. I can't imagine living here for years and seeing these stones every day."

"That's probably why this is so far from the house," I said. "She kept them close, but not too close." I took a deep breath. "Have we seen enough?"

"I think so. Let's go back to the house and admire the furnishings." She paused. "Do we need to tell anybody about what we found here?"

"I'd rather not. But let me know if you find out any more details when you're doing research."

"Of course. And I'll look for anything I can find about Mary."

We were silent as we walked back to the house, cutting across the lawn to walk through the old gardens, cresting the low hill and descending back into the mansion's gentle valley. We sat for an extended period in the little gazebo, not saying much, each of us daydreaming about what this place might have been like, and what it could become. When at last we returned to the mansion, the sun had passed its apex in the sky and begun its slow descent over the west side of the house. I unlocked the back door, and we walked the central hallway to the grand front parlor, the only sounds made by our feet creaking on the long floorboards.

Once inside, I felt my spirits rise a bit. It was so lovely! Shabby, as one might expect after a century of sitting empty, even with occasional visits from a cleaning crew. It was unbelievably silent—odd how all that upholstery and velvet soaked up sound. Where the sun found its way through the windows, the light was golden and highlighted the dust motes drifting through the air in lazy constellations. Still, it was possible to imagine what life might have been like when Henry and Mary had created their home. I hoped they'd been content here, at least as much as circumstances had allowed.

"Want to take a look at the kitchen?" I asked Carroll. She nodded, and we shuffled down the quiet central hall to the room at the rear of the house. "It'll take some serious work if we're going to make it functional again. Do you have any idea what a nineteenth-century kitchen was like?"

"Only what I remember from my grandmother's house, which had been her mother's before her. And my grandmother died when I was about four, so . . . not much. I remember the stove being taller than I was."

"That's more than I know."

We reached the end of the hall and stopped dumbstruck in the doorway. I had never been inside an authentic Victorian kitchen before this one, and I hadn't paid much attention to it before this moment. I'd studied some photos of modern re-creations—most of which were polished and shiny, filled with pretty copper pans and matching china—but this was different.

The room measured about fifteen by twenty feet, by my rough guess. The stove dominated the space—it had to be at least five feet high, all black cast iron with nickel fittings that cried out for polishing. Three ovens, plus an open grill in the middle, which probably doubled as a burner for boiling things. The whole of the oven was nestled in a large nook that must once have been a fireplace—from the old farmhouse kitchen?—which itself was flanked by shelves and a couple of cupboards and another smaller, lower stove and oven. Could anyone have run out of space in the big one? I couldn't imagine. And just below the ceiling, a deep shelf ran around most of the room, holding an assortment of pottery jugs, mixing bowls, and other items of cookware that were mysterious to me. At the center of the room was a broad wooden prep table that would easily seat eight, with a comfortable chair parked at one end, where no doubt a cook sat to peel vegetables for many long hours in the house's life. I would have dropped into the chair simply to study the layout and the details of the room, but I wasn't sure it would support me. It looked like it hadn't been sat in for a century.

"Okay, I'll say it first. Wow!" Carroll exclaimed, somehow bubbly and reverent at the same time.

"I know, right? I can't imagine using it, though."

"Servants worked hard back in the day. You know, we should think about this."

"What do you mean?" I asked.

"Well, we've both spent time in this house. We know Henry and his wife lived here. But who else? How many servants, and who were they?"

"You're right. I touched on this at the board meeting, actually. There's still a lot to discover. Where did the workers stay? I think I remember some rooms in the attic—let's revisit that later. Would two people have been enough to manage all this? Just think of the number of tasks that had to be done! Hauling in coal for the fire, peeling and chopping food—not to mention cooking it—then pumping water for the dishes, unless somebody had put in running water early. And that's just for this one room! And don't forget laundry, and . . ." I felt tired just thinking about it. "Learning more about Mary and her family might give us some clues. Maybe she grew up as a farm girl and wouldn't put up with people working for her as servants. Or maybe she was lonely way out here and enjoyed the company of another woman in the house."

We fell silent, and I realized we were both gazing out the back window toward the graves, invisible from this distance but very present in spirit.

"I'll admit it's a puzzle," I told Carroll. "There's still a lot we don't know about this house. Josh can help fill in the industrial and economic history, I hope. But the life of the place—that's the real draw, I think. Who should we look for to get the . . . what would you call it? Social history?"

"Something like that. Maybe more than one person could contribute to that. Frances, from the paper? I can probably help too, since I know how to pull records. And then someone with knowledge of Civil War history. Ooh, and someone who knows about kitchen utensils circa 1880. I'll keep my eyes open for anything like that too. Hey, I'm getting hungry—do we have any plans for lunch? Or are we closer to dinner by now? What time is it?"

I checked my phone. "It's getting late, and I'm hungry too. I forget if there's anything in the fridge—I was trying to wrap my head around the presentation to the board members yesterday, so I didn't do any practical stuff. And we've kind of exhausted Cordelia's wine supply. I'm not sure what's open at the moment, but we can find something."

"Sounds good to me," Carroll said amiably.

"Anything else you want to look at while we're here?"

"I should do some more research and figure out what I need to look for. There's no rush, is there? I've got the whole summer."

"I wish I thought this would move quickly, but have you ever known a renovation that did? I still don't even know what needs doing. My first task is to find a renovator who knows Victorian buildings, and I don't even know where to look."

"You don't know any burly do-it-yourselfers around here?" Carroll smirked. "A jack-of-all-trades with a wrench in one hand and a history book in the other?"

"I wish! I haven't been here long enough—or had the time—to meet that many people. It's the big stuff like wiring and plumbing that I'm most worried about."

"I hear you," Carroll agreed. "Don't worry too much, Kate. I just know you'll find someone good. So . . . food?"

"Yes, please. Let's go back to the car and go hunting."

It was a pleasant summer day, now late afternoon, so Carroll and I didn't hurry as we stocked up at the local grocery store. We strolled the aisles at a leisurely pace, occasionally squinting up at the long fluorescent bulbs set high in the ceiling—such a contrast to the dim and dusty elegance of the mansion. We made sure to pick up more wine. We returned to the B&B, and before we got out of the car, Carroll said carefully, "We aren't going to talk about Mary to anyone else, right? Or the . . . well, the babies?"

"Right. Not right away. I suppose people will have to know eventually, but right now, I feel like it would be invading their privacy. I'd rather wait until we know a little more about Mary. Are you okay with that?"

Carroll nodded. "I am. Mum's the word."

"Settled. Hey, look—Josh is here." His battered gray station wagon rounded the bend into the B&B's gravel parking area. "I wasn't expecting him."

"Isn't he teaching this summer?" Carroll asked.

"He is, but it's just part-time for the summer term. Maybe he wants to do some more local research. Well, I guess we'll find out."

"I'll give you two some space—as long as we can eat first!"

"Deal."

Carroll headed for the front door of the bed-and-breakfast, carrying our bags of groceries. I leaned against my car and waited for Josh to approach. I watched with mild amusement as he got out of his car, stretched his arms and legs, removed his glasses and wiped them on his shirt, then started walking my way.

"Hey there!" I said when he was in earshot. "I didn't know you were coming today. Are you planning to stay here?"

"If I'm welcome. Now that things have changed at the mansion, I don't get a free room in the stable anymore."

Joshua Wainwright, my maybe-paramour, had signed on for a year as caretaker of the Barton estate, a position that had been created by Henry Barton in his will. When he took the job, Josh had recently split with his wife and had been looking for a short-term home from which he could commute to his teaching job in Baltimore. And while he wasn't exactly handy with a hammer or a wrench, he had been a careful custodian of the place.

That was well before I'd agreed to come back to my former hometown and attempt to save it from its long slide into decline. But I'd jumped into the work on a leap of faith, having no other commitments in my life at that time—and Josh and I had somehow become involved along the way. He was an intelligent, attractive man—just past forty, bespectacled, bearded, pleasantly scruffy—and he knew a lot about local history and regional industrialization, which had dovetailed neatly with Henry Barton's role as owner of the only factory in Asheboro. I hadn't been looking for a relationship, but Josh was turning out to be a good foil as I fumbled my way back into the community I thought I'd left behind long ago. Josh was curious about details, gruffer than I was, less sentimental; I enjoyed the balance. Was whatever Josh and I had going to go anywhere? I had no idea, but we both had a lot to keep us busy, so our romance was simmering quietly on the back burner. Yet here he was again.

We walked up the front steps onto the B&B's wrap-around porch, and paused together in front of the door. "Did you come all this way just to see me, or do you have an ulterior motive?" I asked, not quite sure if I was joking.

"Some of each. My life in Baltimore isn't as exciting as what's going on here."

"You found an apartment?"

"If you can call it that. It's more like a closet with plumbing, but it's a place to sleep. How are things on this end?"

"Moving right along. We had the first meeting of the board last night. Ryan's submitted our application for non-profit status. Carroll just arrived this morning, and we went out to refresh her memory of the mansion." I briefly debated whether to tell Josh about the tombstones we'd found, but wasn't yet sure how best to handle that discovery. I was feeling protective of the place, and now especially of Mary, about whom I knew so little. "I wanted to look at the kitchen there more critically—I think that should be the first phase of the renovation, because it's going to be more complicated than the other rooms."

We stepped into the B&B and wandered toward its kitchen, arriving there to find Carroll banging pans around, with a big pot of water set to boil on the stove top. "I was wondering if you'd gotten lost," she said. "I voted unanimously for spaghetti. You staying, Josh?"

"I am. Are you just passing through, or are you here for the summer?"

"Looks like you're stuck with me. I convinced my boss

that this would be a good project, and she agreed. Kate wants me to find out more about Mary Barton and the rest of the household, as well as sort through the rest of the Barton documents in the library. Now that we've set aside the business papers, I can see if either Mary or Henry left anything personal behind."

"Sounds like you've got your work cut out for you," Josh said. "Is there wine?"

"Of course," I told him, and retrieved a bottle and glasses.

Once Carroll had thrown together a sauce for the promised spaghetti, we sat around the dining room table as it simmered, each of us with a full wineglass.

"So, Josh," I began, "do you know of any contractors around here who can handle restoring a Victorian home without mucking it up? I want it to look historically accurate but function by modern standards."

"I didn't do much in the way of repairs or construction while I was staying at the mansion," Josh said, "but I can ask around. Didn't Ryan have any ideas?"

"I haven't asked him. And I'm afraid the people I worked with in Baltimore are more accustomed to working on large commercial buildings, and the Barton place just wouldn't appeal to them."

"You want to interview a couple of outfits, see which one you like best?"

"I suppose. I want to get this right, and I honestly don't know much of anything about Victorian kitchens, high- or low-end. I'm open to suggestions. Carroll, let me know if you find a tattered invoice for a cast-iron stove for the kitchen. I could use some clues."

"Will do. More wine?" she asked. We all nodded happily.

After we'd eaten, Josh washed the dishes, and Carroll graciously retreated to her room upstairs. Josh and I took our glasses and ambled out to the small patio in the back. It was a lovely evening—not too hot, not too cool, and not too many bugs. A string of white fairy lights bordered the little enclosure where we sat.

"You look like you're enjoying yourself," Josh commented after a while.

"You mean, being in Asheboro? Or being here with you?"

"I'm not fishing for compliments, though I hope that's true. I meant being here in your old town, with a challenging project in front of you. It seems to suit you. Did you ever give yourself time to mourn losing your hotel job?"

"I guess not. Lisbeth had already asked me to help her, although I probably wouldn't have considered coming here if I hadn't been let go, like, five minutes later. It was definitely hard—I don't like to lose. But in a way, it's been good for me. I have a lot of the skills this town project needs, and I have history with the place. And I do like challenges." I hadn't said all that to myself before, and I realized it was true. I was enjoying the project, with all its uncertainties. I looked at Josh in the fading blue light of early evening. He did look awfully handsome. "Did you finish your book while you were on sabbatical here? You can't complain about too many interruptions out at the mansion, at least before I showed up."

"I actually didn't get very far. The different aspects of this place are hard to reconcile. I was supposed to be writing about the growth of railroads and the spread of new and diverse factories and the influx of immigrant workers, all alone in the peace and quiet . . . but then I'd get distracted by the sunset, or a bird. I never saw myself as a nature lover, but the place grew on me."

"I can understand that. So, what about the book?"

"It's still in the works, but it may be going in a different direction."

"I see," I said, lost in my own thoughts about the work ahead of me. "Say, do you know any kitchen historians?"

"Is there such a thing?" Josh countered.

"Beats me. But we can find out, right?"

"I don't know why not. Can you still use those old appliances?"

"I don't have a clue, but I wouldn't count on it. I'm not trying to blow up bystanders, especially once we open this place to the public. Mostly, I want things to look right, and to cook for parties."

Josh smiled and put down his empty glass on the patio

table, then gazed at me in my chair across from his. "You look chilly."

"Josh, it must be seventy degrees out here. I'd hardly call this—"

"Kate, that was a hint. Let me rephrase: Would you like to come sit next to me?"

I blushed, which I was glad Josh couldn't see in the gathering dark around us.

"Sure," I replied. I got up and arranged myself on the love seat next to Josh. I busied myself tracing the veins on the back of his hand with my fingertips. "Do you have plans for tomorrow?" I asked.

"Trying to pull my notes together, I guess. Don't worry about me—you can go on about your business, you and Carroll, and I'll hang out here and get something done."

"You don't have a class?"

"Not until Tuesday."

"I guess I'll start hunting for a contractor. I think Carroll is going to dig into the Barton papers again, but with a different angle. We both want to know more about what Henry and Mary were actually like as people, even if it's only by inference. I may enlist Frances from the paper to look through her archives, since she struck gold with that newspaper photo of Henry with Thomas Edison. I'm not sure what was covered in the society pages in the later 1800s, if anything. Especially in a small, fairly rural town. But nothing ventured, nothing gained." I paused, wondering what I wanted to say next. Josh was looking down at my hand on his. "I think I'll go up now, so I can get an early start in the morning."

Josh regarded me levelly for a long moment. "Would you like company?"

I hesitated only a few seconds. "Yes, I would."

4

When I woke up, I could hear the shower running, and the dip on Josh's side of the bed was still warm under the rumpled sheets. Last night had been . . . nice. Or maybe more than nice. But I wasn't sure what I wanted from him. What I did know was that I didn't want to be taken for granted, anytime he felt like showing up. Perhaps a conversation was in order. But I had other things on my to-do list for the day.

I threw on some grubby at-home clothes and wandered down to the kitchen. Carroll had beaten me there, and even made coffee. She looked up from the travel magazine she was reading and said, "You don't get a paper here?"

"Not since I've been here, but maybe Cordy used to. Not that she was much of a reader, or had any interest in current events—or at least, not the ones that didn't affect her."

"Meow," Carroll said, wrinkling her nose. "You ever going to get past old grudges?"

"Eventually . . . Probably. I'll think about it." I was sometimes surprised by my own capacity to hang on to resentments. I hadn't been in touch with Cordelia in years, yet the old feeling could still well up at times.

"Right," Carroll said. "Anyway, Ryan dumped her, so you won, right? Or something. Are you still interested in him?"

"Old news. I erased him from my data banks a long time ago."

"So . . . Josh?"

"Maybe. One day at a time." I opted to throw her off the scent with a rapid conversational pivot. "Are you going to the library today?"

"Of course. I'm itching to get going on Barton's papers. Although I could start by looking at the censuses to see if any servants or employees were listed—that data becomes available online after seventy-two years, you know."

"I did not know that, but it's a great idea."

Carroll continued animatedly, turning her coffee cup around and around between her hands on the table. "Oh, and I should probably request Henry's war and discharge records from whichever agency keeps them—they might tell us something, or at least confirm some of the dates. I wonder where he met Mary, and when they married? Did you check with the bank to see if he left a forgotten safe-deposit box? That'd be a find. Or if there's a hidden safe in the house somewhere? Have we felt along all the walls? And what about—"

I held up a hand. "Slow down! That's an awful lot of questions. Of course, I want to know the answers too—but one at a time, eh? Me, I'm searching for building contractors today. I have a feeling that taking the kitchen apart and putting it back together may get messy, and I want to get started, but I also want it done right."

"Good luck!" Carroll said as she left the kitchen, practically skipping off to her day in the archives.

I checked the clock over the sink: just after eight. Too early to call Ryan? Would he be in his office, or en route? Might as well find out. I dialed his number.

"Kate?" he answered on the fourth ring. He sounded like he was chewing a doughnut, but by the looks of him, he was more likely an egg-white-spinach-protein-wrap kind of guy, no butter. Another reason we would never make it as a couple. A plodding sound in the background wherever he was became apparent to me. Was he walking on a treadmill? He went on, still chewing. "You got a problem?"

"No, but I need your advice. I want to talk to a few contractors about remodeling the kitchen at the mansion, only I don't know any around here. I want it to look authentic— I'd love to think we can use the original appliances, but I'm not betting on it. I need somebody who likes this kind of challenge. Do you have any recommendations?"

"I'll make some calls. There aren't any major construction companies in Asheboro, but there are some good ones in my neck of the woods. Unless you want to look in Baltimore?"

"I know some people there, but I think the ones I've worked with are all used to big budgets, and they skew toward contemporary design anyway. I'd like to support local workers if we can—they need the jobs. If you could get back to me with some names by lunch, I can start setting up interviews this afternoon."

"Yes, ma'am! Whatever you say, ma'am!" Ryan chuckled to himself, still chewing and walking, by the sound of it. "How about dinner sometime this week, and you can tell me where things stand with the project?" I thought for a second. Ryan had made a half-hearted pass at me when I first got back to town, which I'd quickly rebuffed. Was he trying again? Not that he wasn't still good-looking, intelligent, a stable guy with a good career—but something about him just didn't feel right, all these years later. The heat was gone—for me, at least. I kept my tone friendly. After all, we were practically coworkers now.

"Dinner? Sure. But only if you get me a contractor."

"I'll see what I can do." He hung up first.

Josh walked into the kitchen just as I rose to pour myself a second cup of coffee. "Morning," he said, making a beeline for the half-empty French press. We met right in front of it at the counter, each with a hand extended; upon seeing each other there, we engaged in a polite standoff, each deferring to the other in a silent and protracted "after you," "no, after *you*" routine. After a few tense seconds, I grabbed the carafe, poured each of us half a cup, and set a new pot of water to boil.

"Good morning to you too," I said. "You have plans for your day?"

"Only vague ones." He removed his glasses, breathed on the lenses, and rubbed them on the front of his Johns Hopkins T-shirt. He looked sleepy but handsome. "I passed Carroll in the hall upstairs. She's doing research today?" He sat down across from me at the kitchen island.

"Yes. But I think she's going back to the mansion, too—she has her own set of keys. She's been wanting to look for secret hiding places for any other documents, just in case we missed something when we cleared out the attic. She loves that kind of thing—but then again, who doesn't love that kind of thing?"

"What about you?"

"I asked Ryan to recommend some contractors, so I can get started on the kitchen. I'd like to survey the local options and proceed from there." *And what if they don't pan out? Back to square one?* I paused and took a sip of coffee as I considered my plans, and wondered for the millionth time if I'd bitten off more than I could chew here. In the meantime, I was curious about how Josh's book was coming.

"What about you?" I asked. "Do you have a time line?"

"Not really, but I'd like to get as much done as I can

this summer, before classes start full-time again. Yes, I know, I had a whole sabbatical year to work on this, but given recent events, I'm going to have to do some serious editing."

"My, we're going to be busy this summer, aren't we? Where do you want to set up to work? Carroll will probably be using the town library as her base, and I've claimed the office across the hall here as my business headquarters."

"Could I use the old carriage house again? Do I need formal permission?"

"That could probably be worked out."

"Great. I'll make sure everything is still hooked up at the carriage house and work there for a while. What's on for dinner?"

"Why don't you cook tonight? You and Carroll can confer about the menu. If I can connect with any contractors, I may be out at the mansion sometime later today."

"Works for me," Josh said, standing up. "I'll check with Carroll."

As promised, Ryan texted me the names of three local contractors before noon. I didn't recognize any of the names, but that wasn't surprising, given that I hadn't lived in this town in years, and had never attempted to hire a tradesman here as a teenager. I called each one in turn and asked him to stop by the mansion that afternoon, and each of them jumped at the chance. I texted Ryan a quick thank-you and put down my phone for a while, feeling satisfied by this small piece of progress.

This Barton house project was a whole new animal for me. My previous construction expertise lay in major metropolitan projects, primarily in the hospitality business. While the hotels I'd dealt with had been high-end, and both structure and finishes had been first-class, they were still a far cry from Henry Barton's mansion, a fancifully detailed living space from another time. I wasn't sure what a fair price would be for a project of this size, or how long it would take to complete, but I was planning to start with only the one room while I explored options for the others, as needed. Maybe I should open up the components of the project to a range of providers, which could give them some fodder for advertising while also giving Asheboro some much-needed exposure to a wider universe of sightseers. And then there was the need for a publicist, eventually. I wished I could hire at least one person to serve as office staff for me, because I would be juggling a lot of balls in the air, and realistically, I knew I wouldn't have time to do everything.

Don't get ahead of yourself, Kate! So far, I'd raised some money and put together a committee to help, but that was about all. The rest of the project was still in my head. *One step at a time,* I told myself. Right now, I needed to go out to the mansion and try to visualize what I hoped the kitchen would look like, before the contractors arrived.

I ate a quick toast-and-cheese lunch and headed for the mansion and my three meetings of the afternoon. When I arrived, I went straight to the kitchen at the back of the house to get a good look at it by harsh daylight—and without the rose-colored glasses. Was I crazy? It was a perfectly preserved Victorian kitchen, but what would it really take to make it work? Could the antique spirit be preserved if all the pieces actually had to function? Would it be worth the expense, or should I just find a good caterer and let them bring everything in themselves? I realized that caterers would still need an electrical supply for some elements of their work, and running water was a basic sanitation concern. And then, if there was a bar—which would certainly facilitate the writing of generous checks—there would have to be ice, and a way to keep wine cold . . .

The possibilities were like a swarm of bees, darting through my mind faster than I could consider them. Maybe I was overreaching. But for this afternoon at least, I'd simply let the contractors make their own suggestions. Maybe I'd hate them all. Or find out that what I wanted was impossible. Ah, the impossible dream: it was fast becoming an old friend.

5

P ushing complicated catering thoughts out of my head, I settled in the kitchen to wait for the first contractor. I was glad I had installed an intercom for the front gate so I knew when someone was arriving and could activate the mechanism to let them in. When a man called, his voice over the intercom a hash of approximate syllables, I pressed the buzzer that would slide open the long electric gate, and directed him to follow the driveway and meet me at the front door.

I opened the door to find not one but two guys, who both seemed immediately stunned by the opulence of the house's interior. Both of them—one young, one middle-aged; both blond and pink-faced, perhaps father and son, or uncle and nephew—stopped dead in the front parlor, wordlessly looking around them. *Well, at least they've got good taste.* It took some persuasion to get them down the hall to the kitchen, but I couldn't fault them for being impressed.

"So, what do you want to do with this space?" the older one asked.

"I want to make this a working kitchen, while still retaining the Victorian appearance to fit with the rest of the house. Can you do that?"

"What's the state of the wiring? Plumbing?" he asked.

"Assume the worst. This place was last remodeled in the later 1800s—the original owner was an early advocate of electrical power, and he ran a few lines through the house himself. I think a caretaker in the '50s might have made some updates, but not many. So, the technology was probably state-of-the-art when it was put in, but I imagine it's in pretty rough shape by now. As far as plumbing goes, that's above my pay grade. See what you can figure out."

"Huh. I can already say, it's going to cost you," he said, and blew a short stream of air out through his front teeth as if to punctuate his point.

"I know that," I said, swallowing a spark of annoyance. I wanted someone working on this space because he wanted a challenge, and appreciated my goals. "Can you make it work?"

"Yeah, but we might have to take it down to the studs to fit everything in. Gotta be up to code, you know."

"I've handled bigger projects in Baltimore. I know what it takes. Have you worked on other Victorian buildings?"

"Not a lot," he admitted. "Mostly, people want to modernize, not retrofit. It's faster and easier."

"I'm not interested in getting it done over a weekend, and certainly not if it means destroying the details. It's important that it look right. I know we're going to have to rewire the building, and I'd be interested in hearing your thoughts about that. Keeping in mind that we want to preserve as much as possible of the original. But I wanted to consider the kitchen first."

"Got it. Mind if I poke around a bit?"

"Go right ahead," I told him.

He and the younger man conferred briefly, then split up and started inspecting the kitchen—the ancient appliances, the lone overhead light fixture with its single bulb. I kept reminding myself that a simple farmhouse had formed the core of this building. Had Henry torn it down, or maintained the original elements and built around them? The boundaries of the old house's walls were visible in the basement, but I didn't know much more than that.

The older guy interrupted my thoughts. "Basement under here?" he asked. When I nodded, he said, "Mind if we take a look?"

"Go ahead." I showed him where the door to the basement was located, but remained upstairs and let him and his younger colleague explore on their own. I couldn't tell them much of anything about it anyway. When I went back to the kitchen, I could hear low muttering coming from the two men beneath my feet.

I wasn't very impressed by them. Maybe they were good at their jobs if they were presented with a modern site, or even a twentieth-century one, but they showed no enthusiasm for the handsome old Barton kitchen, even if they did respond to the velvet-filled opulence of the parlor. Maybe I was kidding myself, but I knew I didn't want a bunch of guys to come in and rip things out and slap drywall over the studs, add a few store-bought moldings, and call it done. These guys didn't have the right attitude. I sighed. But this was only the first team—I hoped numbers two and three would be better.

When the two men emerged from the basement, I made polite noises, and they promised to send a plan and an estimate of costs. I said I'd look forward to seeing it and shepherded them out the front door. The younger man tipped his baseball cap to me as they exited, taking one last backward look at the parlor. When I returned to the kitchen, I found Carroll there.

"Oh, you're here!" I said, pleasantly surprised.

"I am. I hope that's okay. I got a good start at the library, but I realized I was daydreaming about this place. I parked out front and walked around back, and then just . . . stared at the backyard for a while. I love all the possibilities! Mind if I poke around the upper floors for a bit?"

"Go right ahead."

"Were those guys who just left contractors?" she asked.

"Yup."

"Any good?"

"No. I'm sure they'd be fine for a modern home, but not for this place. They're going to send an estimate, so at least we'll have something to compare other contractors' estimates to. Am I being unreasonable? I mean, trying to make this one room look the way it did more than a century ago, and still work today?"

"Maybe. It can take a lot to bring places up to code, especially if there's any chance you'll be serving food to the public. I understand why you want to do it, but I can't say whether it will work—or if this group can afford it."

"That's what I'm afraid of," I told her. "And I'll have blown a large part of the budget on one small part of the project, when there's so much else to be done. I just want it—the whole house, I mean—to be memorable, and to make people really see what life was like back then."

"I hear you. The kitchen is the center of the house—and it can tell us a lot. So what's next on your schedule?"

"I've got two more contractors coming, and I'll see how that goes. Ryan gave me three names, but I can go farther afield if I have to. Or I can just give up and hang pictures of Victorian kitchens around the room and tell visitors to use their imaginations."

"Hey, don't give up so easily!"

"I'll try not to. I just want everything to work out. What have you been up to?" I asked.

"Mostly poking around, looking for secrets. I keep wondering why Henry and Mary Barton were so reclusive. They didn't come from money, so I don't think they were snobs. He seemed energetic, from what we know. He certainly did a lot in his time. Maybe she was hideously ugly, or had a terrible disease and didn't want to be seen in public—or she was insane? So far, I don't have a lot to work with."

"That's a pretty grisly list of options you've come up with, Carroll. What if she was just extremely introverted, or both of them were? I guess we'll learn more as we go anyway." I checked my watch. "Still half an hour to kill before the next contractor is due. Maybe I'll take a walk."

It was a warm early afternoon, and the bright sun shone starkly against my rather pale skin. I felt better just being outside. It was such a lovely piece of land. Hard to imagine these grounds as a working farm—there were no traces of that left. If there had once been a barn, it was long gone. It might have sat where the carriage house was now, but that building dated from Henry's remodeling of the place. I sat on the back steps outside the kitchen and wondered idly if I should plan for a parking lot. I quickly vetoed the idea. I couldn't abide the thought of paving over any of this open land just now—and besides, I was going to provide carriages departing from the center of town, right? Another pie-in-the-sky idea on a list that was long and still growing. But if we could arrange for carriage transport, modern visitors would arrive at the mansion and see it the way Henry had, in his day. I liked that thought.

The sound of a truck pulling up to the front signaled the arrival of Contractor Number Two. I reentered through the back door and walked the length of the house's main hall to let him—and not one but two assistants—in by the front door. The leader of the crew was fastidiously clean, with an expensive-looking fountain pen protruding from his shirt pocket and a faint Polish accent. His assistants— both baby-faced young men with neat haircuts—never said a word, but took in every detail matter-of-factly, nodding and typing occasionally on their phones. Our discussion followed much the same outline as the one I'd had with the first candidates, although this man was not as dismissive, and actually seemed interested in the structure of the building itself. That was good. But his face fell when he looked around the kitchen.

"Plumbing and wiring are original?"

"If you mean later nineteenth century, yes. I want to preserve as much of the building in its Victorian condition as possible."

"That would be expensive, you know," the man said. "And time-consuming as well."

"I realize that," I told him, "but this is one of the more interesting rooms in the house, and I want visitors to see what living here would have been like after the Civil War. That's the whole point. Have you done anything like this before?"

"Only in pieces—a stove here, a sink there. Mind if we look at the basement? I need to see the wiring and pipes."

"No problem." Once again, I led the way into the hall and pointed to the cellar door. The group descended, and

I rocked back and forth on my heels for a few minutes, hearing their shuffling footsteps and murmured conversation drifting up from below.

Then Number Two and crew came trudging up the cellar stairs, shaking their heads collectively. When the leader saw me waiting, he said, "You'd be better off replacing all the plumbing and wiring, and that will be messy. We could subcontract for the other trades, but the layout in your kitchen doesn't work for modern appliances, even if they're made to look old. You don't want an electric stove, do you?"

"No, absolutely not. What did people use for cooking in 1880? Wood? Coal?"

"Both, probably. And you'll have to put in ventilation, so whoever cooks there doesn't suffocate. I admire your idea, but it would be a lot of work. Not so easy. Summer is our busy season, and I don't think we're the right guys for this job."

I was glad for his honesty. "I understand. I appreciate your coming out to take a look." I shook his hand and led the crew back out the front entrance.

Two down, one to go. I was a little surprised that the first two outfits hadn't appeared very interested, since I had kind of assumed that the people around Asheboro would be eager to get some work. Apparently, construction wasn't in that category. Maybe the locals were only looking to spruce up their homes to sell them and move on. Maybe I shouldn't have started with the kitchen in a building that most people in town didn't even know existed. Maybe I should have chosen a more visible structure in the community to whet the appetites of local builders and convince them that the project wasn't just a crazy plan dreamed up by an equally crazy lady . . . Perhaps, perhaps, perhaps.

Carroll appeared from upstairs, looking for something to drink. While we had a classic icebox in the kitchen, it was just a box set into the wall, and not cold. I made a mental note to get a cooler and fill it with ice and cold drinks for whoever was working in the house. "No luck with Number Two?" Carroll asked, having apparently given up her search for secret drawers in pieces of furniture upstairs.

"Nothing there either. He seemed interested, but on further inspection downstairs, it was a hard no. I guess I'm too used to working in a big city, where people expect elaborate renovations. Or maybe nobody around here likes Victoriana. Or maybe I'm just insane."

Carroll made a snorting noise. "Seriously? You're giving up after talking to all of two people? I expect more from you, Kate. Whoever told you this would be easy?"

"Apparently, my imagination," I said glumly.

"Chin up, kid. Maybe Number Three will be the charm."

"I hope so."

"Anyway, I'm parched. I'm going into town for refreshments. Be back soon. You want something?"

"Yes, please, anything." I was fighting off an encroaching foul mood, a result of two rounds of disappointing conversations. Maybe I expected too much of people. I went out front to see if there was any sign of Number Three and was surprised to see a truck with a company logo on it, but no sign of the driver. Where was he? I walked up to the truck: nobody snoozing in the front seat—or in a pile of hay in the bed, for that matter. That was a good sign. I walked around the side of the house to find a middle-aged man standing on the grass and staring up at the side of the building with a half-smile on his face. He wore overalls over a red button-down shirt and seemed to be counting something high above with an extended finger. I called out to him.

"Mr. Wheeler?"

He turned at the sound of my voice. "Oh, hello there. Call me Morgan. You must be Kate Hamilton." He pulled a small spiral notebook and a square carpenter's pencil from the front pocket of his overalls and jotted a few notes as he spoke. "I'm sorry—I got distracted. Those shingles on the second level—three different shapes! Wow. You don't see that anymore. What an incredible building!"

"It is, isn't it? Shows what you could do back in the day if you had all the money you could ever want. You've never seen this place before?"

"Oh, not by daylight." He chuckled. "Not at all, actually—I've heard a few stories. No doubt you've heard tell of some of the other activities that took place here, since I understand you went to high school locally."

I couldn't help but smile. Anyone who'd once been a bored teen in the area knew about the habit of sneaking onto the property at night. "My, you've done your homework. And yes, I knew about the . . . other activities, although I don't think they involved admiring vintage architecture. Are you ready to see the kitchen?"

"I am. I must say I was surprised to hear that was your first priority."

"So am I, in hindsight," I told him. "But I think it might be the most challenging part of the project, and I want to get it out of the way. It could really add value to this place as a teaching institution, if we can get it working. Have you worked on old houses before?"

"Whenever I can—which is not very often. A lot of folks these days just want to tear down and start over. Lead the way."

I winced at the mental image of a wrecking ball ripping into this glorious structure, realizing that this had been the fate of many like it in this area and all over the country. This house, which had stood stalwart on the edge of town for a hundred years, suddenly seemed fragile, precarious, in need of protection. But protect it was what I aimed to do. I shrugged off the image and led Morgan in through the back door, since I was afraid I would lose him in rapt admiration of all the other wonders of the house if we took the main entrance. Then I stepped back and let him explore on his own. He took his time and seemed to absorb the details. After a few minutes, I asked, "Do you want to see the basement? In other words, the out-of-date utilities?"

"I think I can guess what they look like. Right now, I'm a bit perplexed by the proportions of this room."

"Really? As I understand it, the core of the building was an old farmhouse, so maybe the owner just built around it when he remodeled."

Morgan nodded. "That would make sense. But this wall—it looks to be in the wrong place. Why waste space?" He started moving slowly around the perimeter of the room, apparently feeling for joints in the walls, or maybe changes in material. Occasionally, he knocked on part of a wall, and eventually he came to one area on the inside wall that sounded hollow. He briefly walked out to look at the adjoining room, then returned. "Is there any access to this side? Upstairs? Downstairs?"

"Not that I know of, but I haven't been looking that closely. There's a small spiral staircase that runs up the back of the house, probably for servants to use back in the day, but I don't think it has any secret doors that would connect here. You think there's a space behind the wall?"

"Sounds like it. Wait a minute—I have something in the truck that might tell us more. I'll be right back." As he left, I found myself staring at the blank wall he'd just been knocking on. It seemed like an ordinary wall to me. He returned a minute later with an odd machine, like a video game controller outfitted with a miniature screen, and a scope attached to one end. I had never seen anything like it before.

"What is that?" I asked.

Morgan grinned. "It's kind of a spy cam. It's got a lens at the end of this tube here, and you can view what it sees on this little screen. I saw something like it on *CSI* and thought it might be useful for looking inside walls, to figure out where the pipes and wires went, or could go. Besides, I love new toys. My wife thinks it's ridiculous, but hey, it keeps me happy. Do you mind if I make a very small hole so I can look inside this wall? I promise I won't damage anything."

"Sure, I guess. You can fix it afterward, right? And now you've got me curious."

I stood and waited while he went back out and retrieved a small power drill from the truck, then tapped on the wall some more before making a tidy hole, no more than half an inch wide. Then he inserted the tube into the hole and turned on the machine, rotating it carefully so he could see the full image of whatever was behind the wall.

And then he stopped moving. He fiddled with the dials on the machine. His easy smile dropped away, and his expression became somber. He looked again, and finally turned to me. "I think you need to see this."

A few random thoughts flitted through my head. What had he seen? A nest of tarantulas? A colony of rats? Fifty years of garbage? "Don't move the lens," he instructed. "Just look at the screen."

I looked. And I looked again. "You've got to be kidding," I said to myself. I turned back to Morgan. "Will you hand me my phone, on the table over there? We need to call the police."

6

egrettably, I'd had to use the number more than
once. I had first encountered Detective Brady
Reynolds after I found Cordelia's body on the
front steps of this very house, and I'd kept the state police
number saved in my phone ever since. This was Monday,
if I recalled correctly, so Reynolds should be at work, unless he'd taken off on a vacation where there was no phone
service. Unlikely. I hit the dial button.

"May I speak to Detective Reynolds, please?" I asked
politely when a female voice answered.

"What is this regarding?"

"Uh, this is Kate Hamilton in Asheboro. I'm at the
Barton mansion—the detective knows where it is—and
it appears that we've found a body. It's inside the kitchen
wall."

There was a moment of silence. "Oh, hi, Kate. This isn't
a joke, is it?"

"I wish it were, but it looks real. I suppose it could be a dummy, but with my luck, I doubt it."

"You sure the person is dead?"

"Yes, and it looks as if he's been that way for a long time."

"I'll put you through."

I waited on the line for Detective Reynolds. We were sort of friends, now that we'd spent a bit of time together working on other cases. But what would he make of this development? My mind was spinning with questions already. Who was this guy in the wall—assuming it was a man? How long had he been in there? Had someone put a wall around a dead body—or deposited the body inside the wall? Or could it be that some foolish teenager of my generation—or earlier, even—had snuck in, found a crawl space, and gotten stuck?

Reynolds came on the line.

"Hello, Kate," he began. "I hear you've found a body. Want to give me the details?"

"Of course." I was mildly cowed by his professional brusqueness, but tried to keep the details simple. "I've been interviewing contractors to renovate the kitchen at the mansion. My third interview was with a Mr. Wheeler, who's still here. He thought one of the interior walls sounded hollow. He has a machine that can look inside walls—I'll let him explain that to you—so he made a little hole and peeked inside, and voilà, there was a body."

"What can you tell me about the body?"

"Not much, from here. I think it's male, based on the

clothes, but since it's more skeleton than body, I can't give you much more detail. It looks like there's an old staircase behind the wall there—maybe from the farmhouse that once stood on this land—so I guess it's possible that he died in a fall. But then somebody walled him in. I'm guessing the kitchen was remodeled about 1880, based on the utilities, so if he got walled in, he had to have died around then. And that is the sum and total of what I know."

"I can't speculate on the circumstances without examining the scene. Who did you say was with you there?"

"Morgan Wheeler, the contractor." I realized I hadn't actually offered Morgan the job, and we had barely talked about it, before this interruption. I'd need some time to think, which was in short supply at this moment. "A potential contractor, I mean. I interviewed two others today, but they didn't comment on the state of the wall. So . . . now what?"

"It's an unexplained death, so we have to investigate. We'll try to identify the man. That might not be easy, if the body's from the Victorian era. You don't think it's Henry Barton, by any chance?"

"No. We know he lived until 1911, which was long after the completion of work on this house. And people at the time were aware that he had died—he didn't just disappear. Come to think of it, there are a few existing pictures of him. I can dig one out just to be sure. Maybe the poor man has some ID on him?"

"I doubt it, considering the era. But we're getting ahead

of ourselves. The age of the body has not been conclusively determined. I'll round up a couple of my men and come take a look. No one has disturbed the body?"

"No. All we've seen was through that hole in the wall. It's all yours. Oh, and can I make a request? If you plan to remove the poor man from the wall, could you do it without destroying the walls, or anything else? I'm hoping to re-create the kitchen in all its Victorian glory, and I'd hate to lose a big chunk of the house."

"No guarantees, Kate. Our priority is to secure the evidence. But we can keep the integrity of the building in mind wherever possible. Are there any other means of access to that space?"

"Not that I know of, but I didn't even know it existed until a few minutes ago. I can check for hidden doors or hatches—maybe upstairs, or in the basement—but if the old stairs were so carefully hidden, any openings would have been too, I'm guessing. But I won't touch anything."

"That's fine. I can be there in half an hour. And ask Mr. Wheeler to stick around—I want to see this machine of his."

We hung up at the same time. I'd acted without thinking—mainly about what impact the discovery of a body would have on my plans for renovating the kitchen. Was a hidden body a plus or a minus when it came to attracting visitors? I'd have to think about that. But it wasn't as though the state police would have to publicize the discovery. If the poor man had been dead for a hundred

years, nobody was going to remember him. I had to wonder if there was an obscure family story that had been
handed down through generations, about when Uncle
Fred had simply gone missing one day. Then I thought,
rather darkly, that it might be some rich competitor of
Henry Barton's who had to be gotten rid of for some reason. How much did we really know about Henry's character, after all?

I should call Frances at the newspaper. She of anyone
could lay hands quickly on the older records of Asheboro.
But what would I ask her to look for? Would the town have
noticed if a man had gone missing? Had he been local, or
from some other area? Who would have come looking for
him?

"Kate?" Morgan's voice interrupted my circling thoughts.
"What did the police say?"

"The detective is on his way. We've worked together before, over the last few months. Oh, and he asked if you
would stay until he gets here—he sounds interested in that
machine of yours. Does it have a name?"

"Like . . . Archibald?" Though his face was still quite
pale from the shock of what he'd discovered, he gave a
small chuckle. "No, but the generic name is an endo-
scope, otherwise known as an under-door camera. They
don't have to be expensive, but they can be useful. As you
have just seen . . . Well, I suppose I'll be sticking around."
He rolled the brim of his faded green ball cap back and
forth in his hands, worrying its shape into a deeper curve.

At that precise moment, I heard the front door open and close. Surely the detective and his crew didn't move *that* quickly. I turned to see Carroll padding innocently down the main hall toward the kitchen, staring into her phone, a plastic grocery bag swinging from one hand. She stopped dead in the doorway when she saw Morgan.

"Oh, hi. You must be Contractor Number Three? Kate, I got some lemonade at the store . . . but then I drank it all on the way here. Sorry. What's going on here?"

Morgan smiled wanly, and extended a hand. "Hello. Yes, I'm here to speak with Miss Hamilton about the renovations on the house. Morgan Wheeler. And you are?"

"Carroll Peterson. I'm here for the summer doing research on the former owner of this house, but I come from Philadelphia."

"Oh, how nice. 'I went to Philadelphia, but it was closed!'" Morgan cocked an eyebrow and spoke out of one side of his mouth in a jaunty character voice.

Carroll looked at me. I shrugged.

"W. C. Fields? Really, nothing? I must be getting old." Morgan waved a hand in the air as if batting away his failed attempt at a shared joke. He began to fan himself with his cap. The afternoon heat had indeed made the air feel close in the Barton kitchen. Or maybe it was the knowledge that there was a dead body inside the wall, five feet from where we all stood. Morgan cleared his throat. "But this is perhaps not the moment for jocularity."

I nodded, and Carroll looked at me, her eyebrows

raised in question. "Carroll, there's something you need to know," I said. "There's a dead body behind that wall. Morgan found it."

"Are you joking?" Carroll said incredulously.

"Nope. Morgan can show it to you with his little machine here. Don't worry—whoever it is, it looks like they've been in there for a long time. The body is mostly a skeleton now."

"Have you called the cops?"

"I just did. They're on their way. I told them they didn't have to hurry."

"Gee, Kate, it sure is fun working with you. So, Morgan—find many skeletons in your line of work?" Carroll seemed shocked but a little amused. Having just seen the corpse myself, even through the distance of a wall and a digital screen, I wasn't able to share her levity.

"This is my first," Morgan replied, "although you'd be surprised the things you do find in old houses, under floorboards or behind walls."

"You'll have to tell me all about it sometime. What happens now, Kate?" Carroll asked.

"Based on my extensive experience with bodies and police investigations, I would guess that Detective Reynolds and his band of merry men will get here and attempt to remove the body. I hope they can do this without destroying part of the house. We should look for other ways of getting behind the wall, although I suppose nobody expected they'd ever need to. Wow, I've got a lot of questions. Who was this? How did he die? And if it was a murder, who could have done it?"

"Henry?" Carroll asked.

"From what little I know of Henry, he doesn't strike me as a killer. But I could be wrong," I told her, turning to our poor contractor. "I wish I could offer you a cold drink, but we don't have a fridge. Or . . . any drinks."

"That's quite all right," Morgan said, though a fine gleam of sweat had appeared on his forehead. "I've got a thermos in the truck."

"Does Josh have anything to drink out in the carriage house?" Carroll asked.

"Maybe. I think he's out there now. Why don't you check? You don't have any evidence to offer. I should wait here for the police."

"I'll do that," Carroll said, and headed for the back door.

I followed her to the steps. "See if Josh has some cups, or a cold beverage, or send him out to find something. And bring him back here—he might as well hear the story. We can ask if he knows anything about this hollow wall. He must've poked around this place when he was serving as caretaker."

"Will do. I won't be long."

I went back into the kitchen to find Morgan fiddling with the hulking cast-iron stove. He hadn't been kidding when he'd said he liked devices. He straightened up when he saw me. "So, what's the story here? I tried looking up the Barton mansion's history online, but there wasn't much of anything written about it. Are you wanting to live in this place, or is this part of some grand scheme?"

One more thing to add to my to-do list: find a tech person and put together a website for publicity. We were going to need some press coverage—once we dealt with this body and figured out what to tell the public about it. If anything. And find someone to take pictures, or ask Frances for some archival photos, and . . . oops, I hadn't answered Morgan's question. "So you haven't heard about the renovation project? Do you live in Asheboro?"

"No, I'm a couple of towns over, west of here. But not far."

"That's one of our problems. Most people don't know what we're up to, even locally. Here's the short story: This town is dying off, and has been for a while. But a lot of the old buildings have good bones, as they say. We're going to rehab all the storefronts on the main street in town—a lot of them got really banged up in the storm a few months back—and rebrand the place as a 'Victorian village.' Think of Old Sturbridge Village, or Colonial Williamsburg—a living history site, with reenactors, old-timey craft and trade demonstrations, period-appropriate foods, the whole thing. But we're starting on Henry Barton's place, with a chunk of cash provided by Mid-Atlantic Power, thanks to Henry's brief affiliation with Thomas Edison back in the day. That's a long story, but suffice it to say Edison wasn't the only guy experimenting with new lighting systems in the 1880s. So, here we are. With a body in the wall. And

I really want this kitchen to work, and to help people see what life was like a hundred years ago, and—is any of this making sense?" I was starting to sweat. The day's heat, combined with the enormity of the task I'd just outlined to a relative stranger, was feeling oppressive.

"Uh, sort of," Morgan said. "And I hadn't heard about any of that. You should hire a PR guy."

"I agree. But I'm the only one running the show, and I wish my days were thirty-six hours long. It will get better, I keep telling myself. We've got money in the bank, a board, and people working on the plan. I wanted to get the kitchen started just so I had something real to show people. You can feel free to run screaming out the door and never come back—I'll understand."

Morgan laughed. "What, and miss all this fun? I wouldn't dream of it! You've got this incredible building, like something preserved in amber, you've got money to spend, you're getting people in town involved, and you've got a plan. That all sounds like a good start, if you ask me." His level assessment was a balm to my overwhelmed psyche. "But you want to make this place authentic, not Theme Park Maryland, right?"

I nodded vigorously. "Exactly. It's a rare opportunity, and I want to do it right. If the whole thing fails, Asheboro is no worse off than it was when I started. Or we'll take the rest of the money and turn the old Barton Shovel Factory into a museum and stop there. But I'm going to at least try to bring back this kitchen. Are you interested?"

"You know, I think I am." He scratched his head, look-ing around the room with what appeared to be a familial fondness. "This project could make or break us both, but it sure won't be dull. I've got some time free—I turned down some other work this summer to build a new shed out back of my own place, but that can wait. You want me to write up a proposal and a cost estimate?"

Maybe it was the heat, but I was feeling a little giddy. "Sure, why not? But for now, can you stay long enough to keep Detective Reynolds and his henchmen from tearing the place apart to get that body out?"

"Not a problem," Morgan said, smiling.

As if on cue, the police arrived, pounding on the front door.

7

I let the detective in at the front door, making a mental note to lock the front gate next time I came in. "Welcome, gentlemen."

"Hello, Kate," Detective Reynolds said. The man had a square haircut, a square jaw, and a square suit to match—though I had to admit it became him. He stepped inside, and his analytic gaze swept over the library and front parlor visible from the foyer, then landed on the central hallway extending behind me. "The body's in the kitchen?"

"Yes. To be accurate, the body's behind the wall in the kitchen. We haven't touched it."

"How many people are here with you?"

"Well, there's Carroll Peterson—the researcher; you've met her—and the contractor I was interviewing for the restoration project, Morgan Wheeler. He's the one who found the body in the wall. And I think Josh is over in the carriage house, if you need the full manifest. Carroll went over there to find him, but she should be back soon. So, what do you want to do first?"

He almost cracked a smile. "Why don't you show me the basic layout of the area, and we can decide how to retrieve the deceased? You said it was an old body?"

"I think so. From what little we could see, it's like a leathery skeleton with clothes on. But I don't know how long it takes for a body to get that way." I turned and led the way toward the kitchen, where Josh and Carroll had arrived and were making small talk with Morgan. Everyone greeted everyone else briefly, and I was happy to see that Carroll had returned with some peach tea and a small stack of waxed-paper drinking cups. They might have been thirty years old, left in the carriage house by someone several caretakers ago, but at the moment, I didn't much care.

"Show me the deceased, please," the detective said, looking at Morgan.

"Happy to," Morgan said. "I can show off my spy camera again."

The two men conferred over Morgan's device, then moved over to the wall. Morgan inserted the scope with its LED attachment into the hole he'd made earlier, then handed the small screen to Detective Reynolds. "Take a look," he said.

"Ah," said the detective, studying the screen. He took his time before handing the control box back to Morgan. He clicked a small handheld recorder extracted from his suit pocket and spoke into it. "I see the remains of an adult male, essentially desiccated, lying on a wooden staircase that appears to lead from the kitchen to the second floor of the house. It's crudely built, maybe three feet wide. The body's head is pointed toward the bottom of the stairs. From this vantage point, I cannot see any door or other means of exit at the upper end, nor do I see one at the bottom end here. What can you tell me about the history of this house, Kate?"

"As I understand it, this was once a farmhouse, which Henry Barton bought after the Civil War ended. He started up the shovel factory in town, and after a few years, he was wealthy enough to turn the original building into what you see now. He married at some point, although we don't know much about his wife. She died well before he did, and I think he lost interest in the house, although he was successful professionally, as you know. They had no heirs, and the house has been vacant for over a century, until recently. I may be getting ahead of myself, but it looks to me as though that wooden staircase was part of the farmhouse, and it was, well, swallowed by the expansion of the new house, which should provide an approximate date for the death. The body was clearly hidden, if you ask me. And that's all I've got."

"An excellent summary, Kate. Mr. Wheeler, you know construction. Do you have anything to add?"

"From what I've seen of the kitchen wall here, it was built with care, not just thrown together. Nobody was in

a panic to hide the body. I don't know if that means anything. There's plenty of land around here—I wonder why
whoever killed him didn't just bury him in the woods
somewhere. If it was a murder, I mean."

Reynolds kept his eyes fixed on the wall, which had
looked so ordinary a few hours ago, and now held an old
secret—and the potential to derail my renovation plans.
"Our next task is to extricate the body from the wall. Kate
here has asked that we not damage the house itself, for her
own reasons, and I will honor that request insofar as it is
possible. Once we have the body out, we will attempt to
identify the deceased." He clicked the recorder off, returned it to his pocket, and nodded to the staff sergeants
behind him. "Floyd, Eaton, we'll need to check the basement and the second story to see if there is any apparent
access to the staircase." The two young men nodded, and
Reynolds went on staring at the wall a few seconds longer,
until I spoke up.

"Thank you, Detective. That works for me. But I have
to ask: Are we all coming? I have a certain responsibility
for taking care of the property, so I'd like to be there."

"I have no problem with that. I doubt you'll be destroying any evidence," the detective said. "Let's start in the
basement."

We all trooped out into the hall—the detective and his
men, Morgan, Josh, Carroll, and I—to the doorway beneath
the grand staircase that led to the basement, and down the
stairs. When we were all gathered in the basement, I said,

"You can see that the masonry changed when the house was expanded. The kitchen is directly above us, in this corner, and it looks as though the masonry was earlier. Do you agree, Morgan?"

"I do. So, if that staircase predates the mansion, there should be some section that was boarded over, under the staircase—unless of course they rebuilt the whole floor, but that seems unlikely." He pulled a small flashlight from a pocket and walked slowly toward the corner, peering upward. "Here," he said.

We followed his lead, and there was indeed a solidly built patch in the subflooring over our heads. "Is it the same age as the rest of the house?"

"Most likely. Certainly not much newer—the lumber matches, and it was secured with cut nails, as was the rest of the subfloor. So in my opinion, the staircase was walled in about the time the kitchen for the new-and-improved house was built."

"We can assume no one pushed the deceased up into the stairway space from down here," Reynolds remarked.

"It would be difficult, but not impossible," Morgan told him. "Shall we see what's above the staircase?"

"Follow me," I said, and led the way back up.

The second-floor hall was wide and high-ceilinged, with richly molded doors spaced every ten feet or so. Clearly, no expense had been spared on this floor, despite the fact that few people would ever see it. Once again, we took a moment to orient ourselves. The main staircase, with its handsome mahogany railing, came up from the front of the main hall beneath, so the kitchen below would be at the far end on our right. We knew from what we'd seen in the kitchen that the upper end of the old staircase had to be at the rear, so that was where we headed. The bedroom door opened onto the hall at the near end of the room, so we walked in and continued along the wall until we reached the corner.

Morgan's eyes glowed like those of a hunter. He laid his hands gently on the wall and searched with his fingertips. "In case you're wondering, I'm looking for where a door might once have been. This would have to have been the outer wall of the staircase, else the hall up here would be significantly narrower. I'd bet they built the bedroom up against the staircase, but nobody ever noticed that the bedroom was a bit small." He started knocking on the wall, and yes, it too sounded hollow, like the space beneath.

"No door?" I asked.

"Not that I can see. Whoever did the construction work did not intend to use that staircase, it seems, but for whatever reason, he was too lazy to tear it down."

"Or he knew the body was there and was in a hurry to make sure it stayed hidden," I countered. "What do we do now? Since this wallpaper is both lovely and in excellent condition, I would suggest removing the body from below—the cellar patch will be no loss to architectural history. Detective, will that work for your crew?"

"Since any forensic evidence is no doubt long gone,

I think that would be the easiest approach. If there were bloodstains on the stairs, or any artifacts, it would be easy enough to retrieve them from below as well."

"Are you going to do that now?" I asked, hating how anxious I sounded.

"I think it can wait until tomorrow. I'll leave an officer here to keep watch, in case anyone is curious, and I know you've replaced the security system recently. You weren't planning to spend the night here, were you?"

"With a dead body in the place? No, thank you. Carroll and I are staying at the bed-and-breakfast in town. I told Josh he could stay at the carriage house if he wanted, but he's welcome to join us at the B&B. And, Morgan—you said you live nearby?"

"Right, a couple of towns over, so it's not hard to come back and forth. I'd like to do a bit of research on local houses of this era, in case there are any other surprises. Detective, would you like me to come back tomorrow?"

Detective Reynolds eyed him. "It wouldn't hurt, in case there's something crucial caught on a nail, or a pool of blood in the wrong place. Say ten o'clock?"

"I'll be here." He tipped his cap to the detective, then turned to Carroll and me. "Ladies, are you leaving now?"

I looked at Detective Reynolds. "Do you need us?"

"No, but you should be here tomorrow. And I know where to find you if anything else turns up before that."

Carroll and I fled before he could change his mind.

It wasn't as if I were squeamish about bodies or blood.

And the poor dead man hardly seemed human—more like a piece of leather. I didn't know him, and he didn't mean anything to me, at least not in any personal sense. How this might affect the renovation phase of my grand project remained to be seen. The presence of a hidden dead man could work for or against me—it added a thrill of ghoulish excitement, but a tale of historical murder might become a distraction from the glory of the building itself and its potential as a tool for learning. I'd have to give that some thought. Would this man, whoever he was, become part of the official narrative of Henry Barton and his marvelous mansion?

Morgan, Josh, Carroll, and I had all convened on the front porch and stood in awkward silence for a moment, without a clear image of what to do next, separately or together.

"I don't feel like eating at the B&B tonight," I announced to no one in particular. "Can we eat out? Josh, you up for it?" He nodded. "Morgan, do you want to join us, or do you have someone to go home to?"

"The missus is at book club this evening. I'd be happy to join you, if you know of a decent restaurant nearby."

"It's slim pickings, but I think hunger beats gourmet food tonight. Just follow me."

We found a fast-food place on the highway outside of town and ordered lots of hot, greasy food. Forget about calories and cholesterol: we'd spent a couple of hours investigating a dead body who definitely should not have been where he was, so we didn't have the energy to question our junk-food extravaganza. And the investigation wasn't over yet.

"So," I said, my mouth full of fries, "tomorrow the police drag the poor man out of the staircase. Think we'll learn anything?"

Carroll answered, trailing a fry lazily through a small lake of ketchup on her tray. "We know he's dead. We know he's not Henry Barton. We think somebody put him there and covered up the evidence. What we don't know is how he died. Accident . . . or *murder*?" She stabbed the fry straight down into the tray for emphasis.

Josh had been uncharacteristically quiet since he'd joined us, but he piped up now, compacting an empty wrapper into a tight ball in his hands. "Henry seems to have been a law-abiding kind of guy. If someone had fallen down the stairs and died, wouldn't he have reported it to the authorities?"

"Or, even if it was an accident but he didn't want to call the cops," Carroll added, "why wouldn't he remove the body from the house and bury it somewhere? I can't imagine living in that house for years knowing there was a body next to the kitchen. Too creepy. No, thank you."

"If Henry left the body there on purpose, does that imply he knew the guy, or that he *didn't* know him?" I wondered out loud. My eyes scanned the brightly lit menu on the wall across the room. We needed some apple pies if we were going to crack this case. I stood, intending to indulge the collective sweet tooth, then sat back down as a new thought occurred.

"Maybe it was someone who had a long-standing grudge against Henry, dating back to the war, and he came back to exact his revenge, and Henry was forced to kill him?"

Carroll's eyes widened as she sucked bright orange liquid through her straw. "Or the guy had gone broke and lost the farm that Henry bought, but still thought it was rightfully his and came back to reclaim it?"

Morgan chimed in, "Any chance he was a former slave?"

"How would that figure in the story?"

"I can't say with any certainty, but maybe there was some conflict involved. I can well imagine the ill will an enslaved person might bear toward a wealthy white man—even a stranger, even years after the war. Old memories die hard." He took the last bite of his veggie burger and wiped his hands on a handkerchief produced from a pocket.

"Well," I said, my head now thoroughly spinning with opposing notions, "it should be possible to at least figure out his skin color when we get a better look at the body."

"Ick," Carroll said. "I don't think I need to be standing around in the room when that happens, if it's all right by you. I'll get back into research mode tomorrow and start on the genealogy side of things. I've got my work cut out for me, tracking down details about Henry, Mary, their families, and also the property itself. Not to mention making another pass through the house to check for any personal documents we might have missed. Six bedrooms could contain a lot of nooks and crannies." Her eyes went dreamy in a way I recognized—the house's secrets had led to many flights of fancy in my own mind, often in the minutes just before falling asleep. After a moment, she snapped back to our conversation. "Kate, what are your plans?"

I took a long swig of soda before answering—I was still feeling dehydrated from earlier. "Well, first, I need to officially ask Morgan here if he'd like to work on this project with us—assuming your prices are fair, of course. You definitely know your nineteenth-century buildings, and more importantly, you seem to like them. That's what I want for the mansion. Of course, I'd still like to see a proposal from you, if you're interested. But if you're in, and the police drag their feet tomorrow getting the body out, maybe you and I can do a more detailed walk-through of the mansion, while we have the time?"

"Miz Hamilton, I would be delighted to work with you." He nodded sagely, like a monk. "I'll try to be fair, but you already know this is going to be expensive. I think it will be worth it, though."

"Good! One more thing I can check off my list. Has everybody finished eating? Because I'm having trouble keeping my eyes open." They all nodded in agreement, and we stood to dispose of our trash by the exit. I lingered by the swinging door, letting Morgan and Carroll go through first, and then buttonholed Josh. "Hey. Are you coming back to the bed-and-breakfast?"

"Happy to, if I'm welcome."

"Of course you are. I just like to know your plans. And at least I can promise you breakfast. We can all rendezvous at the mansion before ten tomorrow morning, and see who comes out of that wall."

8

I had crashed early the night before, and I woke up feeling good . . . for about five seconds. Then I remembered my plans for the morning: meeting up with Detective Reynolds and his crew to observe the removal of a body from the house I was working on—or trying to work on anyway. It was going to be an unusual day, to say the least. But I still wanted to know who the guy was, and why he was there. Which reminded me that I should call Frances and see if there was anything in the old Asheboro newspapers under her care that might shed some light on missing persons in 1880-something. But I wasn't going to hold my breath.

Josh bumbled his way in from the bathroom, vigorously drying his hair with a towel. "Hey, you woke up. No nightmares?"

"No, nothing murder-related—just the usual final exam for a class I forgot to attend all year."

"That old chestnut," he chuckled. "Listen, I'm due back in the city to teach this afternoon. It slipped my mind last night, after all the day's excitement."

"Josh, you really don't have to be at the mansion for this. I know you're busy. I'll be fine. Today is the detective's project anyway—I'll just be standing off to the side chewing my nails if anyone scratches the antique wallpaper."

"Really? You don't mind? I do want to be there—it's just that I haven't taught this class for a few years, and I could use the extra hours to brush up on my lecture notes."

"Don't worry about it! Go—I've got this under control." Did I really mean that? Of course I didn't *need* Josh to be there; I'd overseen bigger projects than the Barton kitchen in my days working hospitality. But I enjoyed having him around to bounce ideas off of—when he was available.

We made it down to breakfast eventually, to find Carroll sitting at the kitchen table busily scribbling notes on a lined pad. She had the buzzy look of a person who's been up drinking coffee since dawn. "Hey, guys—I wondered when you'd wake up. Any brilliant revelations overnight?"

I answered first. "Nope. I'm sticking with the known facts: there's a dead guy behind the wall in the kitchen of the Barton house, and . . . Well, that's all I'd swear to. I suppose it's not impossible that it's a dummy someone left there to freak out whoever found it. We know the place has been a snooping ground for local kids for a long time—it's a wonder it's still in such good shape. Anyway, I'll wait for the police pathologist to tell us more. Josh has to head back to the city today. Are you coming along, or would you rather go right to the library?" I didn't want to say it, but I was hoping for a little company in the strange span of hours ahead.

"Oh no, I'd better head to the library and get going on those documents," she replied, almost vibrating with caffeine and a researcher's excitement. "I've got a lot to look for: Henry's family, and Mary's story, possible servants, not to mention tracking down prior owners of the house itself. But I could stop by later? To look at the maid's room like we talked about."

"Right—sure, that's a good idea." My face fell a little, but I hoped it didn't show. "I'll expect you sometime later on." *Onward, Kate! There's work to be done.* I took a deep breath and pulled my hair back into a low ponytail. It was a potentially dusty day at the Barton mansion.

Josh, Carroll, and I left the B&B, locking up carefully, and split up in the driveway for our separate vehicles. I headed for the mansion, uncertain what the day would bring. I managed to arrive there ahead of the police and the pathologist, and on entering, I checked in with our police guard, who had nothing to report. Once in the Barton kitchen I looked around carefully to see if anything had changed or if my perception of it had changed. But everything was the same, as far as I could see. It was a large, pleasant, high-ceilinged room with rear-facing windows and a body behind the wall. *All perfectly normal,* I thought dryly. I spied Morgan on the back lawn through a window; he seemed to be studying the outside of the building from all angles. I imagined the morning light might reveal details that had been invisible yesterday. I opened the back door and called out to him.

"See anything new?"

"No, but sometimes it takes a while."

"I'd offer you coffee, but there isn't any. Or water, for that matter. I'm working on it. Say, how many houses have hidden staircases?"

"I think 'hidden' might be overstating the case. There are a fair number of secondary staircases in homes of this era—for servants or nannies in charge of small children who should be seen but not heard, or to enable a quick escape from unwanted visitors. This house, as you know, has a back staircase apparently added at the time of the 1880s rebuild. Cover up one staircase, build another—go figure. And of course there were secret spaces in some homes—holding places for travelers on the Underground Railroad . . . But I haven't seen anything of the sort here so far." He furrowed his brow, casting his gaze toward the building's stone foundation.

"Was the Underground Railroad active in this area?" I asked.

"That I can't say, but I'll wager either Carroll or Josh could find out easily enough."

"Josh isn't with us today, and Carroll is working at the library for a while. Are you coming in? The detective and his crew should be here soon with the pathologist."

Just then, I heard more than one vehicle crunching its way down the driveway on the other side of the house. The police had arrived.

I went to the front to let them in. The detective—Brady—led the way, followed by a woman I didn't recognize, who turned out to be the pathologist. A couple of men in uniform brought up the rear, I assumed to do the heavy lifting. We all traded introductions, and then I took them to the kitchen. They glanced around at the walls as we walked, and I was glad to see that nobody was carrying a sledgehammer.

Meredith, our pathologist, got right down to business. "Where's our victim?"

"Behind that wall there." I waved vaguely. "Before you all get carried away, I'd like to ask you again to try not to destroy anything. This is a historic building, and I've formed a committee to try to preserve it and open it to the public later this year. I'd like to keep things as intact as possible. Please."

"Do you have a floor plan for the house?" Meredith asked.

"No, I haven't found one. We talked yesterday with the detective about going in through the basement."

"Kate," Morgan broke in, "I hate to say it, but I've been thinking over that plan, and it may not be our best bet. I believe we'd compromise the structural integrity of the building by removing a patch of ceiling of that size from the basement. You saw what it looks like down there—it's substantial stuff. I think we'll do best to go through this wall here, same way we found him."

I swallowed a small lump of disappointment. "That's fine, if it's what you need to do." I shot a glance over at Detective Reynolds, looking for confirmation. His face was stony as he spoke.

"I agree. Let's go in here."

"Now, these walls are lath and plaster, keep in mind," Morgan continued. "It's not like modern drywall. Which means it will take some work to get access to the body."

"I'm well aware, Mr. Wheeler," the detective replied. "We'll do whatever we need to."

"What condition do you think the body is in?" I asked.

Meredith considered this for a moment. "Is the house damp?"

"No," Morgan replied. "Not unusually so."

"That bodes well," Meredith said. "While this isn't exactly ancient Egypt, odds are the body mummified, rather than rotted."

"How does that work?" I asked, intrigued in spite of myself.

"If the circumstances are right—which mostly means dry—it can happen very quickly, in weeks or months. If this kitchen's oven was in use, or the furnace lies beneath this part of the house, either might have sped up the process. So far you've been basing your estimate of the time of death on the architecture, rather than the state of the body?"

"Right," I replied. "No one's seen the body up close yet."

"We can change that," Meredith replied, faintly smiling. She nodded to a man behind her, who laid out a large duffel of tools on the kitchen table.

I turned to Detective Reynolds. "What will you do with him, once you get him out of there?"

"Take him back to headquarters, so we can get a good look at him. Determine cause of death. Meredith may run some labs to determine if any unusual chemical agents are present. Look for identifying marks—not that they'll be of much use, if he's been dead a hundred years. But it all needs to be looked at and recorded."

"I see. You're taking this very seriously, aren't you?"

"A death is a death, Ms. Hamilton, whether it happened last year or a century ago. We'll do what we can."

"How long should we leave the scene intact?" I asked.

"You mean, when can you begin your renovation project? Let me get a look at the body and the space once we open it up, and I'll be able to give you a better idea. A week, perhaps?"

Meredith had covered herself in protective gear and now held a small electric handsaw that oddly resembled a lamprey. She looked around at the people standing in the kitchen.

"We're ready. We've got a gurney to move the body, and a photographer to record what we find. Kate, Morgan, if you're squeamish, now's the time to clear out. But you're welcome to watch from over there."

I was torn. I felt very protective of this house, as though it were a living thing whose welfare had been entrusted to me. I didn't want to see it damaged. But I knew this was happening either way.

"I'm going to step out for a few minutes, but I'll be nearby. Just shout if you need me."

"I think I'll stay," said Morgan. "I've heard the plaster in Victorian walls could include horsehair, among other things—I'd like to see firsthand what's in that mix."

I wandered out to the dining room to clear my head. The room was dark, the heavy draperies drawn mostly closed, so only thin strips of white sunlight slotted in. The dense Persian rug underfoot made dry scuffing noises as I walked on it. I had so many questions, and no idea whether we'd find answers. Who was the man? Why had he died? Was local business magnate Henry Barton—who by now was coming to feel like a friend—a killer? Had whoever was using the kitchen to prepare meals for the next twenty-plus years been aware that there was a dead man in the wall? I sat down in a high-backed dining chair and looked down at the rich wood of the table, where many meals must have been served and eaten, many conversations had—all now lost to time, reduced to silence and a darkened room. I hoped I'd still get my chance to bring the life back into this place.

There were ominous cracking noises coming from the kitchen, as well as the squealing, grinding sounds of a powerful saw, but I thought it wiser to stay out of the way.

After a few minutes, Morgan came into the dining room. "They've opened up a panel big enough to get the body out, but the police want some pictures before anyone tries to move him. It'll be a while."

"Any surprises?" I asked as I stood up.

"Nothing obvious—yet. Were you expecting a note or something?"

"Maybe. But this house and its occupants didn't seem to work that way. Is it—he—disgusting?"

"Not really. More like your typical Egyptian mummy. Dry, and no bugs or goo."

"Thank goodness—I'm not in a mood for goo today. I guess I'd better come watch."

We turned and headed back toward the brightly lit kitchen.

9

There wasn't room in the kitchen to get too close. Besides Detective Reynolds and Meredith, the medical examiner, two uniformed cops had made their way in, along with a tech Meredith had brought to assist, a photographer, plus Morgan and me. We made quite a crowd, and the room was heating up, as much from the activity of heavy equipment the group had brought in as from the Maryland summer now ramping up to full effect. I was glad to see that the people handling the body were being careful—they moved slowly, examining every angle before making a decision—and the hole in the wall didn't look too bad. Maybe we'd want to take out this wall anyway in the final assessment—would tourists want to come through and see the "murder staircase," if that's what it was? Or could we appeal to a niche market of architectural historians who'd be thrilled to see a piece of an old farmhouse preserved inside the Victorian manse?

I pushed aside those thoughts and focused on the action in front of me.

Meredith was holding the gurney in place while two men—her assistant and one of the uniformed officers—jockeyed for space to reach into the staircase and get ahold of the body. It seemed to move easily, so it hadn't been tied down or anything. Had he just lain where he fell, for all of the last century? The head end emerged first, and the guys slid the rest of the stiff body out easily, while Meredith maneuvered the gurney to receive him. It was done quickly, and we all got our first glance of the Dead Man in the Wall.

The photographer snapped more pictures, and then Meredith measured the body. She described what she was observing, probably for the benefit of Detective Reynolds, but we all leaned in to hear the updates.

"Looks like he was about five feet eight inches, though he might have shrunken a bit over time. Appears to be wearing ordinary clothes, possibly work clothes." With gloved hands, she deftly felt assorted parts of the body. "Visible skull fracture, and a possible broken neck. There may be other breaks, but it's hard to tell before I get his clothes off. Either the head or neck injury could have killed him, but I'll have to look more carefully to see if I can determine in what order they happened." The sweat on my forehead suddenly felt cold.

"Can you tell how old he was?" I asked from across the room.

"I'll have to check his teeth and bones. Not old, but past his teens, I'm guessing. For the moment, we can guess between twenty and forty. But don't quote me on that."

"Anything in his pockets?" the detective asked.

"What, you want to see if he has a driver's license?" Meredith smiled, then felt in the man's jacket and pants pockets. "Sorry, no. Look, I'll be able to tell you more once I get him back to the lab. Kate, do you want to come meet the man in your wall, up close and personal?"

I hesitated. No, I didn't, but I felt I should. *Now or never, Hamilton.* The policemen stepped back and let me approach, until I was standing at the near end of the gurney. The man looked small, shrunken. His hair was reddish, and he had what looked like the beginning of a beard. No jewelry—or at least, no rings. When had wedding rings for men become popular? In short, there really wasn't much to see. I didn't feel much for the man—not disgust, not pity, not sympathy. Shallow of me, but at the moment, he was an inconvenient object getting in the way of my plans. I promised myself that Carroll and I would work toward giving him a name and a reason for lying dead in front of me.

"Seen enough?" Meredith asked.

"I think so. How long will your autopsy take?"

"A couple of days, maybe."

"I've got a friend working on the genealogy and histories of the people who lived in this building in its heyday. If you find anything notable about this man, or if we can offer you any clues, please let me know."

"Will do." She turned to the other policemen, and then to Reynolds. "Okay, guys—let's get him back to the lab. Brady, I'll be in touch." Then she followed the gurney out the door.

The tech set to unplugging the stand lights that had been placed around the hole in the wall, and the photographer fiddled with his equipment on the large kitchen table, fitting a very expensive-looking lens into a foam-lined case. Morgan and I stood looking at the hole, not saying much, and eventually the workers left and we found ourselves alone in the kitchen again. I was about to open my mouth to suggest we get a Shop-Vac on-site sooner than later, when Detective Reynolds walked back into the room, surprising us both.

"Thank you for letting us barge in on your project space today, Kate," he said. Like I'd had a choice. "We'll let you know if we discover anything of interest."

"How far back do your records of missing persons go?" I asked.

"Not far enough for this gentleman, unless he was a former president, or something like it. I'm afraid you're on your own."

"We'll manage. I hope you're not going to make some announcement to the public."

"There's nothing to be gained. No one alive today is going to remember him."

"That works for me. I want to get my mind around the history here before I start getting calls about this. Or we could think of it this way—let me write it up when we know more, and we'll both benefit. But anyway, thanks for your help. That went as well as it could have, I guess."

"You're welcome. Try not to find any more bodies this week."

"I'll do my best." I followed him to the front door and watched him march to his unmarked car in the driveway, then returned to Morgan in the kitchen. He was poking minutely at the exposed plaster in the wall with a pocket comb, and looked up when I came in.

"Everybody gone now?" he asked.

"Yup. That didn't take as long as it might have, but I'm exhausted."

"I understand."

I turned on my heel and walked back into the dining room, then took out my phone and called Carroll. She picked up on the third ring, sounding a bit dazed.

"Hi, Kate. How's it going over there?"

"They're gone. With the body. There was nothing awful or disgusting, and the poor man didn't fall apart when they extracted him from his hiding place. He had both a skull fracture and a broken neck, but nothing that would identify him. The pathologist will get back to us if she finds anything, and I said you might be able to help if she hits a dead end." I paused, feeling a little dazed myself, wondering what our next move should be. Everything felt uncertain. "Speaking of which . . . find anything interesting?"

"Hold on to your bonnet, Hamilton, because I've got some news. Mary news."

"Do tell! I could use some good news right about now."

"I told you before, I think we have a pretty good handle on Henry's overall story, although there were a lot of blanks for other parts of his life. Since we know he started in Massachusetts, I figured I should work out how he ended up in Maryland and then stayed."

"Makes sense to me. And?"

"I started with two questions," Carroll continued. "One, was it the war that brought him here? And two, how and when did he end up with this property? So I looked at war records, which are available online. It's a little harder to pin down deeds when you're starting with not much information, but I made a few phone calls to friends who were likely to have access to that information. And I got answers." I could hear her grin through the phone. "I'll start with his war records. I can give you Henry's unit and so on, although he never made it past corporal. So if you were hoping for a three-star general, you're out of luck. His unit was posted down this way for some of the major battles you hear about, and he was wounded in one of the last ones, close to the end of the war."

"I assume there's more?"

"Of course. Henry's injuries were serious enough that he had to spend some time recuperating, and by the time he was well enough to travel, the war was pretty much over. So he ended up recuperating in Maryland."

"Here?" I breathed.

"Bingo. *Right* here, in fact—that is, not just in Asheboro but in the very house where you stand. Of course, it was a shabby farmhouse back then. The owners took in wounded soldiers to make a bit of money from the government. The only child at home was a young woman, who did the nursing and such. And—"

"Her name was Mary," I whispered.

"You got it."

"Wow." I sat with that thought for a moment. There was something almost cloyingly romantic about it, but I liked the story anyway: young Mary nurses wounded soldiers in her family home, falls in love with one of them, marries him, and becomes the lady of the grand house, which just happened to have been her own house, before the boom. Of course, it was a romance story largely composed in my own mind—but the facts were coming together. "That does shift the perspective a bit. Anything you can tell about her personally? More details?"

"You don't get much sense of someone's personality from a census. But reading between the lines, I have some guesses . . ." She trailed off.

"Well? What?"

"It's not about Mary, exactly. But her family—her father, specifically. By the end of the war, he seems to be gone from the house, with just Mary and her mother, Annelise, running the place."

"Where's the father?"

"I found a death certificate. Cause of death is given as 'acute mania.'"

"Mania?" I furrowed my brow. "Like what? He got so excited, he ran into a wall?"

"No, not exactly. It can mean a few things—medical terminology was a little fuzzy in Victorian times, and certain terms were politely used to avoid saying certain other terms. Mania might mean mental illness, alcoholism, DTs. Hard to say. But it's *where* he died that's the kicker." She seemed to pause for effect, but I heard a shuffling of papers in the background, so perhaps she was only finding her reference. "Clear Brook. Mary's father died in 1872 in the Clear Brook Hospital for Mental Diseases, a little ways west of here. It seems to have been a pretty big place. I couldn't find any records about his time there—there was a fire in the '20s—but the time line seems to indicate he went in there when Mary was a teenager and never came back."

"Oh, that's terrible." I put my hand to my mouth. "So it was just the two of them, Mary and her mother, running the place?"

"For some years, it looks like. That's probably why they started taking in wounded soldiers—subsistence farming was pretty tough with no man in the house."

"Mary didn't have any brothers who could help?"

"Nope. It looks like she was the only child. Unusual, for that era."

"And then Henry came along. I'm glad they found each other."

"Me too." She sighed and didn't immediately say anything else. She sounded tired, and that was how I felt too. I walked back to the door I'd come through and angled my head toward the kitchen. Morgan was in there taking measurements with a long tape and furiously scribbling into his notepad. I was glad to see the project was still on his mind.

"Listen, Carroll, I'm beat. You want to meet up and eat lunch?"

"Capital idea. My eyes are glazing over anyway. Shall I meet you at the mansion? I can grab something for us on the way over—unless you've magically installed a mini-fridge stocked with pop and cold sandwiches since I last saw you."

"What do you think?"

"Very well, then. How about I stop by Ted's lunch counter and get us some burgers?"

"Perfect. Or—no, wait. That fast food from last night is still too much with me. Do you think Ted does salads?"

"He might have . . . coleslaw? Or baked beans. Is that a vegetable?"

"Do your best to find some vitamins on the menu. Really, though, I'm famished—whatever you show up with, I'm eating it. And Morgan's here too. Just get a pile of food, and we'll figure it out." I hung up and looked around the elegant dining room I stood in. How much of this had been Mary's creation—a chance to make a beautiful place as an adult, after a strained and impoverished childhood? Had she relished the finials and fine draperies, or were her tastes more modest? And how long had she gotten to live in this jewel box before she died and left Henry here with his money and his inventions, all alone?

10

I resolved to make some phone calls while I waited for Carroll to appear. I walked to the far end of the dining room, skimming my finger through a fine layer of dust on the deep mantelpiece, over which an enormous mirror rose, gilded around its perimeter and reflecting darkly the other side of the room. Several stuffed velvet chairs sat by the windows, but I walked around them to stand just behind the curtains, pulling one aside to see the afternoon sun baking the grass outside. I dialed Ryan's number. I wanted to talk particulars with him: who would have keys to this place, who could write checks, the status of our non-profit application—all the details swirling in my mind, just behind the day's larger drama. And I should probably tell him about that too. I wondered if a special board meeting was necessary.

He didn't pick up. Maybe he was in a meeting, or

maybe he psychically sensed my administrative questions coming his way, and ducked. I left him a message, quickly saying I wanted to talk when he had a chance. He *had* asked me about dinner this week, after all.

Next I called the number for the local paper, hoping to confer with Frances. A male voice answered, sounding very young and not terribly chipper.

"Hi, uh, *Asheboro Gazette.*"

"Hello, this is Kate Hamilton. I'm trying to reach Frances." A long pause ensued. "Is she in?" I heard a whirr in the background, suggesting a scanner or an industrial copy machine.

"Frances . . . ? Oh, you mean Mrs. Carter? Yeah, just a sec." He put the receiver down with a clunk, and I could half hear a conversation across the room. I looked out at the grass on the lawn, crisping in the sun. *Should I hire a groundskeeper?* Frances picked up.

"Kate! Oh, I'm so pleased to hear from you. That was Troy, one of my interns—isn't he charming?" I sensed a tinge of sarcasm.

"Hello, Frances. Charming? I guess you could call it that."

"Well, he and his young cohort keep me from having to learn graphic design software, and he's marginally house-trained, so I'm happy to have him around. Plus, they're digitizing the paper's archives, so everything will be available online and searchable. One of these kids is even talking about getting into *metadata*—isn't it thrilling? I can't say I know what that is, but thrilling nonetheless. Now, how are things going over there at the estate?"

"Well, things are a little odd, to be honest. I'll tell you about that later. But I found a contractor, so that's something. Morgan Wheeler—he's here now actually, taking some measurements."

"Morgan . . . did you say Wheeler? He's leading the charge? I think I know him—or his family."

"You do? Wow, small world."

"You might think so, dear. But keep in mind, young people of your generation and a bit older have been moving away from this area in droves, finding work elsewhere, never coming back. But before that? Folks stayed put. This town used to have a lot more to recommend it. The Barton factory provided jobs for a lot of able-bodied men in town, and the stores on Main Street used to be something. Essentials, but also gifts, tailored clothing, handcrafts. My mother was one of a small collective of women who operated a sewing and quilting supply shop not far from the *Gazette*'s offices. They passed on the skills of many generations to young women growing up in Asheboro."

"But not anymore. That's sad. What does that have to do with Morgan?"

"I can't say I know the man personally. But his family's been in the area quite a long time. You hear names go past enough, they start to seem familiar. Memories are long in quiet places—old loves, old feuds, they tend to get handed down through generations." She trailed off. This sounded a bit ominous to me, and I wasn't sure what to make of it. After a few seconds, I spoke.

"Right. Anyway, I was hoping we could get together and look through some old copies of the *Gazette* to see if there's more about Henry Barton—or Mary. We've got a bit of a lead, but if there's more, I want to see it."

"What are you hoping to learn?"

"Well, we now know Mary was from Asheboro and grew up in the farmhouse that Henry remodeled into what is now the mansion. Apparently, she stayed there with her mother after her dad went into an asylum, and the two of them tended to wounded soldiers at the end of the war. But I've never seen an obituary for her, or anything personal. What was she like? Is there something like a social register? Mentions of the couple in the gossip pages?"

"Dear, have you been to Asheboro? We don't have gossip pages."

"Ha, right—but what about in Victorian times? Do you think Henry and Mary ever made appearances? Or hosted events?" I was grasping at straws, but hopefully.

"We can always look. I'll have Troy pull from the archives. When are you thinking—1880s?"

"We think Mary died in the early 1880s, so maybe more like the early 1870s?"

"I'll have him pull what we have. Is there anything else, dear?"

"No. Thanks, Frances—I'll try to stop in tomorrow to look at those."

"I'll see you then, Kate."

I hung up and walked back to the kitchen. Morgan had produced a large sheet of drafting paper from somewhere and was sketching out a scale model of the room, with copious notes around the margins. He looked up and smiled.

"Kate, you're back. Any news?"

I filled him in on the new details about Mary, and the approximate plan for lunch. He was glad to hear of the imminent arrival of food, but otherwise sounded energetic, glad to be in the thick of the kind of work he clearly loved. It occurred to me that I didn't know what the process would look like moving forward.

"Morgan, now that you're on board to work on this house, I realize you'll need some help. Do you have a crew you usually work with, people who know different trades?"

"I don't, not exactly. But I have a handful of contacts. I'll make some calls today, see who's available for the next few months."

"That would be great. I'd like it if we had some consistency—keep the number of new people tromping through here to a minimum, before it becomes a public place."

"I hear what you are saying. And it's best for the quality of work to have the same few hands on deck throughout. It's not everybody who wants to work on old houses, much less knows how to, but I'll see who I can get."

"Thanks, Morgan." I meant it. It was a real comfort to have found someone else who liked this place and cared about its details the way I did. I strolled over to the hole in the wall, a new ominous presence in the room, even without the century-old dead body in it. "Did they find anything else of interest in here? Besides . . . that guy?"

"Nope. I guess whoever left him there didn't feel like leaving a cedar trunk filled with winter clothes in the under-stairs storage. They'd just have to come back for it later, eh?"

"That's true." I gazed into the dark space in the wall. It didn't look like much: a set of rustic wooden steps, bowing slightly in the center, with no railing. How long were they in use, before this grand house grew up around them? Centuries? The floor below them was made of long wood planks, a bit dusty, with—white pebbles in one corner? I stepped closer.

"What's this? These . . . stones?" Morgan looked up from his work and came over, crouching down next to me. We both squinted into the hole in the wall. A few small, white . . . things rested on the floor beneath the stairs. Morgan withdrew a pocket flashlight from the bib of his overalls and pointed it at the objects.

"Huh. The crew didn't see anything in here. And that's because . . . well, there isn't anything, really. Except those." I leaned forward and extended a hand, picking up one of the objects. It was about the size of a pea, very pale beige, and had a slight ridge running around its circumference.

"I think it's a . . . cherry pit?"

Morgan looked closer as I turned the tiny object between my fingers. "I suppose that could be. Now what do you think that means?"

"I don't know. Maybe nothing. To be honest, I might be imagining a wild significance to everything around me in my state of hunger. But . . . I'll hang on to it for now." I slipped the thing into my pocket. Morgan nodded at me gravely, laid one finger beside his nose in a joking spy gesture, then turned back to his work at the kitchen table, whistling faintly. I resolved to wait for Carroll outside.

The day was fine and bright as I stepped out onto the front porch. I looked to my left, where the structure wrapped around the building, creating a whole extra room in the open air. I wondered if Henry and Mary ever took their afternoon tea out here, the sinking sun casting floral shapes against the outer wall through the decorative brackets. Had they sat in wicker chairs, reading aloud to each other—George Eliot, the Brontës? Or was Henry, being business-minded, more of a John Stuart Mill fan? I found myself wishing they had kept diaries; even with the abundance of physical objects left in the house, it was so hard to get a feel for the texture of daily life in this place.

I craned my neck a little farther to get a view of the driveway, but saw no car approaching. Noting a slight cover of clouds appearing over the sun, I decided to walk the grounds of the estate as I waited. Carroll could always call my cell when she arrived. I walked along the side of the house and then strode onto the broad lawn behind it, taking in the vista stretching before me. The carriage house stood about fifty feet beyond and to my right, and the crest of an enormous chestnut tree rose just behind it, alone in its great height.

Carroll's car horn jolted me from my contemplation of the grounds, cheekily bleating out the "shave and a haircut, two bits" rhythm. *Very funny, Carroll.* I turned and walked back toward the front of the house and found her peeping around the corner at me, holding a bag of food that looked as large as a carry-on suitcase. I grinned and followed her into the house.

We took up residence in the kitchen—which seemed like the room with the fewest precious objects we might get stains on—and I told Carroll all the details of our morning. Carroll nodded as she produced from the greasy paper bag a miraculous bounty of grilled chicken sandwiches, spinach salads, coleslaw with sesame-peanut dressing, and even small tubs of faintly spicy creamed corn; I felt a new respect for Ted's humble luncheonette in downtown Asheboro. Morgan ate quickly and excused himself to make phone calls; I was glad he was taking our time line seriously and trying to assemble a team as soon as possible.

"So there was nothing else in the staircase?" Carroll asked, gesturing with the remaining half of her sandwich.

"What, like a murder weapon? I'm afraid not—no candlestick, no vial of poison, no bloody knife. Judging by the injuries the ME described, it seems like he just . . . fell down the stairs."

"And then somebody built a new wall around him. Nothing suspicious there."

"Right. Now, as to the matter of whether he fell on his own or was pushed—that's an open question." I wondered what could have brought violence into this idyllic setting—a business deal gone wrong? An old enemy, returning to make good on a grudge? Or a madman, come howling out of the night from the woods beyond the property line? I crunched into a spear of orange bell pepper, lightly dressed in vinaigrette. "But I did find something in there, after everybody left." I produced the small round object from my pocket. Carroll furrowed her brow, and then her eyes widened.

"It looks like a fruit pit!" she chirped.

"That's what I thought."

She wrinkled her forehead in thought, and then her eyes popped open and she turned to face me directly. "I'm remembering now, in the stacks of business correspondence from Henry's estate, there was a whole pile of household receipts—handwritten, of course. A pretty interesting inventory of stuff coming into the house. Tools, horse and carriage equipment . . ." She seemed momentarily lost in the recollection.

"And?" I demanded, polishing off the creamed corn and barely restraining myself from licking the container.

"One of the first things he brought in, once they were flush with shovel money, was a big shipment of fruit trees to be planted on the property. Including, if I remember right, half a dozen cherry trees. Maybe that's where your pit came from."

"Huh." I tried to picture the grounds of the estate, where I had just been strolling, lined with the cheerful stalks of young trees. And what else might Henry have put in? Vegetables, an herb garden, leafy ornamentals—a bounteous array of flora, to ensure his beloved Mary would never want again? Suddenly, I felt a little silly. The whole romance of Henry and Mary was an invention of my own mind. What had they really been like as people, as a couple? I had to admit I didn't know. It was just as possible that Henry, the shrewd businessman, had been a domestic tyrant, keeping his poor wife cooped up in their lonely mansion on the outskirts of town, never taking her to the music halls and playhouses in the nearby city. Maybe he forced her to do all their washing by hand, to save money. I shuddered at the thought, never having ironed a shirt in my adult life. But that thought reminded me: Weren't there servants' quarters in the attic?

I turned to Carroll, who had balled up our empty food wrappers, placed them tidily back into the bag they'd come in, and was now squatting in front of the hole in the wall, as Morgan and I had been doing earlier.

"Compelling, isn't it?" I asked. "Who knew that thing was there?"

"Somebody did, but they aren't talking."

"Hey, are you suitably refreshed by that delicious lunch? If we've both got our strength back, there's something I want to show you in the attic."

Carroll turned to me and grinned. "I thought you'd never ask."

11

Carroll and I trooped up the grand front staircase to the second-floor landing, then rounded the corner, shuffled past several closed bedroom doors, and approached the attic entrance. I extracted from my pocket the extensive ring of keys that came with the house, and when I unlocked the old wooden door, it immediately swung open. We both gazed up into an ascending blackness.

"No light up here?" Carroll asked.

"A couple of bare bulbs hanging from cords," I said. "Remember, when we had the high school football team load all the Barton documents out of here and into the public library, how we had to have several people stationed up there as flashlight holders so nobody would fall and break their neck? It's not wired for much, still—and I can't say that's high on the agenda. I don't imagine we'll want the public to view this part of the house as an exhibit."

"Depends on how you angle it," she replied. "It might be an interesting reference, especially for kids, who don't remember a time when a lot of people—even middle-class people—regularly employed servants in their homes. Very *Upstairs, Downstairs*, don't you think?"

"I guess so. Except it's not a grand estate with dozens of servants, just two or three people, we think. Plus, the maid's bedroom is in the attic, not the lower level, so it's more of an *Upstairs, Upstairs* situation." I fell silent, and we both stared up into the dark passage. "You know more of this history than I do. Was it customary then for servants to be living in people's homes?"

"For wealthy people, yes," Carroll said. "Although the quarters generally weren't very appealing. After all, female servants were supposed to be working from dawn to dusk and beyond. You know, emptying the slops, cleaning out the ashes in the fireplaces and starting new fires in the morning, preparing meals, cleaning up—which wasn't exactly easy in the past. Whoever lived up there might have gotten off work on Sunday mornings to attend church, but otherwise, it was all labor. So the bottom line was, she didn't need more than some blankets to sleep on, and probably no light—she'd have to bring her own candle. People made do on a lot less back then—especially if they didn't have Barton-level wealth, which was basically everybody." She took her phone out of her pocket and turned on the flashlight function. A little white circle of light appeared on the dark steps in front of us. "But enough talk. Let's get up there!"

The stairs were steep, made of unpolished wood, and creaked as we climbed. Once we got to the top, I had to reorient myself—besides standing in near-total darkness, I hadn't been up here in a while, and I'd lost my bearings. Shafts of white light came in through the dormer windows at the front and sides of the house, but they were only bright patches peering into utter blackness. I couldn't make out much.

Suddenly, Carroll pulled the string hanging at the center of the ceiling, illuminating the single bare bulb that hung there, and the attic was bathed in a dusty gold glow. She pointed toward the gable at the back end of the house. "I think that's the door there. When we first came in here, I assumed it was only a storage room of some sort, but if I remember right, it's a rudimentary bedroom."

Finding the door locked, I took out my ring of keys once more. I was fumbling among a dozen or so, my body casting a shadow over them as I stood facing the door, when a thump came from below us. And then another. Footsteps. Carroll and I both startled, looked at each other, and peered down the dark stairway. We couldn't quite see the bottom from where we stood.

"Hello?" My voice was a croak.

"Hello, ladies? Are you up there?" The cheerful figure of Morgan Wheeler bounded up the tall steps, change and small tools audibly jangling in his pockets. "I thought I'd lost you. Taking a look at the upper floors, are we?"

"Hello, Morgan. Yes, we were just going to check out the maid's room. I haven't seen it in a while. Now, if I could only find the right key. Was this locked before? I don't remember having to open it last time." I felt a prickly annoyance rise in me. It was stuffy on the third floor, and I was beginning to sweat under my clothes.

"Don't worry about that," Morgan said, fishing some tools from his pocket. He inserted a thin metal rod into the lock on the door, then another at an angle to the first, and after a bit of jiggling, the lock popped, and the door swung open with a drawn-out creak.

There was no lighting inside the room beyond a small window in the far wall, allowing in some dusty sunlight. A row of hooks hung on the wall to our right, presumably for clothes, and there was, too, a tin basin that might have been used for a rather minimalist sponge bath. A bed frame with a sadly thin mattress stood along the left wall, and there was a battered Bible on the floor next to the bed. A chamber pot protruded slightly from under the far end of the bed. And that was all. No light, no heat, one window, and a coating of dust on every surface.

"Henry wasn't particularly generous with the hired help," I commented.

"It could have been his wife who dealt with a servant," Carroll replied. "Hard to say right now; I haven't come across any specifics on the help in this household. But honestly? This was probably as good as it got in those days. This place wasn't exactly Downton Abbey."

"Hardly," I said. "Well, at least there isn't a body lying on the bed. One a week is plenty."

"Right," she said. "Let's not make a habit of that." She walked to the end of the small room, pointing her phone's flashlight here and there. She lifted a corner of the thin mattress with one hand, and, seeing nothing under it, let it fall back to the frame. A small puff of dust issued as it landed. She produced a pair of thin cotton gloves from her pocket—the mark of a true librarian if I had ever seen it—and put them on, then picked up the Bible from the floor. It looked heavily dog-eared. She flipped through it carefully and then opened it to the page marked by the crumbling ribbon placeholder. She paused, and the room felt heavy as she read.

"Whoever lived in this room underlined in pencil this little passage from Isaiah. *Also I heard the voice of the Lord, saying, Whom shall I send, and who will go for us? Then said I, here am I, send me.* What does that mean?"

"I don't know," I answered. "I've never been much for Bible study, honestly."

"It means you don't always choose the work that comes to you," Morgan volunteered. "But when a task is presented, you go where you are called. At least, that's how I hear it."

"I can understand that," I said. In fact, it sounded a lot like my whole sojourn here in Asheboro. "Are you a religious man, Morgan?"

"*Spiritual* might be the better word," he replied. "Quaker."

"I see." Carroll leafed through the book a bit more and didn't seem to find anything of interest. She replaced it carefully in its spot, a crisp, dustless rectangle on the floor. Perhaps that spot hadn't had a particular significance in the life of this room's inhabitant, but when something's been sitting in one place for a century, that place can seem like hallowed ground. The sun was turning gold and sinking outside the small round window at the end of the room. We all looked at it for a moment.

"I should head home," Morgan said. "The missus requested fried chicken for dinner, and I am but a humble servant." He smiled and began to exit, but turned back to face me. "I assume you won't be needing me in the morning, what with the police investigation. I can put together my estimate and some rough ideas about what to do with the kitchen, and when you get the go-ahead from the police, we can recommence, what say?"

I smiled back at him, grateful that Morgan was still on board after our rather morbid morning, and that he seemed as dedicated to this project as I'd hoped our contractor would be.

"That makes sense," I replied. "I think we've all had a long day, and we can regroup tomorrow or the day after. I don't think Detective Reynolds will have any reason to hold us up. But I'll be in touch. And please let me know when you've got the crew lined up, so we can arrange a walk-through of the site as soon as it's cleared."

"Will do, Miz Hamilton." He tipped his faded green ball cap to me and to Carroll and then all but bounded down the attic stairs. Carroll and I remained standing in the maid's tiny bedroom a bit longer, both of us seemingly uncertain as to the next step. Finally, we walked back out into the attic's main space, and I locked the door behind us, though there wasn't much of value to protect in there.

"So, what have we learned here?" I asked, turning to Carroll. She gave a little shrug, casting her eyes around the mostly empty attic space.

"Well, there's a bedroom, and someone lived there. Someone who subsisted on very minimal means inside this lavish house, and who was perhaps religious. Although, you know what . . ." She trailed off, looking back toward the closed bedroom door in thought.

"No, Carroll, I don't know. What?"

"Why wouldn't she take that Bible? That would've been the only book many people owned, back then—working people anyway, not highly educated, not people of many possessions. The clothes are gone, which makes sense, and I didn't see any keepsakes, but why didn't she take the Bible?"

"Maybe she left in a hurry," I said.

"Huh. Maybe."

"Is there any chance that man in the staircase was the person who lived in there?"

"I doubt it. It was much more common for maids or other women servants to occupy the upper quarters in a house of this size. She'd have to be up at dawn and working long past the bedtime of the house's owners, so it was to everyone's advantage to have her on-site up here. The servants' stairs in this house probably saw a lot of traffic: hauling water, laundry, supplies. I bet she was up and down all day. A hard life, for sure. So, no—I think if the guy in the wall were a servant, he would more likely have been quartered in the rooms above the carriage house."

"I guess that makes sense. But we don't know who he is yet, in any case. He didn't look expensively dressed, if that's any hint. He seemed to have a beard. Was that typical for people of a certain social rank back then?"

"This may shock you, but historical facial hair is not actually an area of my expertise, Kate." She smiled at me in the dim light. "But I've seen illustrations and photos of various different types of men in history, and I will say that *lots* of them had beards. The beards on rich guys were just . . . better combed. But if this guy was killed, and if there was any sort of struggle, he might naturally look a bit unkempt. And thus any beard-grooming clues would have been lost to history."

"I suppose so. Did you find anything in your research identifying the help in this house?"

"Not yet, no. I'll dig some more tomorrow."

"Good." I struggled to think of what else to ask. My eyes were perhaps glazing over a bit. "Well, shall we call it a day? I'm exhausted."

"Fine by me."

Carroll pulled the cord in the ceiling, and the room went dark. We stalked back down the steep stairs, tracing along the walls with our hands for balance. Once back on the second floor, I locked the attic door, and we descended to ground level. Carroll took my keys and stepped out to wash up in the carriage house, which stood empty with Josh back in the city for a few days.

Still feeling a bit groggy—that garret bedroom was not fabulously well ventilated—I strode into the house's front parlor. What did we know? Someone lived up there, two people lived in the rest of the house, and there had been a dead guy walled up in the kitchen. *Clear as mud*, as my mother liked to say. I ran my hand along the arm of a sofa in one corner of the room, feeling the dense pile of its fabric shift under my fingers. I stepped out of the parlor and exited the house onto the front porch. I paused there, closing my eyes tightly and wishing for a wicker chair and a bit of ease to end the day, but nothing appeared. I saw Carroll approaching on the lawn, striding through the shaggy grass—there was no one to cut it lately, with Josh's term as caretaker completed. Carroll stooped to examine the thin stalks of native flowers here and there, and crouched over low patches of wild strawberries, the fruit as tiny as pearl buttons. I tried to picture that same lawn crisscrossed

with rows of fruit trees, their branches bounteously full
and leaning toward the ground, toward the reaching hands
of . . .

Then I remembered that there had been no children
here—none who survived, anyway. What had happened to
them, the small, lost people now resting with their parents
in the far back lawn of the property? And how would we
sum up the complex life of this house to show it to the visiting public? Carroll finally got close enough that I could
see the handkerchief she clutched daintily in her hands,
the corners gathered up to contain something inside.

"Did you know there's a grapevine out behind the carriage house? I never noticed before. This house sure is full
of surprises."

"You are right about that."

"I'm tired, and I need a real shower. Let's blow this Pop-
sicle stand!"

"Gladly."

We locked up, piled back into my car, and headed into
town.

12

Carroll and I passed an uneventful evening at the B&B, scavenging a light dinner of sliced cucumbers bathed in the last dregs of several different flavors of salad dressing, along with cheese and crackers. High living, indeed. I fell into bed before 10:00 p.m., drifting off while thinking about that tiny bedroom in the Barton attic and the life of its inhabitant. I startled awake when my phone rang just after seven the next morning.

"Kate, it's Morgan. Hope I didn't catch you too early. Got to rise ahead of the heat around here, as I'm sure you know." I scratched my head, rose creakily from the bed. How did servants manage going up and down those stairs all day?

"Oh, hi, Morgan. No, it's fine. What's up?"

"I've got some workers for you. I think it'll be a good team." He paused briefly. Did he want me to whoop in

congratulations, or was he a bit uncertain about his statement? I couldn't tell. Also, I needed some coffee if I was
going to have civilized conversations with anyone today.

"That's great, Morgan. Can we meet up with them tomorrow, tentatively? I need to get word from Detective
Reynolds that it's okay to proceed with work on the house."

"Sure. I'll let them know. I got the estimate typed up
last night, and I'll email it to you. There're a couple of good
sites for salvaged antique parts and fixtures too—I'll send
you the links. And I know a guy—no online presence, God
bless him—but we can go check out his warehouse sometime."

"That sounds amazing, Morgan. My, you work fast,
don't you?" I thought about what I'd done last night—
mostly a haze of snacking and dozing off in an armchair,
before actually hauling myself upstairs to go to bed.

"They say idle hands are the devil's workshop, Miz
Hamilton."

"I guess that's true. You're an example for us all, Mr.
Wheeler. Steadfast American industry!" I was perhaps feeling a bit loopy in my pre-coffee mentality.

"Well, I wouldn't go that far. But I'm glad to be on the
job. Let's say tomorrow if I don't hear otherwise from you.
Have a good day, Kate."

"Thanks, Morgan." I hung up and stared into the space
above my head. There was a slightly gaudy ceiling medal-
lion at the center of the room, a decorative oval with inter-
locking floral motifs. I wondered if it was original to this

house or if Cordelia had added it as a way to class up the joint. I lay down and drifted off again, thinking of decorative finishes.

I awoke what felt like minutes later to another phone call. The clock said it was 8:30, so I must have really fallen back asleep. It was Morgan again. He sounded oddly strained.

"Kate? Sorry to call you again so soon. Listen . . ." He paused. Was something wrong? He was usually quick with words. "Can we meet up today to look at the job, rather than tomorrow?"

"Sure, Morgan. I have some time. Is everything all right?"

"Yes . . . mostly. It will be fine. One of my contractors is just balking at the wait. I guess he wants to get going, or he has some commitment tomorrow that he didn't see fit to mention when we first spoke." There was a slight edge in his voice, which I wasn't expecting—although I had to remind myself that we had met just a few days ago. I thought I had a read on who Morgan was—but did I? I certainly felt like I could trust him, so far.

"Okay, no problem. What time do you want to meet?"

"Say around three today? I do apologize for the short notice. It doesn't have to be long. We can just give them a general impression of the job."

"That works for me."

"Much obliged, Kate." He hung up quickly. *Well, that was odd. Is this too good to be true? I thought the body in*

the wall was our main problem, but . . . I stood and began
to dress and think of coffee downstairs, hoping to escape
those troubling thoughts. *Get out of your head, Kate.* I
needed to keep moving.

❧

Arriving back at the mansion that afternoon, I stepped
into the cool front parlor, shaded by its thick drapes. I
opened an east-facing window to let in the faint breeze. I
still had more than an hour to kill before the meeting with
Morgan and his crew, so I sat down and looked around
me. I wondered if Henry and Mary had done this very
thing—passing the idle afternoon hours together, sitting
on the plush sofas and wingback chairs. I looked around
the room, and as my gaze passed by the door that led out
to the main hall and the library on the other side, the
tall bookshelves caught my eye. I had never really stopped
to look at Henry's collection. Not being terribly literary
myself, I figured his choices of books wouldn't mean all
that much to me. Should I have hired a literary consultant, to get some insight on the house's intellectual life?
I made a mental note. But now my interest was piqued,
and I stood and walked into the library, pulled out the first
book my hand landed on, and sat to read. It was a novel
by Anthony Trollope, a Victorian author about whom I
knew exactly nothing. I read the first few pages. The story

concerned the lives of several civil servants, their loves and professional pursuits, and . . .

I must have drifted off, because a loud rapping on the front door was the next thing I heard. I stood and replaced the book on the shelf, wondering if this 1850-something edition was perhaps worth real money, and smoothed my clothes as I walked to the door. Out on the porch, I found a woman, about my age or a little younger, dressed in a black T-shirt, work pants, and boots, a dense ring of keys dangling from a carabiner on her belt loop. She was staring up at the underside of the porch roof, which was painted pale blue—a Victorian custom, to mimic the sky above. As I opened the front door, she looked down to meet my gaze and smiled.

"Hi. Are you Kate?" She stuck out a hand. "Bethany Wallace. I handle the wiring. Morgan said to be here at three, but I guess I'm early. Nice to meet you."

"You too," I said, shaking her hand. My gaze followed where hers had been, and we both looked up at the porch roof in silence for a moment.

"It's cool, right?" I said. "Looks like the sky. That's some kind of Victorian tradition."

"Well, it is and it isn't," she said, still looking up, her mouth wrinkling into a smile.

"What do you mean?"

"I can't say as to your original builder's specific history and intentions in choosing this color, but the tradition of blue porch ceilings actually comes from Gullah culture. They called it 'haint blue.' My grandmother's people were Gullah, from West Africa way back when, and she told me about this when I was a kid. You can see the influence more as you go farther south—she grew up in Georgia— but the traditions pop up all over. Like right here. Gullah people believe that evil spirits can't cross bodies of water, so they paint porches blue, sometimes front windows and doors, and the spirits are supposed to get confused and pass on by. My sister lives over on the other side of town, by the grocery store—she and I painted her front door blue a few years ago when our grandma passed, as a tribute to her." She fell silent, both of us staring up at the peeling blue paint. "I wonder if there were some bad things in this house that needed keeping away."

I looked at her. She didn't seem to mean anything serious by the remark, and it remained to be seen how much of this house's history she was aware of. I thought of Mary's three lost babies, resting quietly in the family plot out in the back field—to say nothing of the dead man in the staircase. But I'd explain that part when the rest of the crew got here.

Soon two more trucks appeared at the far end of the long driveway, the one behind driving slightly too close to the one in front, as if anxious to get where it was going, though they were both perfectly on time for our appointment. They parked, and Morgan stepped out of the first truck; two men emerged from the second, the larger one slapping the smaller on the shoulder as they walked— whether in a gesture of comradeship or impatience, I couldn't quite tell.

When they reached the porch, I beckoned all of them into the house, where Morgan introduced the new faces. The larger of the two men looked mildly peeved, although maybe that was just the resting appearance of his face.

"Kate, this is Steve, our plumbing lead, and Lars, his assistant. It looks like you've met Bethany—she'll be our head electrician. We'll have more of a crew when we get going, but I thought these folks should come through first, since they're leading the charge." The peeved-looking man stuck his hand out first, stepping forward and angling his body past the others to face me.

"Steve Abernathy," he said, staring hard at the space between my eyes. "This is Lars, my little brother. I'm teaching him everything I know. Nice place you've got here." He looked around the room appraisingly, then past my head toward the kitchen at the end of the hall. He was a stocky man, a little older than I was—probably early forties—with sandy hair and a pink complexion. The other man, thin and reedy, sheepishly put out a hand, and I shook it without saying a word. He had a curious look and was less pink in the face than his brother; he nodded and smiled as we shook hands.

"Hi, Steve. Hi, Lars. Nice to meet you. Yes, I just met

Bethany a few minutes ago. She was just telling me something I never knew about the porch ceiling—"

"Well, well," Steve broke in, "the electric lady's an expert on that stuff, isn't she?"

Bethany smiled at him, but the smile had a bite to it.
"Steve here had never worked with a woman electrician
before we met. Isn't that right, Steve? But I can hardly
blame him—not too many of us around here. I'm always
telling the guys I work with that small hands are better for
feeding wires through small spaces." She shot a jesting
glance toward Steve, who didn't seem to get the joke.
"Anyway, I'm glad to be on the job. Thanks for meeting us
on such short notice."

Steve snorted, and then spoke again. "Yep, we had to
get in right away and see what's what. The kitchen's this
way?" He gestured with his chin toward the back of the
house and started walking that way before anyone could
answer. Bethany raised her eyebrows at him, but followed
him toward the kitchen, looking around her with interest
at the details of the rooms. Lars drifted after them like a
boat in tow. Morgan stayed behind.

"You said you'd worked with these three before?" I
asked when they were out of earshot. "Can you trust them
to respect the building as it is? I mean, even I know it's
tricky to feed wires through walls without tearing the walls
open, much less make sure that pipes won't leak, but I
don't want them to look for shortcuts. Or at least, can I trust
they'll make the holes invisible before they leave?"

"Don't worry—I'll keep an eye on them." He looked like he wanted to believe what he was saying, but wasn't sure.

"Did we ever settle on a schedule? I seem to remember that the plan you sketched out for me involved totally rewiring the house first, and *then* getting to the kitchen."

"Yes, that will be necessary, just to bring the place up to code. Let's put it this way: it would be possible to get it all done in, say, three weeks, if you were willing to hire a lot of extra people and pay them overtime for long hours. But the rest of the house wouldn't be ready for the public by then, would it?"

I shook my head. "When I started all this, I was hoping for a splashy fall opening. Now maybe I should start thinking about Christmas."

"Everybody loves a holiday!" Morgan said, which I interpreted as *It's definitely going to take at least six months.* I sighed.

"It is what it is, I guess," I said ruefully. I tried to turn my thoughts around, to face what was possible in the moment. "Well, let's show them the place, eh?"

"Yes, ma'am," Morgan said, smiling as he removed his cap.

Once we were all gathered in the kitchen, I quickly outlined my original plan and the changes that had occurred over the past couple of days—acknowledging the large hole in one wall, and why it was there. Steve, Bethany, and Lars all stared at it, and Bethany laughed quietly at the strangeness of it. I wrapped up my introduction, cautiously watching their faces for reactions.

"So, I want to preserve the style and ambiance of the house, but I also want to be able to use it in the modern world. I know it'll be a juggling act for you, trying to maintain the best of the old while still making it functional, but I hope you'll do your best. If you run into any problems, talk to me. Now, you know better than I do what you need to look for, so I'll leave you to walk through for a while and make any notes you need. You might want to start with the basement, where pretty much everything is exposed. By the time you get to the attic, there's only one hanging bulb, so I hope you have some flashlights. Sound okay?"

Everybody nodded, so I directed the workers to the cellar stairs. As they descended, a thought seemed to occur to Morgan, and he turned to me.

"You planning to leave the staircase in the kitchen there?"

"I don't know." I had been mulling it over privately and honestly didn't know the right answer yet. "It's interesting and it's creepy at the same time. I'm not sure I'd want to live with it in my own home, knowing what had happened, but this is going to be a public building, and the story might appeal to people. You think you'd want that extra three feet of space for the kitchen?"

"Not necessarily. Kitchens were for servants in those days, so they weren't always large. There had to be room for a big table in the middle, because that was the main working surface. Of course, you could pull a stunt with it—install a retractable panel over the staircase, push a button, and give the crowd a before-and-after view of the room. But that's a little silly. Anyway, you've got some options to think over here. Do you want to keep the layout?"

"I think so, unless you tell me there's a good reason not to. What about lighting? Nowadays, we're accustomed to recessed spotlights everywhere you might be working in the space, but I assume things weren't like that in 1880?"

"No, they weren't. Even for the rich, there were limitations. Your Henry worked with light bulbs, didn't he?"

"Among other things. He was an industrious kind of guy." But enough chitchat—we were supposed to be doing business. "Morgan, give it to me straight: Do you think your people can handle this renovation?"

"I wouldn't have brought them here if I didn't. I've worked with these two before—Steve and Bethany, I mean. I can't say I know Lars well, but he seems to have a good head on his shoulders. Anyway, they know my standards. They'll bring in a few other apprentices, but I'll keep an eye on them too."

A personal recommendation was always encouraging, and I didn't think Morgan would lie to me. "Do you think they'll start with the basement?"

"Most likely. They need to map out where the main circuits will go first. Would you happen to have the original plans for the house, at the time of its rebuilding?"

"I'll see if I can find any—I don't know how much

Henry did himself, or if it was all done in one continuous operation. Or who he hired to work on it. I'll ask Carroll to check."

Morgan smiled. "Don't worry—we'll figure it out. When do you want us to start?"

"As soon as you can, I guess. Do you have a contract?"

"I'll put something together. Don't worry."

So unlike Baltimore! I thought. I was used to looking out for sharks, budget inflators, and corner-cutters, so this exhibition of small-town trustworthiness was almost confusing.

"Thank you, Morgan. Should we shake on it?" The idea seemed both old-fashioned and appropriate—Asheboro really was a little world unto itself. We shook hands.

So, one small step accomplished. Having said that to myself, of course I realized there were a lot of other issues, things I hadn't even contemplated tackling yet. What did our insurance cover, with these new people coming through the house? Should I have Ryan look at any contract before signing it—or even write up the contracts himself? Would Morgan know where to find vintage fabrics and such, or did he have a counterpart who handled interiors? Did I need to approve each design choice as it came up—or did I need a new research consultant for this?

Calm down, Kate, a voice said, and I realized it was my own. Out loud. Luckily, Morgan had wandered off down the basement steps after our handshake, so he didn't have to hear me giving myself a pep talk. I continued, just for the heck of it. *One thing, and then the next. Make a list. Ask someone. And remember—you can't move the mountain in a day.*

It was oddly comforting. I shifted my weight forward and proceeded straight ahead to the next task at hand.

13

Steve, Lars, Bethany, and Morgan poked around the house for the next two-plus hours, longer than I had expected for this first walk-through. I was getting a bit tired, but I was also glad to see the team investigating the place so thoroughly. I mostly let them be, pacing in the library and making my own lists of tasks for the days and months to come. The light turned gold and began to fade in the hushed parlors. After a while, I stepped out onto the front porch for some air, only to see Carroll's car wending its way down the long drive leading to the house. I approached once she had parked and stepped out.

"Hey, stranger. Had enough of primary sources for one day?"

"You said it. I had to get out of there. What's going on here?"

"Morgan and I were planning to meet up with his crew

and look at the house tomorrow, but he called and changed it to today. They're in there now. It's been a while, actually, and I don't know how much more day I have in me."

"You want me to go in there and check their progress? I can pretend I'm the boss-lady foreman and tell them to get the lead out." She looked slightly giddy at the prospect.

"I don't know if all that is necessary, but feel free to check in and meet the new people. I didn't talk to them much, but Morgan brought them on board, and they seem to know what they're doing."

Carroll nodded. "Very well, then. I'll pop in, *not* boss anyone around, and let you know how it's looking."

She disappeared into the house, and I sat on the front steps, looking out at the yard and the road beyond it, stretching back toward town. The house was nestled in its own shallow valley, with gentle hills rising on three sides. I imagined floating above the place like a bird, looking down at the house and its grounds. From that imaginary vantage, the mansion's placement among the swells of land gave the impression of a heavy box placed on a cushy pillow. And it was something of a mystery box indeed, though we were learning more about its history and inhabitants with each passing day. The thought of history put Josh in my mind. I pulled my phone from my pocket and dialed his number. No response. I hesitated as his voice mail message played, and hung up before the beep.

After about twenty minutes, Carroll came back out,

leading Steve, Bethany, Lars, and Morgan behind her. She seemed to have marshalled the troops after all, for which I was quietly grateful. Carroll and Bethany were chatting amiably about town history—not that Carroll was from around here at all, but she was a quick study—and Steve grumbled about some detail of the house's layout while Morgan nodded, somewhat grimly, though he didn't seem to be engaging with the conversation. Steve and Bethany waved goodbye and headed out to their respective trucks, and Morgan stayed behind.

"Well, we're all done here, Kate. Thanks again for re-arranging your time. Much obliged."

"Is everything okay with Steve? He seemed kind of brusque."

"Oh, he'll be fine, I think." Morgan looked out at the driveway, where Steve's and Bethany's trucks were now receding toward the street. "We can get under each other's skin sometimes, is all. But he's respected around here—his family has been in the building trades for generations, in fact—and I know he'll do fine work. Don't you worry."

"I just hope you'll let me know when there's something I need to know about." I looked him right in the eye as I spoke.

"You bet, Miz Kate." He returned my look and nodded. "Shall we speak tomorrow and set a date to start work?"

"That sounds great."

"You take care now." And he was off.

Carroll and I looked at each other and I meekly said,

"Pizza?" She nodded. We locked up and headed back toward town in our separate cars.

❦

Back at the B&B, Carroll and I sprawled on sofas and ate generous slices of Florentine pizza from a local shop, talking over the day's events. I realized that I was due to update my board members on recent developments—hiring Morgan, finding and removing the body, the imminent commencement of work on the house—and climbed the stairs to the bedroom to make some calls. Could everyone get together at the house to get on the same page, meet Morgan, and save me having to tell seven different people the same story? I could only hope. I called Frances, Mac, and Lisbeth; sent quick emails to Mayor Skip, Ryan, and Ted; hemmed and hawed about Josh, whom I hadn't heard from, finally dashing off a text message; and bellowed down the stairs to Carroll, who responded with a thumbs-up. Miraculously, everyone except Mayor Skip and Frances were available to get together the next day at lunchtime. Frances had an unmovable doctor's appointment—I hoped nothing serious—and would call me later for the updates. Skip was busy attending the town's budget committee meetings all week, but said he was happy to be informed of anything significant via email. I said a silent word of thanks for level heads in public service, and went to bed.

The next morning, I woke from dreams of pipes and copper wire rising like shoots and branches all around me. Surprisingly, I felt very well rested. As I brushed my teeth and dressed, I remembered that I also needed to confer with Morgan about whether we could salvage the original appliances—at least the sink and the humongous stove—or if we'd have to start over. Obviously, we'd have to come to some decision about the staircase space—just open it up and tear it out altogether, or leave it, if a bit more open, to show the building's architectural lineage? I decided I would hold out for keeping the staircase, but making it more visible. It might be an unforeseen delight to lead visitors up the stairs from the kitchen and magically appear in a back bedroom. I made a mental note to have Morgan make sure the steps were still structurally sound after all these years.

I plodded downstairs and found Carroll at the dining room table, papers spread all around her. I cleared my throat, and she jumped about a foot in the air.

"You scared me! I didn't hear you come in."

"You must have been really interested in what you were reading. Anything good?"

"I've been working up a family tree for Henry. We know he had brothers, that they were all reasonably successful, and that none of them had a claim on Henry's property when he died. So they might've been dead already, I figured—or maybe they just hated Maryland and didn't want to own a house here? From what I've seen in the Civil War records, they weren't all part of the same army unit or anything, but they did serve. So what I just figured out this morning is that Henry was the baby of the family, and he outlived most of his brothers. The oldest seems to have visited once, around 1880, but for some reason he never came back, and then he died at home in Massachusetts. That would explain why no obvious close relative was on hand to deal with the estate."

"No sisters?" I asked.

"None that I've come across. They would've had different surnames if they'd married, of course, but I don't see birth records for them anyway."

"I see." I scratched my head, thinking of my overfull to-do list scrawled on a legal pad upstairs. "Carroll, do you think once we get organized, we'll be able to plan our days better?"

"'Organized'—what's that? Ha. But . . . maybe? I have a friend in Philly who can set up a basic web presence for us at a reasonable rate, if you want to get that rolling."

"Oh, right. Yes, that's a good idea. Morgan's from around here, but he didn't even know about this project! I guess news travels slowly sometimes. Do we need to have social media accounts for a historic mansion?"

"It probably wouldn't hurt. Just think of it all as communication. You want people to know about something, you have to tell them. In this case, with pretty photos and some punchy copy attached." She wrinkled her nose. "Speaking of communication, where is Professor Josh? Is he on the project or what?"

"I don't know, really." I sighed. "He's been off at his summer teaching gig. Which I know is important, but I can't tell if he's really interested in this project. I need a commitment one way or the other. But he'll be at our meeting today—I *think* that's what his text said—so maybe we can hash it out this afternoon."

"That's decisive talk, Ms. Hamilton! Well, you've got your work cut out for you. Want to eat breakfast and head over to the mansion in a bit?"

I nodded and proceeded to raid the fridge for the remaining eggs and bacon in our stash. As we ate, Carroll outlined the basics of her genealogical research methods, and I nodded as if I knew what she was talking about. My eyes drifted to the clock. It was still early, but I was itching to get back to the mansion.

We drove out of town and along the winding local highway leading to the Barton property. I opened the gate to let us in, then drove slowly down the sweeping drive. There was mist lingering in the hollows. I could understand why Henry had fallen in love with the site, and I hoped Mary had been happy here. Carroll's phone rang just as I was parking, so she stayed outside for a few minutes to deal with what sounded like a student loan administrator, while I went on inside. I let myself in by the front door. Inside, I paused for a moment to enjoy the opulence of the interior. And then I heard noise coming from the kitchen. Morgan? Josh? An early-rising thief? Or, God forbid, a raccoon? I slipped quietly down the hall toward the back of the house, hugging the wall and scouting for blunt objects close at hand—and I was surprised to find Steve poking around the room.

"Steve, what are you doing here? And how did you get in?" I reminded myself to talk with Morgan about access for the workers; I had given him a set of keys for when we started work, but I didn't want people just wandering in at will.

Steve snorted. "I grew up around here—I know the back ways. Could be you know them too, if you went to school in town." His face formed a smile that was part snarl. Was he trying to mock me? And what did he mean to say, exactly?

"I'd prefer it if you came in the front," I said stiffly. "I'd like to maintain security here; there are some valuable items in the house." I thought of the antique book I'd been reading yesterday, sitting quietly on the shelf, waiting to walk away in somebody's satchel. "Were you looking for something in particular?"

He shrugged. "If this room was a retrofit, even in the 1880s, you're likely to find some surprises inside the walls. Besides that dead guy, I mean. I want to get a head start, be prepared."

"Right. Has Morgan talked to you all about a schedule?"

"We're starting next week, he says."

"But you just thought you'd pop in before that and . . . look around yourself."

"Yup." He looked placidly around the room, almost as

if he owned it. Then he snapped his gaze back to me. "That a problem?"

He was making that face again, a sort of lizard smile. I wasn't sure how serious he meant to be, whether or not to read this interaction as dangerous, or if I should feel ridiculous to even think that. We were only two people talking in a kitchen—weren't we? I did some quick math: the distance from where I stood to the back door, Steve's weight and build, what shoes I was wearing. I decided to stay put, for now. Carroll was just outside, after all.

"So you're from around here, Steve? Had you ever been inside the house before this week?"

"Nah. People talked about the place some, but I never came here. Well—been on the lawns a few times actually, hanging out, but never in the house. I wasn't much interested in this place in high school. Spent more time looking for beer, and girls." He paused, as if waiting for a reaction. I didn't bite. "The house is in good shape, even though it's old."

"I'm glad to hear that, since I want it to survive. I hope you'll all be careful. I don't want to replace any more than I have to—it's supposed to be a historic site. The old systems are important to its educational value."

"Yeah, I get it. You want it old. Might cost you more, though. Not everybody these days knows how to work with these materials."

"Morgan knows what he's doing. You've worked with him before?"

"On and off."

"Well, if you and the crew do a good job with this place, there might be more work in the future." I wasn't about to lay out an offer on the rest of the town's renovation, but I thought the man should know what was on the table here.

"More work, that'd be good. Been slow around here." He paused, looking at the gaping hole in the wall. "Say, was there something *you* came here looking for?"

"No, I just wanted to look at it all again, before you started making changes. The board members for the town renovation project will be coming by for a walk-through in a few hours."

Steve tilted his head, suddenly at attention. "Oh, really? I'd like to meet these 'board members.'" He had a way of pronouncing words one syllable at a time, as if holding them up to show me.

"Morgan will be at the meeting, so I'm sure he'll fill you—"

Steve cut in abruptly, starting to move as he spoke. "I'll get out of your hair, then. My truck's out back. I came in through the back fence. That's a vulnerability of the property you should know about, if you are a 'security-minded' person."

"Okay, Steve. We'll be in touch, then."

"Right." He turned and left by the kitchen door.

I still wasn't sure I was comfortable being alone with him out here. Did that bode well for our future working together? Maybe it was the lingering effect of finding a body only a few feet away. Maybe it was the comment about what the house had been used for when I was in high school. I didn't have many happy memories of those days. Maybe I simply didn't like the man. But I didn't have to like all the workers, I reminded myself, as long as they did a good job.

I walked to the back of the room and pushed the door halfway open, poking my head out into the sun to watch Steve recede across the broad field toward the property line.

14

I didn't tell Carroll about the encounter with Steve when she came in from her phone call. Instead, to keep the mood light for our upcoming meeting, I showed her the library, which neither of us had spent much time in before. She took a researcher's interest in the array of subjects represented on the shelves. We chatted as we each moved around the room.

"I'm glad you've got Morgan on board for this project," she mused. "He seems like a conscientious guy, and he really likes Victorian stuff. Not everybody does." She paused to squint at a gold-lettered spine. "Did you grow up in a Victorian house? Or neighborhood?"

"No, just an ordinary midcentury colonial, nothing fancy. But I didn't know any better then."

"What is it you like about this style?"

"Well, for the well-built houses, their sense of space, I guess. Not that anybody *needs* ten-foot ceilings, but they're pleasing. The big rooms are notoriously inefficient to heat, but I guess they had servants to put up storm windows and such. And they must have been kind of dark, before electricity. Gas lighting is not very bright."

"You do realize you just told me several reasons why you *don't* like Victorian houses."

"I guess I did." I hadn't noticed. "Plus, they were ostentatious and self-indulgent and hard to keep clean—think about dusting all those carved moldings! Or cleaning all the velvet draperies and lace curtains."

"I get it! They're big and fussy. Fair enough. Well, at least they provided a lot of jobs for poor people."

"There is that. Probably not very fun jobs on the whole, but jobs nonetheless. But obviously, I do like these houses. And Henry's place is special. Starting with electric lighting— that would have made a real difference to the quality of life. And I'm coming to believe the place was a labor of love. I have a hunch he built it to make Mary happy—I've never known a guy who was all that into ornate interiors, even if he wasn't responsible for cleaning them."

"That's a nice thought."

"It's speculation, but I like to think it's true. How do you get to know historical people in a personal way—more than what you can glean from vital records and a few press clippings?"

"It's hard, honestly. Unless they left some kind of personal account behind. You know Samuel Pepys?"

"I can't say that I do."

"English guy, member of Parliament, mid-seventeenth century. He famously kept a very detailed diary for about ten years of his life. It got published much later, and it contributed a lot to historians' understanding of that period. Without that kind of account—and surviving artworks, of course—cultural history involves a lot of guessing."

"Great. Well, guessing it is, then. Hopefully, we can cobble together some kind of interesting narrative to sell this place to the public."

"It's got a lot to recommend it. And if all else fails, you can fall back on the 'murder house' angle, right? People love a murder house. Just look at—"

At that moment, we both heard a jangling of keys, a door opening and closing. It was the back door. I braced to meet whoever might be coming down the hall, though Carroll seemed fairly calm about it. Then again, she hadn't had the ominous meeting with Steve I'd just experienced. Josh walked in.

"Hey there," he said.

"Hi. I wasn't sure I was expecting you this morning."

"Oh. Well, I'm here." Did he seem distracted? "You know, I came in through the back door, and it wasn't even locked. You should be careful about that."

"I know." I felt a surge of peevish annoyance. As if I wasn't paying attention to security? "And I'd forgotten that you had a set of keys still. We need to establish some protocols around comings and goings in here—between us and the new workers, a lot of people have access now."

"Are you saying you don't *want* me to have keys to get in?"

"I'm not saying that, exactly."

"Hey, you two," Carroll piped up. "Maybe this would be a good conversation to have . . . later? It's ten of eleven, and everybody else should be here soon. I mean, keys are definitely important to talk about, but . . ."

"You're right," I said. "Let's talk later. I'll start over. Hi, Josh. Thank you for coming to our board meeting."

"Yup," he replied. "Glad to be here." He didn't quite smile, but there was a softening in his expression. Soon I heard a rap on the front door, and we all decamped into the hallway to let in the crowd.

The Asheboro town liaisons arrived first. Lisbeth, Mac, and Ted strolled in together, talking about a home-gardening movement that had swept the townspeople this season. They waved to me as they walked past, and continued talking in the parlor. I heard a voice nearby, and, poking my head out onto the front porch, I found Ryan pacing back and forth and talking sternly into his phone. I watched him with amusement, reflecting on the comforting quaintness of other people's problems, until he hung up, said a brief hello, and walked inside.

That just left Morgan. I stood on the threshold with the door open, letting the light breeze rolling in from the fields play over my skin as it flowed silently into the mansion. Then I saw Morgan's truck crest the low hill and begin the winding descent toward the house. I squinted as he approached. Was there . . . someone else with him? When his vehicle reached the house, I saw that he'd brought Bethany along in the passenger seat. That was odd—not that I minded her being here, but we hadn't discussed inviting the subcontractors to this meeting. I stepped onto the porch, closing the door behind me, as the two of them walked up the front path.

"Hi, Morgan. Bethany, you really didn't have to be at this meeting—I hope you're not missing anything for this. We're just getting together with the board to talk business."

"Oh, it's no problem." She looked sideways at Morgan. "I got the call about an hour ago, but I wasn't busy. My wife and I had just finished breakfast, so the timing worked out."

"Why don't you head on inside," I said to her, trying to keep my voice neutral. I wasn't mad at her, just . . . confused. "Carroll's in the parlor there, and she can introduce you to the other board members." She nodded and then crossed behind me and disappeared into the house.

"Morgan, it's okay that Bethany is here, but you didn't have to—"

"Look, Kate—it wasn't my first thought either. I apologize if I've made a misstep here. But I got a call from Steve this morning saying that you'd invited him to come to the board meeting, and I figured if he was going to meet everyone, she should too. Honestly, I don't know why you'd invite one and not the other."

"I . . . didn't." I furrowed my brow in confusion. "I'm

sorry you had that impression. No, I absolutely did not invite Steve. He's not here. What did he tell you?"

Just then, the telltale crunch of the gravel driveway announced Steve's arrival, small rocks flying beneath the wheels of his silver pickup.

"Well, I guess it's a party." I threw up my hands. What was happening to this day, which had begun so innocently? Morgan looked at me with a mix of apology and confusion in his eyes. "It's fine. I'll tell you about it later. So, we're all here. We can make it work. When we go in, I'll introduce you around, and then you can brief everyone on your vision for the place so far, the approximate budget, and our plan of action. Sound good?"

"Can do, ma'am." Morgan tipped his hat at me. We both turned to regard Steve, stepping out of his vehicle and walking up to the house. Behind him was Lars, stumbling to keep up, looking slightly embarrassed. Steve said nothing about having crashed the party, nor about bringing his brother, who may have been an unwitting accomplice in the matter. I offered the two of them a tight smile, just to keep the day moving along, and we all walked in together.

Morgan performed splendidly for the assembled team—I was surprised at his professional bearing among this diverse group, considering the rusticated demeanor with which he usually presented himself. He walked everyone through the important elements of the kitchen: its new dimensions (taking into account the revealed staircase), a period-authentic lighting plan, which of

the appliances could be saved and which would have to
be approximately replaced, and at what cost. Then, to
my surprise, he walked us upstairs and showed everyone
where the hidden staircase would emerge on the second
floor, gave an impromptu lecture on wall-building materials of the late nineteenth century, and even described a
cooking demo we could try as programming for visitors,
using the giant fireplace left intact from the bones of the
old farmhouse kitchen. I hadn't realized his interests were
so thorough and so wide-ranging.

Morgan then passed the focus to Bethany, who described her plan for rewiring the place from top to bottom,
demonstrating an impressive grasp of historical materials
and modern techniques. Steve didn't say much, but threw
in comments here and there, and Lars was as silent as a
church mouse, though he nodded enthusiastically as the
others spoke.

Listening to Morgan and Bethany talk about the house
and its potential with such interest, intelligence, and hu-
mor renewed my own confidence in this huge undertaking. I was practically floating by the time we adjourned to
the first floor. The group chatted about this and that, with
Morgan and Ryan pulling off to the side to go over some
budget items. Carroll and I stopped in the library to confer about plans for the evening, and some of the others began to file out to their cars, waving goodbye as they went.
Josh came in.

"Hey," he said. "Do you mind if I stick around here

for the night? I want to get a leg up on grading and sort through some thoughts for my book. I could use a little quiet time in the carriage house."

"Sure," I replied. I wasn't sure why he was asking me, since it sounded like he had made up his mind already. I pushed down a spark of annoyance. It had been a long day, but a good one. "You've got the keys, of course. Carroll and I were just talking about dinner plans anyway. Do you want to eat with us before you retire to your quarters?" I offered a hopeful smile.

"No, thanks. I think I'd better get in as much work time as I can. But things went well today. Thanks for inviting me in."

"Of course. I'm glad you could come."

There was a silence between us, not quite charged but holding in it a sense of something unfinished, a cloud of anticipation. Carroll broke it by clearing her throat.

"Well, friends . . . I'm going to head out to the car. See you there in a minute, Kate?" She raised her eyebrows suggestively in my direction.

"Yes. I'll be right there."

Carroll left through the front door, leaving me and Josh staring at each other in the hushed room. He spoke first.

"I think that went well—really. But I'd like to talk to you about my ongoing participation in the project. Do you have some time, maybe tomorrow?"

"Sure," I said, somewhat warily. His participation? *Oh no, Kate, have you got a dropout on your hands already?* I shrugged off the twinge of fear. "Yes, it would be good to talk about some things. Let's say tomorrow night, if you're free."

"Great. We'll talk then." He hesitated for a fraction of a second, then leaned forward and kissed me on the cheek before retreating. I wasn't sure what to make of that—or the whole conversation, for that matter—but I resolved to speak with him honestly tomorrow, no matter what he wanted to say. I hoped he wasn't going to cut and run from the Asheboro project; his background in industrial history in the region was valuable, and his academic affiliation gave the project more legitimacy as a small-town under-taking.

I looked up from my thoughts and realized that every-one seemed to have left. I walked back down the long hall to the kitchen to lock the back door and heard voices. Mor-gan, Steve, Lars, and Bethany were all standing around the big kitchen table, talking. I didn't catch anything they were saying before I walked in, but they all stopped speak-ing and looked up when I entered the room. I felt like the out-of-town cowboy who's just strutted into the saloon, and suddenly the player piano screeches to a halt.

"Hi, folks. I'm going to head out—I need dinner. Mor-gan, you've got your set of keys, yes? Do you want to lock up whenever you're done here?"

"Absolutely." He glanced quickly at Bethany, who re-turned his look, and then at Steve, who did not. Lars stared mutely at his own feet as if wishing his way out of this room. I waited another moment to see if anyone would speak again, but no one was forthcoming.

"Well . . . I'll be going. Thanks for today. That went really well."

"I think so too," Morgan said, looking weary. "You've got a good team behind you, Kate. We might take another trip through the basement to make plans, but I'll be sure to lock the place up. Let's talk in the morning." He nodded to me and turned back to his crew, standing expectantly around the big kitchen table.

15

I exited the house, puzzling over the mood I'd just walked in on in the kitchen after such a satisfying meeting with the larger group. Had they been arguing? Was I imagining the tension in the air? Carroll was standing out front, looking at the orange sun beginning to drift beyond the hill. Without speaking, we both began to walk and moved not toward my car but into the mansion's backyard, admiring the tall grass and various native wildflowers taking over the lawn in absence of a caretaker. We reached the back of the house, and Carroll went on ahead, looking down at the ground where the rows of the old orchard might have been. I stood alone, breathing the cooler evening air, thinking over the day's events. Then I heard a voice. Muffled from some distance, but a raised voice. A man's voice. I looked around. No one was nearby. I realized it was coming from inside the house.

I turned and walked to the back entrance and stood

just below the short stoop leading up to the kitchen door. I thought I could make out two voices, probably male. A white linen curtain over the back door's glass panel kept me mostly out of view, even if someone happened to glance my way. I leaned in as far as I dared, hoping to catch the gist of the conversation without interrupting it.

Bethany's higher-pitched voice cut through the rumblings, and I could make out most of what she was saying. I stepped closer.

"Get over yourself, Steve. Morgan's in charge. If you don't want to work under him, you can quit. I'm sure he can find someone to replace you."

"You won't get rid of me that easily," the other voice growled. Steve, no doubt. I thought Bethany had a point: there were probably a few other plumbers in the area who would appreciate a substantial job for the coming weeks or months. Steve had no right to complain, I thought. Had he been mistreated somehow? Was there a history between them I hadn't been informed of? I hadn't seen Morgan behave toward anyone as a despot, or even a pedant, just an interested party charged with leading a small team. I'd hired Morgan based on our conversations, and Steve had mostly rubbed me the wrong way so far. If it came down to a choice between the two, I knew where my sympathies lay. The other male voice, which must have been Morgan's, cut in. It was louder, angrier than before.

"Steve, I gave you an assignment. We need that ADA information if we're going to open to the public—it's basic consideration—and you didn't even bother to look up the statute."

"It's a historic building, Wheeler," Steve shot back. "Doesn't matter. There's an exception. We don't need a wheelchair ramp anyway, so why bother?"

"That's really nice, Steve," Bethany replied. "Just because we don't legally *have* to do it, you're not going to make any effort at all?"

"Oh, Mr. High-and-Mighty Wheeler, you know so much better, do you?" Steve said, ignoring Bethany's response. "Just like your daddy. I don't need this from you. I can do the work just fine on my own. You'll see."

Bethany wasn't going to be ignored. "Stop it with the ancient history, Steve. Whatever you think about Morgan's family is not what we're doing here. Can you work on the team or not?"

When Steve answered, I heard him pick out his words as if he were plucking fruit, one at a time, just as he had done in our conversation that morning. "I intend to work on this house," he said, rather ominously. "But there is no need for a ramp."

"Did you even cost it out? It's not as much work as you might think, and it really helps people. This back entrance would work fine, actually—it's pretty wide already . . ." For a moment I didn't hear anything, and then the door swung wide open, with Bethany behind it. She continued talking until she saw me. "Look, you wouldn't even have to take down the—oh . . . Kate. Hi. Do you—"

"Hello, Bethany." I felt a little sheepish being caught eavesdropping, but I reminded myself that I was the boss lady and had every right to be here. Carroll had evidently heard what was going on, because from the corner of my eye I saw her approach and stop just behind me on the lawn. I went on, speaking to Bethany, along with the others behind her, all of them looking a little shocked to find me there. "Is there a problem here, Morgan?"

"A small disagreement. Nothing you need to worry about." Morgan spoke calmly enough, but I found myself wondering if his teeth were clenched. Should I trust this man's assurance over the evidence of my own senses? I let the silence hang between us for a long beat.

"Carroll and I are heading home. Morgan, why don't you and I talk about this in the morning?" I looked pointedly at him as I spoke. I wanted to trust him, but it was hard to read this room.

"Of course," he said, looking crestfallen. "I'm actually going to take off for a spell—the wife expects me at the dinner table—but the others have some work to do. I'll come back and lock up at the end of the night, if that's all right with you." He looked at me with uncertainty on his face.

"I guess that will have to do." The silence between us returned in full force. Then Steve spoke up.

"Say, Wheeler, if you're heading through town, can you drop Lars here at the train station? He's going into the city to see his girlie for a couple of days." He turned to me.

"That's why we had to move our meeting up earlier. This one's got dates to keep, you see." He gestured with his head toward Lars, who turned red in the face.

"That's not . . . ," Lars said, but he trailed off without finishing his protest.

"Sure," Morgan said curtly. "Lars, pack up your things, and I'll meet you at the truck in five minutes."

Lars, Bethany, and Steve turned and exited the kitchen toward the front of the house. Morgan turned and stepped carefully into the kitchen doorway to face me. "Kate . . . I'm sorry. There will be no problem with the team, really. Just a negotiation of terms, you might say. Different temperaments . . . But we're working through it. I think we'll get a good sense of what we need to do tonight."

I stared at him, his kind face framed by shaggy hair going white at the temples, tamped down under his old cap. His eyebrows furrowed in concern.

"All right," I said finally, releasing a breath. "We'll talk in the morning."

I descended the back stoop and walked around the house with Carroll, neither of us speaking. I started up my car as a fine seed of worry germinated in the corner of my mind. We drove in silence for a few minutes, heading toward the grocery store before we returned to the B&B for the evening. She spoke first.

"That was kind of weird, right? I didn't hear what they were saying, but you could cut the tension in there with a knife!"

"Yes, that was . . . something." I chose my words carefully, not wanting to gossip about what we had just witnessed, but also hoping to make some sense of it. Carroll was ten years younger than I was, but I considered her a peer, and she seemed to have a good sense about people. "Let me ask you this, and please answer as honestly as you can. What's your feeling about Steve?"

"Steve the plumber? Honestly? I just met the guy, but . . . I don't know. He seems a little—what's the word?—handsy?"

"What do you mean?"

"Well, you, me, and Bethany are the only women on the crew, you know? Lisbeth was there today too, come to think of it, but I didn't really see them interacting. You're the boss, so Steve was careful around you, probably on best behavior. I don't know Bethany's story, but she's a woman in a trade, so she's probably seen it all, and I don't think she'd put up with any funny stuff. Which left me. He kept following close behind me while we looked at the house, and he would brush up against me more than necessary. Like when you're on a crowded train—but we weren't on a train. He was just . . . too close. And I wasn't encouraging him or anything—I was hardly looking at him, and we were definitely not having a conversation at the time. He just seemed, like, sure that his presence was welcome. But it wasn't."

"Ugh. I'm sorry that happened. What about Lars?"

"I didn't really get a vibe off Lars. He seems fine. Quiet."

She was less effusive than her usual self, looking out the window as she spoke in short bursts.

"I thought so too. It's probably hard to be a little brother to a guy who's, well, kind of a blowhard, if you ask me. But I don't want you to feel unsafe in the house while Steve's working there. Is he going to be a problem?"

"No . . . I don't know. I wasn't planning to spend much time at the mansion anyway. I've still got plenty of archival work to do at the library—on our house servants especially. We don't even have names for them yet."

"That's true," I replied, weighing my words. "It's just . . . I don't know Steve yet, and I'm not sure what to make of him myself. Let me know if anything else happens, okay? I'm sure we can find another plumber if we need to."

"Yeah, okay," Carroll said, staring out the window at the low houses and lush trees flying by just beyond the glass.

I gripped the wheel and stared straight ahead at the narrow local highway. As much as I was glad to have Carroll at the library doing her research, I didn't want her to be avoiding the mansion—the heart of this project—because one of the workers made her uncomfortable. But Morgan had said it would be fine, hadn't he? I felt stuck. Were things falling apart so early? We pulled into the grocery store parking lot, and I put the car in park just as a light rain began to fall on the windshield. Carroll and I looked at each other, and I smiled, still uncertain what to do, but resolved to eat a good meal, sleep on it, and see what I thought in the morning. I handed Carroll a sheaf of newspaper from the car's back seat, took another for myself, and we held them like small tents over our heads as we dashed across the lot toward the brightly lit store.

16

Carroll and I cooked and ate a quiet chicken dinner, then made a brief stop at the town library to retrieve some books on Victorian interiors I had been meaning to look at. She and I sat in the parlor of the B&B for a few hours, reading our respective tomes. It had been an interesting day, and I wasn't quite ready to let it all go. I sat in a plush armchair next to a standing lamp, a magnifying glass in my hand, and pored over old photos of stately homes, hoping for any hint of kitchen or bathroom furnishings in the background. We finally made it upstairs and into our beds, rather later than usual.

I awoke what seemed like minutes later to a banging sound somewhere downstairs. I picked up my phone and, blinking into its small illuminated screen, noted two things: first, that indeed, only half an hour had passed since I'd gone to bed, and second, that I'd missed six calls from Josh in the last several hours. Oops. I hadn't exactly been paying attention to my phone as I was reading and imagining the mansion's possibilities. The banging continued, and as I crept from the bedroom into the hallway and peered down the stairs, I ascertained that the sound was a particularly aggressive knocking at the door. What now? Should I preemptively call the police station? *Hello, Officer, there's someone pounding on my door, could you just stay on hold while I ask what he wants?* But I didn't make the call. I had a hunch.

Grabbing one of Cordelia's golf clubs from the bedroom closet at the far end of the hall and brandishing it like I knew what I was doing, I snuck back to the staircase, crept down, and peered through the front door's peephole. Just as I'd suspected: Josh. Why was he here now, unannounced, and pounding on the door in the middle of the night? I put down the club, unlocked the door, and flung it open, not sure if I should be frightened or annoyed.

"Can I help you?" I said as the door swung open, trying to land my tone on the droll side of exasperated. Josh's fist was up, caught in mid-pound. He froze, looking shocked to see me.

"Kate! Are you all right? I was so worried. Can I come in?"

"Yeah, of course," I said, stepping aside. He walked in, taking the long, loping strides I so liked to watch when he crossed the broad lawn of the mansion. "Why were you worried? What's happening?"

"You didn't get my messages?" He walked past me and into the kitchen, pacing fitfully in front of the tiled counter as he spoke.

"No," I said, feeling a little sheepish. "Carroll and I were doing some research, and I just crashed not that long ago. What's going on?"

He held his breath, then let it go in a short puff. "There was a death at the mansion."

"I . . ." My mind couldn't seem to form a sentence, or even a thought, about what Josh had just said. I managed to sputter, "A new one?"

"Yes. I don't know when exactly, but it can't have been that long ago. I was in the back of the carriage house writing, and when I went out to stretch my legs on the lawn, I saw a bunch of police cars, and the back room of the house was all lit up."

"The back—you mean the kitchen? Are you sure this isn't just some follow-up to the body in the wall? Maybe they needed more samples from the staircase?"

"I thought that might be it too, but I walked over and looked in the back door. It wasn't Reynolds or the medical examiner. It was the local guys, Asheboro PD. Now why would that case have gotten bumped down to them? Somebody saw me standing out there and asked me in for questioning—"

"Well, yeah," I interrupted, "a strange man appearing at the back door of a possible crime scene, saying he's been hanging out in the barn nearby this whole time? I'd want to ask you some questions too. Did you find out anything? Who was it?"

"They wouldn't tell me. I heard someone across the room muttering something about a worker, so it could have been a member of your crew."

"Oh no." My eyes widened. I didn't know what else to say. "How can we find out? Do I need to go over there right now?" I started scanning the vicinity for the shoes I had kicked off earlier in the evening, and my hand began patting my pockets for car keys—but I realized I was wearing pajamas. Josh put a hand softly on my forearm.

"Kate. You can't do anything right now. Can you go back to bed? I can stay—if you don't mind, I mean. It's feeling a little spooky over at the Barton place lately."

"You can stay—of course you can stay, Josh." I took his hand in mine, tentatively. "But . . . I know you wanted to talk. Can we do that in the morning?"

"Yes. I'd be useless for conversation right now anyway. Let's go to bed." He looked a little uncertain, then added, "Your room?"

"Yes." We locked the front door behind us and ascended the stairs to the lacy guest bedroom I was calling home. I flopped back onto the bed and stared at the ceiling, feeling flummoxed by this new development. I was asleep by the time Josh finished brushing his teeth.

❖

I woke feeling fantastically well rested, clear sunlight streaming in through the bedroom windows. I began to mentally tick off what I needed to do today—and then my heart sank as I remembered Josh's words from last night: *There was a death at the mansion.* What an odd phrasing. A *death* as a new fact in the landscape. Because what was a death, in fact, but an erasure, a removal, the disappearing of a life? Now here it was like a great dark smear across the day. I took a deep breath and got out of bed, then dressed quickly, wanting to get down to business. Walking into the bathroom, I almost bumped into Josh, who was standing in front of the mirror and brushing his teeth.

"Didn't I just leave you here a few hours ago?"

"I haven't been here brushing this whole time, I swear. I'm not *that* into oral hygiene." He put an arm around me as I grabbed my own toothbrush. "You sure went out like a light last night."

"Long day. Several, actually. And no sign of that stopping, apparently."

He nodded. We both finished dressing and headed downstairs, with few other words passing between us. Josh was making a distinct effort at friendliness, but given his rather distant tone the last few days, I couldn't shake the feeling that he was about to bail on this project. I looked at my phone and saw a missed call from a few minutes before: Detective Reynolds. I'd figured it would come sooner or later. When we landed in the kitchen and Josh set to making coffee, I called Reynolds back. He picked up after three rings.

"Kate. I'm going to need to see you at the mansion. There's been a death."

"People keep saying that to me," I muttered.

"What?" Reynolds almost barked. Maybe he was tired of bodies turning up on my work site too.

"Nothing. Sorry. I haven't had coffee yet. I heard there was . . . well, I don't know. 'A death.' What does that mean? A murder? Accident? Did someone break in? Who is it?"

"Why don't you come on down here and I'll tell you as much as I can. Half an hour?"

"Okay."

He hung up before I could say anything else. He sounded gruff, but I figured he wasn't going to arrest me, whatever may have happened over there. I had an alibi. As if summoned by my thoughts of last night, Carroll plodded down the stairs and into the kitchen, looking slightly bedraggled.

"I slept *terribly*," she said. "I had this dream that someone was pounding on the door at midnight."

"Sorry about that," Josh said sheepishly. "I was just worried about you. Both of you."

"Why?" Carroll cocked her head at Josh.

"There's been a . . ." I searched for words and found only the one I'd heard two people ominously say already. "A death. Something happened at the mansion, I don't know what, but I have to get over there and talk to Reynolds. Now."

We three ate a fast breakfast, and I headed out to my car.

Josh called out from the door. "Hey! Want company?"

I nodded, and he grabbed his boots and followed me into the car. We drove in silence. I wasn't unhappy to have him along, but the idea of a mysterious new body at the site I was desperately trying to oversee was causing considerable stress. Neither of us brought up the conversation we'd agreed to have when Josh showed up last night. If he was planning on skipping town for his real job and bailing out of the Asheboro project just as it got going, I didn't want to hear about it this morning.

When we arrived at the mansion, we found a uniformed officer standing by the front door. I briefly introduced myself, and he let us pass without argument. Once inside, I wasn't sure where to proceed. I noticed that the door to the library on my left was shut. That was new—we usually left the house's interior doors open for airflow. I walked straight ahead toward the kitchen; that seemed to be where the activity was taking place. Josh followed behind me. The hallway felt impossibly long. Just as I reached the entrance to the kitchen, Detective Reynolds appeared in the doorway, a boxy silhouette against the light spilling from the bright room into the dark hall.

"Kate." He put up a hand, literally stopping us in place. "Please, join me in the parlor." How formal. Josh and I followed him into the front sitting room. Ensconced in an elegant blue wingback chair, the detective sat back, steepled his fingers, and spoke.

"How well do you know Steve Abernathy?"

"Steve? He's the plumbing lead on this project. I can't say I know him well. Morgan hired him. Oh no—did he do something?" I thought back to my interactions with Steve, which had ranged from mildly annoying to unsettling, even leading me to question my safety with him. And I remembered Carroll's discomfort with his behavior toward her, a complete stranger. How had I been so stupid? Had Steve actually killed someone? My mind spun.

"I don't know what he did or didn't do, Ms. Hamilton, but whatever it was, he's dead at the bottom of the basement stairs."

I blinked at the handsome man in the gray suit seated across from me. His words didn't make sense. All I could think to say at first was, "Oh." Josh and I looked at each other blankly. I didn't know what to think—I hadn't gotten a good feeling from Steve, had found myself actually disliking the man, but I certainly didn't wish him dead. Had someone else? I turned to face the detective again. "What happened to him?"

"That's uncertain at the moment. We're still analyzing

the scene. But I'd like you to take a look in the basement and tell me if anything seems out of place. Would you feel comfortable doing that?"

"I . . . guess so." I wasn't thrilled at the prospect of seeing another dead body, and a fresh one at that, but I wanted to help—and I certainly did want to know if anything was out of place in that basement too. This was still my work site, after all. Could someone have broken in to rob the place and a tussle ensued? Had Steve actually been a hero in this situation? I decided I'd better reserve judgment. Maybe he'd done us a good turn after all, or tried to. We all stood, and as I began moving toward the hallway to head down the basement stairs, Reynolds put up a hand again.

"I'll need you to come in through the outside entrance. The body is still where we found it."

"Oh," I said again intelligently. "If you'll just unbar the door from inside, we'll come right around."

Josh and I walked back out the front door and circled the house. The day wasn't yet at its hottest point, but the sun felt crisp on my neck as we walked. I wanted to drift into a reverie of some future time, sitting peacefully on this lawn, kicking off my shoes and reclining on a lawn chair— but I knew that a man had died in this house. Recently. And now Josh and I were about to confront the scene of it. When we reached the back cellar entrance, a ground-level double door, Reynolds's assistant, another young uni- formed cop, was just swinging the big doors open. The dark stairs descending into the basement came into view. I stepped aside and gestured for Josh to go through first. He obliged, affording me a few extra seconds of not having to look at a freshly dead body. Then I was following his blue Johns Hopkins T-shirt down the steps, ducking to enter the low passage, putting up a hand to steady myself on the wall while my eyes adjusted—and then we were standing side by side in Henry Barton's basement. It was a rough-hewn space, unfinished, but there was a grandeur in its sheer size, stretching the full length of the house above; it could have been midnight or a hundred years ago, so well did the thick foundation block out the day. Just as I cast a glance back to the double door we'd come through, the young officer was shutting it again, closing off any available sunlight.

I looked around. The police had brought back their stand lamps from the other day, and shocking fields of white light flooded the far end of the basement, where several technicians were hovering around the base of the stairs. Nothing seemed out of place, though I had to admit I hadn't been spending that much time in the basement prior to this. Reynolds beckoned from the bottom of the staircase, across the room. I walked toward him, and as he stepped out of the way to give me a view of the body, I stopped cold. It was Steve, all right, but his neck was bent at an angle not found in nature. I took one long look at the body and turned away. Reynolds met me by the wall halfway across the room, where I was avoiding the scene of the crime—if it was a crime—by examining some chalk marks left on the stone wall by one of the workers. I hadn't the slightest idea what they meant, but I convinced myself I was engrossed, so baffled was I by the scene at the other end of the basement.

"Anything leap out at you, Kate?"

"No—other than the dead body over there, the place looks normal. Honestly, there's not much going on down here yet. We've only just started work. Or tried to." Reynolds, to his credit, seemed to sense my frustration, and relaxed his face as he nodded. I continued, trying my luck at extracting some details from this conversation. "What can you tell me about the scene?"

Reynolds obliged. "Well, his injuries are consistent with a fall. There are no major signs of struggle. His fingernails are clean and intact, nothing out of place on his clothes or hair. But he reeks of alcohol. You said he was on your work crew—were you ever aware of him drinking on the job?"

"Not that I'd ever noticed. But I'd only met him a handful of times. He was technically working for me, but we've barely gotten started. It was Morgan Wheeler who hired him—hired the whole team, actually—and he said Steve was a good plumber. That's about all I know." I considered whether or not to go into what I'd heard about Steve's character. Maybe Reynolds needed to know. "And, well, I don't know if there's a polite way to say this, but he may have been a little handsy in mixed company. He made one of the women on our board uncomfortable."

"Who?"

"Do I have to tell you?"

"It may be relevant to the case."

"Carroll Peterson, my lead researcher on the Barton papers. But if you're thinking she pushed him down the stairs or something, I can assure you she had nothing to do with it. Besides being a slip of a girl who probably couldn't punch her way out of a wet paper bag, she was with me at the B&B all last night."

"I see. Thank you, Ms. Hamilton." He made a note on a small pad, which he returned to his pocket before looking back up at me. "I think that's all we'll need from you for now. You're free to go."

"Thanks. When can I get my work site back? Do you know how long this investigation is going to take?"

"We'll remove the body by end of day, but we may need another day or two before we clear the scene. I'll keep you apprised." I had a sudden feeling of déjà vu.

"Okay," I said, feeling a bit defeated. "How much of this can I tell the rest of the crew? I'll need to let them know not to come in to work, but they might want to know why."

"Would this be, uh"—he consulted the small notepad again—"Morgan Wheeler, Bethany Wallace, and Lars Abernathy?"

"Yes, that's them. Why?"

"I don't think you'll have to tell them not to come to work. I spoke with Lars to break the news early this morning. And Morgan Wheeler is down at the Asheboro Police Station now. I'm headed over there to speak with him."

"What? Why? Is he under arrest? And where's Bethany?"

"No one has been arrested in this matter. We just brought Mr. Wheeler in for questioning. It appears both he and Miss Wallace were in the house at the time of Mr. Abernathy's death. We have yet to locate Miss Wallace to speak with her, however."

My face went white. Could my crew—the good Quaker Morgan, and Bethany, who'd taught me about the spiritual qualities of paint colors—have had some part in Steve's death? I didn't want to think so. But there had clearly been some enmity among the group when I'd walked in on their heated conversation the day before. I thanked Detective Reynolds and turned to go.

When Josh and I had almost made it back to the outer door, Reynolds called out, "Oh, Kate—there's one more thing. Does this mean anything to you?" He approached me and produced from a manila folder under his arm a leather-bound book not much larger than a deck of cards. Its gilded spine looked vaguely familiar. I took it from him and turned to the title page. Trollope.

"I'm not sure," I replied, "but I'd bet this came from the library of this house. It looks like the right vintage, and Barton definitely had some of this author's works. Check for an empty spot on the shelf by the big mirror, east side of the room."

"Will do." He took the book from me and returned it precisely to the folder.

"But . . . what does that have to do with anything?"

"We found it in the deceased's back pocket."

"Huh. I see." I distinctly did *not* recall saying Steve could borrow antique books from the mansion's library. There could be some items of real value in there. I kicked myself for not having installed security cameras in this place.

Josh and I said goodbye to the detective and climbed back up the steep outer stairs, emerging onto the back lawn. It was a fine day outside, clear and calm. I wished I felt the same. *You're out of your depth, Hamilton.* I tried my best to shrug off that thought. I needed to know what had happened here. I took out my phone and called Morgan. No answer. I tried Bethany next, and she didn't respond either. Josh and I rounded the house and climbed back into my car, and I mutely started driving back to the B&B.

When we arrived, Carroll had just showered and was looking over some scans of Henry Barton's financial documents on her laptop. As I explained the events of the past hour, her eyes grew wider and wider. She was mildly alarmed to hear that her name had come up in connection with Steve, but I reminded her that I was her alibi for last night—and we were probably visible on the library's security camera, if it came to that—so any call Reynolds paid to her would likely be only to confirm what I'd told him. We shared a plate of cheese and crackers, brewed a fresh pot of coffee, and stared into space together for a few minutes, mulling over the strangeness of this latest development. Josh headed upstairs for a nap, not having slept well after his run-in with the police and subsequent worry over my safety last night.

Carroll returned to her research, and I sat in the kitchen, feeling stuck. What was I supposed to do now? I couldn't work on the mansion—heck, it seemed like I couldn't even set foot in the mansion without finding a body there. I needed to talk to Morgan. What was really going on with his crew—and was he a person of interest in Steve's death?

Just then, my phone rang. I looked at the screen, wondering if the device had read my thoughts—but it was Lisbeth. What could she want? I let it go to voice mail. Feeling defeated, I walked back into the parlor, plopped down in a chair, and tried to focus on my research.

17

A few hours passed, in which I was able to concentrate very little on the task in front of me. Then Lisbeth called again, and I picked up.

"Hi, Lisbeth. Is everything all right?"

"Oh yes, no trouble here. It's just that Phil's gone out with the kids for the afternoon—I thought you might like to come over for a late lunch. Are you free? Carroll can come too. And I've just spoken with Frances from the paper—since she missed the board meeting at the mansion, I figured we could fill her in too. Oh, it'll be a girls' lunch! I can make *gougères*, fruit salad, mimosas . . ."

I listened to her speak, her tone almost giddy at the prospect of the gathering. If I were to be honest, I'd tell her I felt terrible, that things were *not* going well, and all things being equal, I'd most prefer to curl up in a ball and go back to bed. But I thought better of that. A change of scenery might help. I took a deep breath.

"Sure, Lisbeth. How about an hour from now? I'll see about Carroll too." I hung up and practiced my best cheerful face for the luncheon ahead, but it quickly crumpled. Oh well. I walked into the parlor to find Carroll seated in an armchair, squinting at her laptop. On the screen was what appeared to be a blown-up scan of a historic document. Carroll was focused intently on a particular marking on it.

"Who could read that? That is not useful, Mr. Record Keeper," she grumbled.

"What's this now?"

"I found a ledger from Henry Barton's household accountant, back in the boxes from the library. It lists two servants living in-house; one of them it doesn't bother to name at all, and the other is called . . . squiggle."

"That's not helpful."

"No, it's not. We're looking for *names* here, people. This may be a dead end, but I'll keep searching. Based on this document, it looks like he at least paid them pretty well, for the time. Must've been hard work, but that helps."

"That's something. Hey, Lisbeth just called and invited us to lunch. Want to go? This day is beyond weird, but a good meal and some distraction might help."

"Sure. Just let me wrap up here."

I did a few errands to keep myself busy—contacting Carroll's web designer friend, doing a desperately needed load of laundry—and the next time I looked up, it was time to head over to Lisbeth's. I collected Carroll, and we piled into my car. As I drove toward Lisbeth's house, I tried to remember the last time she and I had visited or even talked by phone—*really* talked, as friends. How had I become so obsessed with the Barton project? It had been my sole focus for the last few months in town. The work was a new sort of challenge for me, requiring me to stretch my imagination. I liked that. The swanky hotels I was accustomed to handling in Baltimore were interesting, but the projects had a sameness to them. Not that I hadn't enjoyed that work—I had, and I'd been rather handsomely paid for it, a fact that was enabling this small-town sojourn in Asheboro.

But the Barton house was a different animal. Not only did this project involve historic preservation, but it called for public interaction—in a broader sense of "public" than I'd been thinking about when working on luxury hotels. We wanted families to come here—adults, kids, retirees, history buffs, and novices—and all find something compelling in the display. I knew I felt compelled by the house. But how would I translate all that we'd discovered—and what we hadn't—into an interesting story for visitors?

My mind drifted to Josh too. I looked forward to our talk about his "participation in the project" with a mix of interest and dread. *Just focus on the day ahead, Kate. "Here am I, send me," et cetera.* Carroll, too, seemed to be lost in thought. After a few minutes' drive, we arrived at Lisbeth's house, a modest bungalow-style on a tree-lined residential street. I parked and turned to Carroll before getting out.

"Listen, I don't think I'm going to tell the others about Steve's death—at least not right away. They'll find out eventually, but I don't even know if Reynolds would approve of me divulging the fact of an open case to anyone else at this point. And aside from that, I think having a normal social call might help lift my mood today."

"I hear that. Fine, no Steve talk."

We nodded to each other and walked up the neatly paved driveway. When I knocked on the door, Lisbeth opened it immediately, as if she'd been standing right there waiting all morning.

"Kate—you're here! Carroll, welcome! Come in, come in. I'm so glad you could make it. I love my kids madly, but sometimes I really do like to talk to grown-ups. Are you hungry? Thirsty?" She was going a mile a minute, a quality I found simultaneously endearing and exhausting about her.

"Hi, Lisbeth. Yes and yes." I laughed. It was good to see her. I looked back and saw Frances's car pull in behind mine in the driveway. "Hail, hail, the gang's all here." We waited for Frances to approach, and then we all stepped into Lisbeth's carpeted foyer.

"Iced tea? Mimosa?" Lisbeth offered. "I warn you—I have my position as an upstanding citizen of Asheboro to consider, so if you have more than one adult beverage, I'll have to appoint a designated driver or get Phil to drive you home when he gets back. But seriously, I have champagne."

"Duly noted," I said. "I'm not in much of an imbibing mood anyway. How about just the orange juice?"

"You got it, lady. Follow me," Lisbeth said. And we did, like an obedient flock of sheep.

We sat around the kitchen table, each with a glass of juice or tea in hand, and shot the breeze about this and that. Small-town life in Asheboro. From what Lisbeth and Frances said, I couldn't see that the place had changed much since I was in high school. It made me sad to think about that gorgeous mansion sitting empty and silent out in the country, hiding its secrets. And there certainly were secrets—starting with that body in the staircase that nobody seemed to have known about. But mostly the talk was general. At one point, we meandered into a discussion of the search for a new town librarian, which had been tabled until the fall. Or maybe forever, if Mayor Skip couldn't find some funding for it in those budget meetings. Lisbeth brought out a heaping tray of home-made cheese rolls, fresh fruit salad—the strawberries were just perfect—and small cookies, for good measure. The mood was quietly cheerful, and we were all well fed. It really was a relief to have a casual conversation after such a strange week. The talk turned to town history, and Frances seemed to arrive at something she'd wanted to tell us.

"I think I've mentioned to you before that memories in the country are long," she said, sipping a tall glass of iced tea. "This may not seem like 'country' to you now—it's been quite built up in my lifetime—but a hundred years ago, it was plenty of farmland on all sides. And no, I'm not talking about my childhood a hundred years ago—I'm not *that* old. But it's all in the papers, if you know how to look. After the Civil War ended, there were a lot of poor people, just trying to get by. Subsistence farming, in many cases, not making a profit but surviving, more or less. They might have owned the family land—that was more than could be said for people just freed from slavery—but still, it was hard to make a living, especially if the family was large. Henry Barton was sitting on a nice piece of land here, but at some point, he stopped farming it and turned his interests to industry in one form or another. There may well have been farmers around here who resented that. Who was this man from Boston, muscling in on their town? He wasn't one of them. That could have contributed to his isolation. The men in town welcomed the jobs he created, but they might also have had some hard feelings."

"You're getting this from the town paper?" Carroll asked.

"Not exactly. It's a broader feeling I have—from reading the papers, yes, but also from living here all my life. Hearing people talk. You see the dynamics in the town over generations, though they're hard to pin down with footnotes, the way you might need to for academic purposes."

"So what *did* you find in the town paper?" Carroll pressed on, clearly hoping for some hard facts.

"Well, now that you ask, there was an interesting series

of articles I had never come upon before. I assume you've heard of the Hatfields and McCoys?"

"Only in a general way," I answered. "Some kind of family feud, right?"

"Yes, in the West Virginia–Kentucky area, right after the Civil War and for a good many years after that. It lasted for generations. Family members on both sides died. You don't need to know the details, but you should know that it was not an isolated incident, only the most famous one."

"You're telling me that things like that happened in other places? Places like Asheboro?"

"Yes," Frances said. "Your family arrived too late to have any part in all that, but there are lots of families around here who never left, and they remember. They don't talk about it much, certainly not with out-of-towners—which, for all practical purposes, is what you are, given that you moved to the city years ago. But they haven't forgotten."

"Wow," I said, and fell silent for a few moments. "Frances, I assume you brought this up for a reason, other than it makes a good story. Does this have something to do with our project or with Henry Barton?"

"Not exactly. Barton had no local connections with any feud. It doesn't seem that Mary's people did either, from the little I've read."

"So," I continued, "why does this matter now?" When Frances began speaking again, I thought for a moment that she'd changed the subject, but that wasn't true.

"Since I've had plenty of time on my hands at the paper, I've read through many decades of issues, cover to cover. There were never dramatic stories about shoot-outs or killings on the edge of town, and no names named, but if you pay attention, over time, you begin to notice details. Who was mentioned, or not mentioned—at church, or local events, or even buying a new horse. Who didn't sell a plot of land to whom, and who didn't hire whose brother-in-law to work it. Ordinary, everyday events in a small town—but certain names come up in connection, for years. It's subtle, and most people don't go looking, but it's there. So when I heard that Morgan Wheeler had hired Steve Abernathy to work on the Barton house, it set off a little alarm in my mind."

I finally saw where she was going with this. "You're saying Morgan and Steve are the latest addition to two families like the Hatfields and McCoys?"

"Maybe. I couldn't swear to it, but I do believe Steve's family's been in plumbing and building for generations around here. I don't know Morgan well, truth be told. But . . ." She hesitated, seeming to assemble her words carefully. "There was some kind of an ugly spat between two local men when I was a girl, and it led to an old barn on someone's property being burned to the ground. It was ruled an accident—luckily, no one was in the barn, or it would've made a much bigger story—but my folks always thought there was something fishy about it. So, I turned up a few notes on the incident in the papers. The men in the argument? Abernathy and Simmons—which, if I recall, was the surname on Morgan's mother's side. So that fire might live on, in some form, in the crew you're now working with."

Oh no. I tried to recall all the interactions I'd seen between Morgan and Steve. There hadn't been many, of course, before Steve's untimely end. But there *had* been that strange tone the night before at the mansion—a struggle for dominance in the Barton project? Or was it something older than that? Could things have turned violent? I thought Morgan seemed like a peaceable type, being Quaker and all—or so he said. Steve had struck me as a wild card, but now he was dead, so there was nothing more to be learned about his character. Carroll and I exchanged a glance. I was determined to keep this lunch light and sociable; I didn't want to tell them about Steve's death unless it was absolutely necessary.

"Frances, this is all good to know. I've actually been wondering if there was a personal problem between Morgan and Steve."

"Oh, dear—is there trouble between them?"

"Well . . . it's hard to say," I said, prevaricating. I flashed back on a memory of Steve's arrogance toward the other people around him: disrespect toward Morgan, his rather dismissive attitude toward Bethany, and the sniping jokes he made toward his own brother. "Steve seems like a competent worker, but he rubs people the wrong way." I glanced at Carroll again, unsure if I had her permission to tell Frances what she'd told me about her incident with Steve. "He made some women on the project uncomfortable, and he was having a shouting match with Morgan and Bethany last night after we left the mansion."

"My. What about?"

"I didn't get the whole thing, but it seemed to be about authority, in part—who was giving the directions, and who had to take assignments."

"That sounds about right." She clucked her tongue. "You see some strange battles for power in this sleepy little town. I wouldn't think there was so much to fight over, but there's always someone with not enough, and someone he thinks has more."

I wanted to say something dismissive, to consider this notion frivolous—could anyone care what happened between some farmers a hundred years ago? But Steve's body at the foot of the basement stairs might speak otherwise. To say nothing of the older body, walled up in the kitchen.

"Frances, are you thinking about the body we found in the wall in relation to this old feud?"

"Maybe. We don't get many murders around here."

I gulped. The scenes of the two deaths in the mansion tangled together in my mind. Were they related? And was Steve's fall a mere drunken accident, or was a killer now at large?

"Maybe there's more we can learn here," I said. "Carroll?"

"Yes?" she said, about to crunch into a cookie. She looked attentive, but confused.

"When you get back to the library, could you look up Steve Abernathy's family in or around Asheboro and see who the family members were? I bet there's something in the genealogical records in that town history room. If his family has been here in the trades for generations, there must be some records of them. We should have his date of birth on the work papers Morgan sent me."

"Sure thing. But why?"

"Well, I think Frances has proposed the idea that the body in the staircase is somehow related to Steve. Or his family."

"Wow. Okay, I'll see what I can find."

"Try to do it discreetly. There's still an investigation open on the old body, though it's something of a formality, but I don't want to publicize that we're pulling documents related to existing families in the town. Luckily, the library's not open to the public these days—or rather, that's lucky for us, unfortunate for the townspeople. But at least it means you won't run the risk of meeting up with any town gossips in the stacks. But see what's up with the Abernathy family—as far back as you can find. Were they dirt poor or comfortable? Where did they live in relation to the Barton mansion? I'd like to know if he's been trying to sabotage the project because of some ancient blood feud, for instance."

"Happy hunting, ladies," Frances said. "It sounds like

you've got plenty to look into. Now, I'd better get to the office. It wouldn't be the first time I've discovered Intern Troy asleep at the scanner."

"Perish the thought," Lisbeth said, grinning. "Frances, you'll teach the youth of Asheboro journalistic rigor if it's the last thing you do!"

"I will indeed," Frances said, returning the smile. "Kate, do stop on by if you'd like to look through some old issues, will you?"

"Definitely. I can see there's more to be learned here."

After some more mild chatter, Frances, Carroll, and I all hugged our host and made our way back out into the sunshine of the day. Indeed, my mood had lifted a bit, though Frances's revelation had left me with a list of new questions.

18

arroll and I returned to the B&B and to our respective research tasks there. There was no sign of Josh, so I figured he had returned to the carriage house, perhaps feeling less spooked about the place now that Steve's body and the authorities were gone. I would've liked a heads-up, but I wasn't about to call and harangue him about it; we were both adults and could sleep wherever we wanted to, I thought somewhat bitterly. I turned in early, feeling unresolved, and slept a deep and dreamless sleep.

On waking, a single and unshakable thought popped into my mind: I needed to talk to Morgan. The town feud story was too big to ignore given recent events, and based on our previous conversations, I thought he'd be honest with me. But was he still at the police station? I'd heard no update from the authorities on the status of the case. But would Reynolds, an intelligence professional but not an Asheboro native, know anything about the bad blood between Steve's and Morgan's families? Heck, I hadn't even known about it until an hour ago, and I grew up here.

I sat up straight in bed, picked up my phone, and dialed Morgan's number. This time, he picked up, sounding weary. He must've been having a hard week too.

"Hello, Kate?"

"Morgan, are you all right? I heard you were down at the police station yesterday."

"I was. I'm home now." He wasn't forthcoming with further details. I felt a pang of fear—at the strangeness of the whole situation, the new sense that the town and its buildings were haunted, and at the nagging feeling that I couldn't trust the man I was coming to like and in fact depending on for the whole Barton project. But I knew I needed to hear the truth—or Morgan's version of it.

"Morgan, can we meet up? I'd like to talk to you."

"I thought you might say as much. Name the time and place."

I told him to meet me at the Barton mansion in an hour. We wouldn't go in—the house was still an active crime scene—but I wanted to walk the grounds with him, and find out what he knew. I dressed and went downstairs, finding Josh reading quietly in an armchair in the parlor; he must have come over early. Carroll was seated with her laptop at the kitchen island, engrossed in a document. I addressed them both from the hallway between the rooms, hoping to sound casual and slip off to my errand without sparking any worry.

"Hey, folks, I'm heading out for a bit. I have some errands to do. Can you hold down the fort?"

"Of course," Carroll said. "Is everything all right?" Josh looked at me from his seat in the parlor, but didn't speak.

"Yes. Don't worry, it's not a big deal. I'm just feeling stymied as far as actual work right now, with the mansion being off limits for a few days. But I can scout out some businesses Morgan referred me to who might do replicas of antique furnishings."

"Oh, great," Carroll said, returning to her work.

I had almost made it out the front door when Josh approached and caught me lightly by the elbow, his voice hushed.

"All right, Carroll might've believed that story about running errands, but I don't buy it for a second. Where are you actually going, Kate?"

"Listen, I don't want you to worry. But I need to talk to Morgan."

"Morgan, who was *in the house* when someone died less than twenty-four hours ago? Carroll told me about the town feud thing Frances briefed you on. Do you even know what happened the night Steve died? Did the detective call you with news?"

"He didn't, no, but that's what I'm hoping to learn about. Morgan's home now. They let him go after questioning, so—"

"That might not mean anything," Josh nearly hissed.

"I don't think Morgan is a killer," I said, uncertain I fully believed myself. I'd heard those heated voices in the Barton kitchen. "And I appreciate the concern, but I have an appointment soon, so I've got to get going."

"Fine," Josh shot back. "But I'm coming with you."

"Fine." We both stood in the doorway for a moment, each of us hoping the other would crack. No such luck—we were two stubborn people. But I had an idea. "Listen, Josh, how about this: when we get there, you head over to the carriage house and stay put for now. You and Morgan don't know each other well, and I think he'll be more inclined to speak frankly if it's just me. But you'll be nearby, and I can call you if things go south."

"If you've got enough time to make a phone call when things go south, that is."

"What, you think he's going to come at me with a wrench, in broad daylight?"

"Barton's house is way out in the country—who would be there to see it if he did? I don't know him well, Kate. And honestly—neither do you."

That statement gave me pause, but I was undeterred. Josh and I hashed out a rough plan in which I'd speak with Morgan on the mansion's lawn, in full view of the carriage house windows, where Josh could watch for any signs of trouble. We drove in silence to the Barton property, and at the last minute, I took the unmarked side road to approach from the back side of the land—to the same broken patch of fence where local teens snuck in—and dropped Josh there, to hoof his own way toward the carriage house. If anything was up with Morgan, I didn't want him to get spooked and keep it from me in our conversation.

When I had circled back and finally arrived at the house, I saw Morgan's truck out front. I parked beside it, but there was no sign of him. I got out and walked around to the back of the house. About fifty feet ahead, off to the side of the carriage house, I could see a man sitting on a low stone bench at the periphery of where the garden had been. Morgan. When I was near enough to shake hands— though we didn't—I stopped, looking down at him on the bench, and he tipped his cap and stood. I spoke first.

"Morgan. Good morning. Listen, you and I both know you've been a great help on this job so far. Bringing Asheboro back to life through its antique architecture must look like a fool's errand to a lot of people. Some days I have to remind myself what the heck I think I'm doing. The first two guys I talked to for the contractor job all but ran screaming off the property. But not you. You looked at the place with a serious eye and dove in. Thank you for that. Sometimes it just takes one other person to believe something can work, to say yes, to keep things afloat. Beyond that, you really impressed the board members, and I could tell from the way you described your plans that you love old houses. That's rare. I've really been looking forward to seeing what you do with the place. And I think we get along well—"

"Kate, just say it, please." Morgan had been listening patiently while rolling his weathered green cap between his hands, and he now spoke up, sounding resigned. "You won't need me on the project anymore. I'm fired. You can say it."

"What?" I sputtered, taken aback. I was prepared to question the man in front of me about an old town feud in connection to a present-day death, but I wasn't planning to *fire* him. "No, I wasn't going to say that. But there's something I need to know. Or—maybe I'd better tell you some things *I* know first." I glanced up at the carriage house windows again. They were dark. Was Josh in there somewhere?

"Very well, then," he said, eyeing me warily.

"I know about the old local feud going back generations between your family and Steve's—"

"Now, that's something I've never put much stock by, Kate," Morgan interjected. His tone was even, but it was clear this was a subject he didn't care to dwell on. "That's in the past—and I'm living here, in the present."

"That's all very well, but memories are long in the country, I know, and some fights don't just dissolve, or . . . Let me just come out and say it. What happened to Steve on Thursday night? How did he end up at the bottom of those stairs? I want the truth."

Morgan took a long pause, turning his head slightly to the right and left, examining the gently sloping country-side—or looking around for witnesses? I shifted my weight onto one foot, prepared to move quickly if I needed to. The sweat on the back of my neck felt prickly and cool in the still air. Morgan stuffed his old green cap into the pocket of his work pants and then put his hand into his other pocket. What was he reaching for? And did I have anything on me with which to defend myself, if that's what it was coming to? I patted the outside of my pants. A pen? A Swiss Army knife? The big ring of keys to the Barton house was about the best I could do in the moment. Did I really think this man was dangerous? My eyes darted once again to the carriage house. A tall figure had appeared on the stoop leading up to the front door—Josh. And he was heading this way. Had he read a threat in Morgan's body language that had only now become apparent to me? Morgan was still fumbling in his pocket, speaking quietly as he did so. I leaned in slightly to hear him—against my better judgment—while gripping the keys tightly in my own pocket.

"I didn't want to have to show you this, Kate. I was hoping to just let this go past."

And then he withdrew an object from his pocket and handed it to me. I took it without thinking, stunned to see that it wasn't a weapon of some sort. It was a small, dark rectangle, with flecks of gold along one side. It was a book.

"What's this?"

"It's from Barton's library. I was hoping to put it back without having to tell you the whole thing, but next time I got down there, the police had arrived. I didn't think that was a good time to go snooping into some other room under their noses, and they wanted to talk to me anyway. I'm sorry, Kate."

"Why do you have it? These things are valuable, you know. I'd appreciate it if they didn't just go walking out of the building."

"I know that, Kate. I hope you'll believe me. I had no intent to take it for myself, honest, though I have read a share of Trollope in my time—interesting guy."

"Morgan, get to the point. Why is this in your pocket?" *And why*, I still wondered, *was its companion volume in Steve's?*

"After you left us at the mansion the other night, I stepped out for dinner with my wife, as I told you. Well, first I dropped young Lars off at the train station for his date in the city, then a quick meal at home, and I came right back here to make sure all was well before Bethany and Steve wrapped up for the evening. But all was not well. I found Steve in the library. Snooping, it looked to me. He had no business there regarding the plumbing work. And the man wasn't much of a reader, far as I could tell. I saw him before he heard me enter the room, and he was pocketing this. I confronted him, took back the book, told him to get back to work."

"That explains something. He had another one of these books in his pocket when they found him."

"I must've missed that. But I locked the door to the library with the key you gave me, so he wouldn't sneak back in when I went upstairs. Looking back on it, I wish I'd kicked him out of the house right then—something about him wasn't right. Like maybe he'd been drinking. Not in his right mind. Eyes a little too big, speech blurry around the edges."

"What happened then?"

"I went back upstairs and returned to working on my floor plan of the house. Shortly after that, I heard a slam, which I took to be the front door. I walked from the back bedroom to the front and looked out onto the lawn. Someone had just left and was walking toward the vehicles. It was Bethany. It was getting dark at this point, but I could see her. She got into her truck and drove away. I thought perhaps she was heading home—now, I appreciate it when people inform me if they're going to clock out for the day, but I do trust Bethany's judgment. Steve's . . . less so. But I went back to my work, and didn't think too much about it—until I heard the sirens.

"Sirens?"

"The Asheboro PD arrived and parked out front. One car at first, and then more were called after they found Steve. I ran downstairs as soon as I saw them coming. They took me to the station and kept me there all night, until Detective Reynolds could be rustled up to speak with me in the morning. It was an awfully long time."

"So you didn't see what happened? And how did the cops even know to show up?"

"I'm afraid I didn't see it, and I don't know who called

the police. I thought I heard a thud just after the front door slammed, but in that moment, I assumed it was just one of the many sounds an old wood house makes. Now I'm not sure. I don't want to believe Bethany had anything to do with Steve's death, but . . . I don't know."

Josh had made his way to within earshot of us. He was almost panting. Morgan saw me watching and turned; we both stared at Josh as he began to speak.

"Detective Reynolds just called on the landline at the carriage house. He's been trying to reach you, Kate, but you seem to have left your cell phone in the car." He gave me a pointed look as if to say, *Good job, junior sleuth.* "They're still looking for Bethany. No one's seen her since the night of Steve's death. Reynolds wants us to contact him with any information, or if Bethany calls you."

Morgan and I looked at each other. Was Bethany all right—or had she fled the scene of something? I didn't *want* to think Bethany had had any part in Steve's death, but we didn't even know her side of the story. A kernel of memory opened up in my mind. I turned to Morgan and Josh, pulling out the keys I was still unconsciously gripping in my pocket.

"Get in the car. I have an idea."

19

Morgan, Josh, and I piled into my car, and I peeled out onto the local highway, heading for the other end of town. I didn't know the exact address I was looking for, but I'd recognize it when I saw it. When we got close to the town grocery store, I made a sloping left turn into a midcentury housing development, the only residential cluster in that part of town. I slowed down and began scanning the façades of houses as we passed them. Morgan leaned forward from the back seat.

"What exactly are we looking for, Miz Kate?"

"I'll let you know. It might be nothing, but . . . I've got a hunch."

With no luck on the first street, I rounded the looped end of a cul-de-sac, exited onto the development's broad central avenue, and turned right onto a tree-lined side street. The paving was just a step up from gravel—this was not a wealthy area, even for Asheboro—but islands of cheerful flowers in big aluminum tubs separated the traffic lanes. Momentarily distracted by the lilies and mammoth sunflowers peering at us from the raised beds in the median, I returned my gaze to the houses we were driving past—and immediately stepped on the brakes. I pulled over and got out of the car. The sun was hot above us.

"Stay here, you two," I said to Josh and Morgan, who looked too confused by this whole escapade to protest. "I'll scream if I need you. Got it?" They nodded.

I walked across the small front yard, which was planted with more sunflowers, along with several kinds of squash and string beans climbing tall trellises. I walked up to the concrete stoop of the house and knocked on the door. The *blue* door—only one like it among the muted color palette favored by most of Asheboro's citizens. A few anxious seconds passed, and then I heard shuffling footsteps approaching the door. It opened, and a girl of thirteen or fourteen stood on the other side, balancing a baby on her hip.

"Can I help you?" the girl asked.

I almost lost confidence. Could I be in the wrong place? "Is . . . is Bethany here?"

"Oh yeah. Hold on." She turned her head toward the inside of the house and shouted, "Auntie B! Lady here to see you." The baby smiled, reached out a sticky starfish of a hand in my direction. The girl turned her blank gaze back to me. "You can come in, if you want. Wait—you selling something?" I shook my head, and the girl shuffled away, evidently satisfied with my answer, her too-big fuzzy slippers slapping the floor beneath her heels.

I stepped into the front room of the house, a narrow space filled with shoes ranging from tiny to adult size, a variety of raincoats and outerwear piled voluminously on hooks along one wall. I waited, a bit tensely. *Could I take Bethany in a fight?* Probably . . . Maybe? Okay, if I was honest with myself, I knew the woman could snap me between two fingers if she wanted to. But it probably wouldn't come to that, right? I was glad I had brought my two male companions along in case things got serious, though they'd be on the other side of the door if anything went down. I heard footsteps in the hall, and Bethany appeared.

"Hi, Kate. What's going on? Why are you at my sister's house?"

"Bethany. I'm sorry to bother you here, but I need to talk to you. Can we sit?"

She looked confused and slightly guarded, but not unfriendly. "Sure, no problem. How did you even find me? I gave Morgan my normal address on the hiring paperwork."

"Who else in this town has a front door painted haint blue?"

"Oh, right." She looked with fondness at the door I had just entered through, and then waved me in. We walked into a sitting room dominated by a large flat-screen TV playing cartoons on mute. A brimming canvas laundry hamper leaned heavily against a wall in one corner of the room. "You met my nieces, I see."

"I did. They're cute."

"I stop in to hang out with them a couple of times a week. Rekia's old enough that she doesn't really need a babysitter, but my sister just wants to make sure she doesn't burn down the house trying to make mac and cheese or something. I don't mind. So what do you want to talk about?" Her question had a slight edge to it.

I didn't know where to begin. I decided to just leap in. "Bethany, I need you to tell me what happened with Steve."

"On Thursday night? Okay, listen, I'm sorry I went MIA, but I just could *not* with him. I don't know if I can come back and be on the crew if we're going to be working at the same time. Not without an apology, first of all."

I blinked at her a few times. "I . . . Okay. Right. Can you tell me what happened?"

"Yeah, sure." She stared at the mute television screen for a moment. "Morgan left, and I kept working on my plans in the kitchen. I don't know what Steve was doing—seemed like he was just wandering around the upstairs rooms, being nosy, but that's not my business. I let him be. Then I went down in the basement—I was trying to see where I could put a chase. I made a few small holes, but nothing conclusive yet. After a while, I heard someone come into the house upstairs. Must have been Morgan coming back from his dinner. Then I heard Steve and Morgan yelling at each other for a couple of minutes, then a door slammed and Steve wandered down to the basement and found me. He seemed . . . off. He wasn't being careful the way he moved, kind of knocking into things, which isn't cool when you're in a delicate work space, you know? And then I think he was trying to hit on me—but, like, really badly. He knows I'm married—and to a woman—but he kept saying things about my appearance, how I looked so good, and then he'd get in my space, try to smell me or something. It was really gross. I almost felt bad for him—it seemed like he'd been drinking, and he was not in control of himself. But then he grabbed me, and I had to draw the line. I told him to get off."

Bethany's shoulders were pulled up, her arms crossed in front of her, her breaths quick, as if she were reliving this moment while reciting it. She went on, "So I twisted to get away from him, told him he needed to cut it out. And he kind of went berserk. Like he thought he was en-titled to treat me that way and I was denying his rights or something. He started saying threatening stuff—not even about me but, like, wouldn't it be a shame if this place burned down? And how he had a tank of kerosene in his truck outside. Which I doubt was true. But he could re-ally have done something. So I told him I was calling the cops. He didn't care. I called the Asheboro station and told them he was drunk and disorderly, he was making threats about arson, endangering town property. I didn't know if that would stick, but I needed to do something. And then I left. I wasn't about to wait for the cops to show up. Steve started to follow me up the stairs, but he wasn't moving too fast. I got out of there and came here—I've been here since, honestly. I just needed some time to decompress from that whole thing. So, again, I'm sorry I didn't call you—my phone service just got shut off, and things have been tight lately, so I wasn't going to re-up it until I got my first paycheck from Morgan. You're not going to fire me over this, are you? If there's a problem with the crew, I think you should really take a look at Steve."

"Oh, I have." I sighed. Now it was my turn to stare at the silent television, its display showing a garish pink cartoon forest with green mushroom people walking through it on some kind of quest. I tried to digest what I had just heard. So, it looked like Bethany *wasn't* a cold-blooded killer, assuming she was telling the truth. I believed that she didn't even know Steve was dead, and I wasn't looking forward to telling her. But what *had* happened to Steve? No answers were appearing.

I knew what we had to do next. I asked Bethany to wait a minute, stepped into the hallway, and called Detective Reynolds. He said he was in his office at the nearby field station, and that I'd better come over with Bethany right away. I returned to Bethany, who was again staring at the TV while rubbing at a knot in her strong forearm.

"Bethany? I need you to come with me. I'm not firing you, don't worry—but someone else needs to hear what you just told me. People have been looking for you, you know. Can you leave here for a little while?" She nodded, confused but willing, and stepped out briefly to speak with her older niece. Satisfied that no mac-and-cheese fires would occur in her absence, she grabbed her bag and headed with me toward the door. As we left the room, my gaze fell on the heaping laundry basket, atop which sat a dusty pair of work pants and a black T-shirt.

"Bethany, are those the work clothes you were wearing on Thursday?"

"Yeah, why? I haven't gotten around to doing laundry."

"Oh, believe me—no judgment here. Do you have a plastic bag I can borrow?"

She walked back to the kitchen and retrieved a disposable grocery bag, its thin white plastic printed with the logo of the store a few blocks from where we stood. I picked out the pants and T-shirt from the top of the laundry pile and placed them into the bag, tied it at the top, and took it with me. Bethany looked at me as if I had two heads, but she didn't argue. It had clearly been an odd few days for her too. We left the house and found Morgan and Josh leaning against the side of my car.

"Don't say anything, you two. We have another stop to make."

Bethany got into the passenger's seat, the two men climbed into the back, and we made the fairly long drive out to Reynolds's field office without speaking. When we arrived, I led Bethany in the front door and asked her to tell the detective what she'd told me. I handed Reynolds the bag of clothing, telling him I'd explain in due time. He brought Bethany into his office, nodded at me, and closed the door. I went back outside and sat on the hood of my car, looking through the storefront office's glass façade for any signs of movement, though I knew it could be a while. Josh and Morgan stood nearby, chatting, but clearly waiting for some sort of explanation. I took out my phone and dialed Meredith, the forensic pathologist who'd extracted the mystery body from the wall only days ago. To my surprise, she picked up.

"Meredith? It's Kate Hamilton. By any chance, are you working on the body of Steve Abernathy, who was found in the Barton house two nights ago?"

"How did you know? It's not often one gets two bodies in the same house, one hundred years apart. What a strange turn of events! I couldn't resist."

"Listen, I need to know something. Was there any dust on Steve's body? White powder, or some sort of dry residue?"

"There was, yes."

"Where was it?"

"On the man's hands. Palms, fingers—all over."

"Is that the only place?"

"Yes. Well, mostly—a few scuffs of it here and there, probably picked up as he was falling down the stairs. But the palms—I thought that was odd. Residue on a victim's hands can indicate a struggle of some sort, but he's got no defensive wounds. So I figured I'd analyze the stuff."

"Were you able to identify it?"

"Not yet. I sent samples to the lab, but they haven't come back yet."

"Meredith, I'll bet you a dollar you'll find some horse DNA in that dust."

"Excuse me?"

"Never mind. Thank you for the information. And please call Brady Reynolds when you have a chance—he's got a new piece of evidence for you to analyze."

"I will, Kate. And just so you know, equine genetic material was *not* at the top of my list on the workup, but I'll make a note. You have a good day." She sounded confused but a little excited too—the woman was good at her job. I hung up and returned to Josh and Morgan.

"What's going on here, Kate?" Josh demanded.

Morgan looked toward the office door with some concern. "Is Bethany in trouble? Did she . . ." I could see he didn't want to finish the question.

"I don't think Bethany killed Steve," I told them. "If she's telling the truth, she didn't even know he was dead. She left the house before it happened. And from what she and you both told me about the condition Steve was in that night, it sounds like he was perfectly capable of falling down a flight of stairs all by himself."

"I can't say with certainty, but sadly, I think you're right,"

Morgan said, removing his cap to give his damp head some air. "Then what the devil are we all doing here?"

I stared hard at the building's façade, willing Bethany and the detective to talk faster. "Gentlemen," I said, "I'll tell you as soon as that door opens."

20

After about an hour, in which I made several impatient loops around the parking lot on foot, going over what I knew—or thought I knew—the front door of the office building opened, and the broad-shouldered form of Detective Brady Reynolds appeared. He beckoned for me to come in, and I did, with Josh and Morgan in tow. When we got inside, the crisp air-conditioning wrapped us like a chilly blanket. Reynolds handed his business card to Bethany and thanked her; she looked stunned but fairly calm. She gathered up the bag she had brought with her, and as she made her way toward the exit, she stopped in front of me.

"Wow, Kate—I had no idea. I'm so sorry. I didn't like the guy, you know that, but I never wanted . . . *that* to happen. It's terrible. Did he have family?"

"There's Lars, of course, but Steve wasn't married, and

no kids that I'm aware of. The Abernathys go way back in the history books in this town, though."

She looked at me quizzically. "Right. Well, my sister's picking me up in a couple of minutes. Call me when you're ready to get back to work. If I'm still on the crew, I mean."

"You are. Of course you are."

"Thanks. Oh, I meant to tell you something about the house." She looked around at the men in the office and seemed to think better of what she was saying. "Just a little thing. Wiring stuff. Call me and we can go over it later. Bye, Kate."

I put out my hand, and she shook it. She nodded and made her way out the door. I was glad I hadn't had to find out if I could take Bethany in a round of fisticuffs after all— the woman had a firm grip.

Reynolds beckoned me to sit, along with Josh and Morgan, but I found I was too wound up to even stand still. I paced as I considered how to unfold what I knew to the detective.

"Reynolds—I mean, Brady—I don't know if you believe Bethany, but we need to talk."

"Kate, I haven't arrested her, obviously—she walked out of here a free woman. But Ms. Wallace was the last person who saw Mr. Abernathy alive. We're keeping tabs on her while we wait for the full pathology report."

"Detective, let me get down to it. I gave you a bag of

clothing earlier, and I'd like you to pass it on to Meredith to look at. It contains the work clothes Bethany was wearing the night Steve died. You might have noticed that the garments are covered in white dust."

"Yes, I saw that," he replied. "I placed the garments in an evidence bag after I spoke with Ms. Wallace. She wasn't entirely clear on why you had extracted her dirty laundry from her sister's home before traveling here. Kate, your methods are a bit unconventional. You could have called me and—"

"I know that, Detective. But I didn't want to clue in Bethany as to what was going on, and I didn't want to run the risk of those clothes getting washed before your team could have a look at them. Now, as I was saying, they're covered in a fine dust—it's all over the basement at the mansion right now. The kitchen too. The crew has hardly started work, but as soon as you make a pilot hole or cut into a wall, the plaster dust is everywhere. Isn't that right, Morgan?"

"It is indeed. We've got an ample supply of protective masks for the workers. Victorian plaster was sometimes made from lime, and I don't want anyone breathing that in all day."

"Of course not. I appreciate your caution—and your knowledge of the materials. Now, what did you tell me was included in that kind of plaster mix?"

"Well," he replied, stroking his chin sagely, "lime plaster, which was used up until the turn of the century, had

four main ingredients: lime—that is, either ground lime-
stone or oyster shells—water, sand, and fiber. The makeup
of the fiber content varied—horsehair, or cattle, or hog."

"Now you tell me! I just bet Meredith a dollar on horse."

"What?" Morgan cocked an eyebrow at me. He and
Josh were looking at me like I was crazy, and the detective's expression had grown sterner than usual. I decided I
had better get to the point.

"I spoke with Meredith," I continued, "and she told me
that there was white dust on Steve's body, but mostly just
one place—his hands. The palms, specifically. It doesn't
sound like he actually did any work that day, before he took
a header down the basement steps, so it makes sense that he
wasn't covered in lime all over. I'm sure Bethany told you
about Steve's actions at the mansion just before he died. It
sounds like he was pretty out of it and not behaving with
caution or consideration for others."

"Yes. We don't have the tox screen back yet, but there
was a distinct smell of alcohol in the room," Reynolds said.

"I hope she also told you that Steve *grabbed* her, while
he was aggressively making passes at her. And if he grabbed
her firmly—which it sounds like he did—that could have
transferred a significant amount of lime powder from Bethany's clothing onto his hands."

"It seems his grip was very firm," Reynolds said, more
quietly than usual. "She showed me the bruising on her
abdomen."

That image took my breath for a moment, and I fumed

silently at Steve, though I knew he was dead and couldn't be punished for his actions. Reynolds made some brief notes on the pad on his desk and continued. "That confirms, to my mind, that the deceased attempted to assault Ms. Wallace, but it doesn't convince me that Ms. Wallace didn't in some way initiate the fall that killed him. There's a clear motive if he had acted violently toward her just moments before."

"I can see how you might think that—I'd certainly want to shove someone who tried that with me. But don't you believe Bethany? When I came and found her, she had no idea Steve was even dead."

"She's had some time to think up that story, Kate."

I felt exasperated. Couldn't Reynolds see that Bethany had been the victim here and was innocent of any crime—or was I just fooling myself that that was true? I let out a sigh.

"Well, I hope you'll speak with Meredith about the evidence. I don't know what else I can tell you."

"I don't know that you *should* tell me anything else now, Kate, unless you have substantive evidence to contribute. This is my case. I'll speak with Meredith about her findings. In the meantime, we've got all we need from the mansion, so if you need to resume work there, go ahead."

"Gee, thanks," I said, trying and failing to hold back a peevish tone. I turned and walked out of the building, followed by Morgan and Josh.

Morgan looked concerned. "I just hope they'll lay off

Bethany once they confirm that evidence you talked about. I'm sure she didn't do this," he said. "Now, this has been quite a day already—I think I'd better get back home to the missus, if you don't mind."

"Of course, Morgan," I said.

We three climbed once more into my car and made the trip back to the Barton mansion, the afternoon sun beaming thickly through the car windows as my air-conditioning system did its best to keep us comfortable. Morgan sat silent in the back seat, and my occasional glances at him in the rearview mirror showed a man lost in thought. A thought popped into my head just before we reached the mansion.

"Say, has anyone spoken to Lars?"

Morgan piped up from the back seat. "The detective said he'd reached him, that he was still in the city. I gave Lars a call last night and he answered, but he didn't want to talk. Sounded very distraught, poor young man."

"I can understand that," Josh said. "It didn't seem like the two of them got along well, but a brother is a brother."

"Indeed." Morgan looked out the window and fell silent again as we reached the gate of the mansion. I entered the code to unlock it and drove the long path down to Henry Barton's house, where Morgan got out, climbed back into his truck, and was off to dinner with his wife. Josh and I stared at his receding taillights in the gathering dusk. Then we looked at each other.

"Should we . . . talk?" I asked, not sure if I really wanted to.

"Right. I've been meaning to speak to you about the project, but—well, other things keep happening. Why don't we go to my place—the carriage house, that is? I'll order takeout."

"Sure."

Josh was being awfully nice, but I braced myself for his imminent departure from the Asheboro project. I didn't want to be pessimistic, but it had just been that kind of week. I was sure I'd soon be back to square one, looking for a historical consultant in addition to a new plumber, decorators, funders, and everything else this project was lacking. Josh and I walked to the carriage house, a dark form against the sun setting beyond the hill.

I hadn't spent much time in the place, and found I was pleased by its simplicity. It was outfitted with a few sturdy wood chairs, a large table, white walls, and dark drapes, without the elaborate finery of the mansion itself. I sat looking out the window at the waning light while Josh made a call and ordered Thai food. He then went outside to wait by the gate for its arrival—he told me he'd found delivery drivers hesitant to traverse the Barton property's long, winding driveway in his previous time here.

That left me all alone for a while. I looked at my phone. Ryan had called but left no message. I realized we had never had our conversation about administrative details—who would write the checks, who got copies of keys, the

powers of the board, and so on. Exhausted as I was, I figured I might still check something off the to-do list today.
I dialed him back, and to my surprise, he picked up immediately.

"Hi, Ryan—thanks for getting back to me. I have a few
questions for—"

"Kate, I cannot *believe* you." His tone was icy.

"Excuse me? What did I do?"

"My buddy at the Asheboro PD called to let me know
about the body found on your work site. The *second* body.
And when I say 'your work site,' I also mean *my* work site.
I'm on the board, remember? What is going on there?"

"Ryan I . . . I don't know, exactly. Steve fell down the
stairs, it seems, or was pushed . . . and he's dead. No one's
been arrested, but the scene is cleared. Reynolds said we
could get back to work now. Honestly, it looks like it was
an accident, Steve had been drinking, and—"

"Kate. Listen to me. Can this not be normal? Can you
just *do* the work? What kind of murder mansion are you
running here? And your crew is drunk on the job? How is
this going to look to potential investors? You need to get
out in front of this story. This is ridiculous."

I could tell Ryan was in a mood, but I was getting tired
of being interrupted. "Ryan. I need you to settle down for
a minute. We don't know all the details yet. Would you
have preferred that I find that old body in the wall and
not tell anyone? Would that have been the adult solution?
Would that even be legal? You're the lawyer. You tell me.

And of course I don't think it's good that Steve was possibly drinking on-site—but I had just met the man!" The week's stresses were catching up with me. I felt heat rise up my neck and into my cheeks, and my tone grew a shade more sarcastic than good judgment would otherwise allow. "But thank you *so* much for thinking about the project. It means a lot that you cared enough to, you know, *check in* on me. Actually, now that you know the big news, I need to go over some details with you. Since you're our lawyer and a board member, this stuff is actually *your* responsibility to help work out. We're going to need more sets of keys made for the contractors, and probably some contracts drawn up, come to think of it, maybe security cameras, and . . ."

I stopped talking and took a deep breath. In the fever of my annoyance, I was forgetting what I actually wanted to talk about. Reality check: Ryan was an old friend. We were on the same side here—we both wanted the project to go well. I couldn't speak for him, but perhaps I was feeling more stressed than I was admitting to myself. I stared out the window, watching Josh's dark form walking back toward the carriage house, takeout in hand.

"Look, Ryan, I'm sorry to get heated. I can't tell if you're really mad at me or if you're just surprised, but I'm not mad at you—I just need some support on this. This project is my baby, of course, and it's going about as well as it *can* go right now, all things considered—but I can't do everything alone, you know? I know the optics of two bodies in the house aren't great. I don't like it either! There's nothing I can do about that. But you and I can talk more about what to tell the press when that time comes. So, if we could just make a date to go over some admin stuff, whenever you have time, I'd appreciate that."

"Sure, Kate." His tone had come down a few notches but was not entirely neutral. "Shoot me an email. I've got a big case coming up later this month, and there's a lot of prep. Sorry. I can't be on phone calls all day. I mean, I actually *am* on phone calls all day. So one more is sometimes too much."

"Okay, I hear you. I'll send you the details." I took another breath and stared at the wall ahead of me. "So . . . truce?"

"Fine. Truce, uncle, whatever. I just need you to tell me what's going on in a timely fashion without blowing up my phone. And please, no more dead bodies."

"I'm trying! Really. Next time I see one, I'll just leave it there and keep moving, okay?" I thought I could detect a smile over the phone line, but perhaps it was wishful thinking. "Anyway, I'm staying over at the carriage house for the evening. Have a good night, okay?"

"Yup. Bye, Kate." He hung up.

Josh was still making his way down the path back to the house. That talk with Ryan had been unpleasant, but I felt I had defused the tension enough for the time being. I leafed through a book Josh had left on the table on the subject of industrial history, but was unable to focus on the words at all. My mind wouldn't stop its whirring. Finally,

Josh came in from outside, a brown paper bag under one arm. It was dotted with grease and emitted an enticing fragrance, but I wasn't quite ready to eat. Josh had his back to me and was shuffling china in a cabinet over the sink, finding us some dinner plates.

"Josh—" I said, uncertain how to begin. And then it all came tumbling out of me. "I know you're a busy man, with a real, full-time appointment at a prestigious institution, and now you've got summer school, and you've got a book to write on top of everything. And this is dinky little Asheboro, pretty much a nothing town, a blip on the map of history. I know—believe me, I'm from here. This Barton stuff is not your precise area of study, I know that, and you've been more than kind in helping us already. So I completely understand if you need to step away from the project, and . . ." My chest felt tight. Why was I saying all this? "But I just need you to *tell* me if that's what is happening. You don't owe me anything, you don't owe Carroll or Henry Barton or Frances—you hardly know us at all, really. It's just that I've been—*we've* been—depending on you, your affiliation, your academic pedigree and sources, to help this project get on its feet. And it's not your fault, of course, that bodies keep turning up, making it impossible to get any *work* done in this town—but I did like having you here, I always do, to toss ideas around, to compare notes, to keep things moving. But you've been away, or distant, and I can't tell if you want to be here anymore, and if you don't, far be it from me to keep you. I don't know if any of that makes sense to you. I just . . ." I trailed off, a ball of nerves. What did I really mean to ask this man? And then I knew: "I just need an answer. Are you in, or are you out?"

Josh paused, momentarily studying the old china pattern on the plates he was holding. After an impossibly long silence that was probably five seconds, he spoke.

"Kate. I appreciate your candor. And you're right; I am a busy man. I thought this summer class might be easy, but it's kicking my butt, to be honest." He paused, weighing his words, and went on. "So, there's something I've been meaning to ask you. This project at the mansion—the whole town, really—just kind of fell into your lap, didn't it? You didn't go to school for restoration, or sweat through a PhD in a garret apartment studying Victoriana. You just kind of . . . appeared. What makes this particular project feel so important to you? Haven't you made your bones overseeing swanky *new* hotels, in big cities?"

I felt like a cat whose fur was beginning to stand up. The men in my life were asking me a few too many pointed questions today. I tried to keep my tone even, but realized being honest with Josh was more important.

"Okay, Mr. Professor—you want to know why? It's because anybody—with enough money—can put together a new mansion, or a good replica of an old one. I've seen enough rich city people install immaculate copies of Renaissance frescoes over penthouse hot tubs to know that money can get you anything, believe me. But

Henry Barton was special. Look at his life! He was born into a middle-class family. He joined up to fight in the Civil War mainly because his brothers did, and ended up serving far from where he started. He never went home again, but stayed here in Maryland, married, took over a farm—and look what he made of it! He made a family here, as much as he could. He started and grew a business. He knew Clara Barton, and they helped each other. He took on Thomas Edison, the genius of his era, and beat him at his own game. He more or less kept Asheboro alive, without demanding any credit for it. Then his wife died and left him rambling around a gorgeous home, which he probably built to make her happy in the first place. He went on with his business, living a quiet life. And then he died. And now, even the local people have forgotten who he was and what he did with his life! How can that be? Now I have a chance to reclaim a little of his fame for him, tell this amazing story, and do a good turn for my hometown as well. Is that not enough reason to be here? You want more?" I realized I was almost foaming at the mouth. Did Josh not feel what I felt for the house, or was he just poking fun at me?

Josh was silent. He stepped forward and set the dinner plates gently on the table between us. Then he took a deep breath and laughed.

"Kate. Of course I don't need more! You've got quite a spiel about this place—and I buy it all, I really do. I just wanted to hear it from your mouth. Your passion for this job is inspiring—I mean that. The thing is . . . I'm rather impressed by Henry Barton too. I didn't know how to tell you, but I've been thinking of narrowing the focus of my book."

"Your book? What do you mean?"

"I've been working on a history of industrialization in the region for years now, but looking at Barton's story, I'm thinking a more personal focus might be the way to go. It'll appeal to the academic presses—that kind of narrative is in vogue lately, to be frank—but it's more than that. Now, I don't want to tell the romance story of Henry and Mary you seem to be dreaming up in your head"—he smiled sideways at me, a little snidely—"but one man's visionary contribution to industrial and economic life in a depressed postwar town? There's a lot there. I've been hesitant to come out and tell you because the Barton documents are your purview now, and Carroll's, and I don't want to step on any scholarly toes."

"So you do want to stick around? And write about Henry?" I released a breath I hadn't realized I was holding. "That's . . . amazing. But what *about* Carroll? She'll probably end up doing some writing from her studies of Henry's papers too—and not just pamphlets for tourists at the mansion. She might want to write a book herself. Can you two play nice?"

"Absolutely." Josh smiled, more broadly this time, bending his tall form into the chair across from mine and taking my hand in his. "I'll speak with her, person to person. I'm sure we can work something out."

I felt like I'd just put down the big rock I was carrying. There was still so much to be done at the mansion, but knowing Josh would be around to help was a distinct comfort. I took my hand from his and ripped open the bag of food, which we ate with gusto before ascending the stairs and falling happily into bed.

21

I woke early, the blue light just turning to yellow over the hillside through the carriage house windows. I walked downstairs and stood on the front stoop, regarding the mansion across the yard in the sober light of day. There it was, my white whale. We'd get back to work soon, I told myself, and things would settle down. I hoped that was true. I said a quick goodbye to Josh and drove back to the B&B to check in with Carroll. She had taken an early run and was just heading out to work at the library again.

I went back to my car and sat in the driveway with my hands on the wheel, uncertain what to do with myself next. Detective Reynolds had given the all clear to return to work at the mansion, but I'd have to talk to Morgan first to get a read on things. And we'd need a new plumber, I realized. I didn't even know if Lars would want to stay on the project without his brother around to teach him the trade. What, then, was possible today? I remembered

Frances's invitation to stop by the newspaper office and look at back issues for any clues on Henry Barton's personal life. Carroll had turned up some helpful facts about Mary's early years, but the union of Henry and Mary, their real married life together, was still largely a mystery.

I reached the headquarters of the *Asheboro Gazette* in about two minutes' drive—Asheboro being, quite literally, a small town. The paper occupied the ground floor of an old brick storefront of the Civil War era, if not older. Tall, arched windows faced the street, and the front entry was shaded by a red awning—clearly a modern addition—displaying the paper's name in white block lettering. I pushed on the glass door of the vestibule, and it slid open with a wheeze. Frances was seated at a crowded desk in the back, examining something with a large handheld magnifier. She looked up as I shuffled toward her.

"Hello, Kate. How's the renovation business going?"

I told her about Steve's death, our hunt for Bethany, the uncertainty clouding the whole project. She pursed her lips in an expression of shock. If she'd had pearls on, she would have clutched them. "My, you don't get bored, do you?"

"I just can't seem to."

"And Steve Abernathy turned up dead? What a shame. Do you think it had anything to do with . . . ?" She seemed to say *the old town feud*, but just with her eyebrows.

I shook my head. "Well, I don't think so. Morgan says

he wasn't nearby when it happened, Steve was drunk, Lars was out of town, and Bethany—I don't think she was there either. Not that she's from one of the feuding families anyway, as far as I know, but . . . I don't know if I should even be talking about this. I thought you might have turned up something in the newspaper about the Bartons—anything? We've been wanting to know more about Mary, but facts are hard to come by. Carroll found records to indicate that she was raised in the farmhouse that later became the mansion, her father was gone for, uh, mental health reasons, and she was an only child. But what about Henry and Mary as a couple? Were they really so reclusive? Do they ever appear at a cotillion or something? Or was that still a thing in 1880?"

"Cotillions are still a thing today, my dear. I never had one, let it be said, and you don't seem the type either, but they do exist. Now, as to your question: no, Henry and Mary did not step out grandly at town events. That doesn't seem to have been their style. There are a handful of notes in the *Gazette* about happenings at the Barton factory—a new piece of equipment coming by rail, a notice looking for workers when operations expanded, that sort of thing. But if you want to know anything about Mary . . . well, you have to read between the lines a bit."

"What do you mean?"

"Let me show you." Frances spun in her office chair and faced a tabletop machine I hadn't noticed was behind her.

It had a screen like a clunky, old computer, an industrial-gray plastic casing with a series of buttons on one side and a small platform on the bottom, like a microscope.

"Goodness, what is that?" I asked. A dim memory fluttered in the back of my mind.

"This, my dear, is a microfilm reader. These were probably just going out of use when you came of age, eh?"

"I guess so. I might've seen one in . . . middle school? But then the internet happened, and we didn't need them anymore."

"Indeed. Well, some of us are still using them in this world, strange as that may seem. Troy and the other interns are digitizing the collections, as I told you, but a lot of our back issues are still stored in microform. It's not perfect, but it's a stabler medium than newsprint, by far." She swiveled to turn off the desk lamp she had previously been using, then turned back to the microfilm machine. She turned on the device, and nineteenth-century Asheboro flickered to life in front of us.

I stared hard at the film as it zipped past, though Frances was flying through it, so it was hard to make out anything definite. Evidently, she knew what she was aiming for on the reel. Days, weeks, and months seemed to be passing before our eyes, whole episodes of the town's life reduced to images on a squat roll of 35-millimeter film, blown up on the screen in front of us.

"Here." Frances slowed down the pace of her scanning, getting close to the mark. She came to rest on the front page of an issue from 1875. A top-of-the-fold photo showed a large, blocky building with a small crowd standing somberly in front of it. Frances turned to me. "Recognize that place?" The image was a bit blurry.

"I don't think I do."

"It's the Barton shovel factory." She pointed at the text on the lower half of the screen. "This photo is from an event marking the expansion of the factory's production—this is when they moved from just making shovels to producing other small tools, and even light machinery. This expansion was part of what made Henry such a wealthy man."

"I see." I scanned through the article, squinting. It didn't reveal anything personal, at least nothing I could detect. "So . . . what does this tell us about Henry?"

"It doesn't *tell* us anything, exactly. But look at the photo. The caption indicates the event was attended by Henry Barton—and family."

"Oh." I strained to make out the faces in the crowd. There was Henry, front and center, shaking hands with a man the caption named as a senator, and there was . . . a woman, standing to his right. With two small children clinging to her skirts. I gasped. "Is that Mary?"

"I believe so. Of course, she's not named in the caption itself, but we know from official records that Henry only married once. Although these children have never been part of the local lore. I'm surprised to see them."

I bit my lip. Should I tell Frances about what Carroll and I had found in the back field of the Barton property?

Perhaps she, custodian of the town's history, ought to know as much as anyone.

"Well, Frances—" I faltered. "The thing is, they did have children. I don't know why no one talks about that, but . . . we found them. Carroll and I. Out behind the house, in a small plot, with Henry and Mary. Three of them. And Henry didn't have an heir to leave the house to because . . . they didn't make it."

"Oh my. And they never appeared on a census?"

"I'm guessing they were born after 1870, and died before 1880. They look small here—two, three years old? So they must never have been counted."

"Oh, how sad." Frances sighed. "Three children, you say? There are only two here. Look at those faces—they're so tiny."

We both stared at the film in silence for a moment. They were, indeed, tiny people, standing in their Victorian formal wear as close to their mother as they could possibly get, staring dutifully toward the camera. One had a ribbon in her hair, the other a small flat cap on his head. Their expressions looked doubtful, as if the event, the sun above, the day itself were a precarious thing, teetering on a fearful edge. And perhaps it was.

"Maybe the third hadn't been born yet," I said. "We don't know what happened. Just that they died. There's no detail given on the stones."

"You may not find any more, dear." Frances sat back

in her office chair. "Henry had a reputation for being private, and it was well earned. I've scanned through quite a few papers from this decade, and he very rarely appears. Another man of his stature in the town might have milked it, so to speak—made grand appearances, speeches, run for office even. Some people love to make a show of their wealth and power. But not Henry. He created jobs for many people in the town, and he seems to have had a hand in establishing the electric grid for the region, but he doesn't appear in Asheboro's social life. He's hard to track down. We might just have to live with his mystery."

"Say it ain't so, Frances!" I sighed and looked again at the photo in front of us. "Does Mary's face look . . . strange to you? Like there's something on it?"

"That's hard to say, dear." Frances leaned closer and put up her magnifier to the screen to enhance our view, not that it did much. "That could be . . . Well, it could be a smudge or an obstruction on the image, which is frequent enough with these things, or it might be that she had something like a birthmark on her face. Port wine, I think they call that. One of my mother's younger cousins had one—as a child I used to see her once a year, at Easter—and she was always embarrassed, shying away from the group. In fact, she was quite lovely."

"Huh. That could be it. But it's hard to tell. So there's nothing else about Mary to be found here? No splashy feature stories on the rich man's wife?"

Frances shrugged. "I'm afraid not, Kate. I'll keep look-ing through this time period, and I'll let you know if I find anything. But don't hold your breath, my dear."

"Thanks, Frances. This has been illuminating, in its way."

"Well, if you want to come back later in your project and look at images of Victorian storefronts for accurate re-production, you know where to find me!"

"Oh, that's a great idea, Frances. I know nothing about period-appropriate paint colors. Although . . . the newspa-per wouldn't have been in color, would it? Shoot. And do you have anything on Victorian kitchens? Or bathrooms?"

"I can't say I've seen many photos of domestic interiors in newspapers of that time, but I'll keep an eye out. Don't be a stranger, Kate."

"I won't. Thanks again." I stood and walked out, the glass front door closing with a soft plunk behind me, and then I was back on Main Street, in the bright yellow sun-shine. Shabby, dear old Main Street Asheboro. I looked at my watch, and saw that it was almost noon. I walked down the block to Ted's lunch counter and ordered a ham-and-cheese sandwich, which arrived with a zesty garnish of pickled onions. Delicious. Ted himself was staffing the reg-ister, and asked how work on the house was going. I de-flected, telling him about my research into cast-iron stoves of the late Victorian era; he narrowed his eyes in thought and kindly didn't ask any follow-up questions. I'd fill in the board members on our latest development soon, but not until I had answered a few questions for myself. As I was finishing up lunch, my phone rang. I didn't recognize the number, but I picked up. It was a woman's voice.

"Hi, Kate? It's Bethany. I know we're not back to work yet, but there's something at the mansion I thought you should see. Can we meet up?"

The hairs on the back of my neck stood at attention. She wanted me to meet her at the mansion? I didn't really think Bethany had killed Steve, but what could she possibly want to show me in the house—just the two of us, way out there in the sticks?

"Well . . . okay," I replied carefully. "Do you want me to call Morgan in too? I know he's been working on the floor plan—"

"No, I wasn't thinking to show Morgan. Yet, I mean. I thought you should know first."

I stared ahead at the menu board mounted on the wall in front of me. Was this advisable? Josh was probably still in the carriage house, working on his book. I could give him a heads-up that I'd be nearby and might need backup. But then again, Bethany was innocent, right? I decided to take a leap of faith.

"Okay, Bethany. Meet you there in half an hour?"

"See you then."

I hung up the phone, took a long last swig from my glass of lemonade, and stood from my chair. *Well, here goes nothing.*

22

As I drove out to the mansion, I called Carroll on speakerphone. She answered with a grunt, clearly engrossed in something else.

"Hi, Carroll. I just wanted to let you know I'm heading to the mansion to meet up with Bethany. She has something there to show me."

"Hmm, okay," she said, half listening. Then a pause. "Wait, what? Are you back to work there already? And what is she showing you?"

"I don't exactly know. But give me a call in about an hour, okay? Just in case."

"Huh. I don't know if I like this, Hamilton. That house has not felt like the safest place lately. But . . . sure. I'll call you in a little bit." She hung up just as I arrived at the mansion's front gate, rolling down my window to punch in the security code. When I arrived at the entrance, Bethany was sitting on the front steps, appearing to enjoy the blazing summer afternoon. She stood up when she saw me and didn't waste any time on pleasantries.

"Kate. Thank you for stopping by. I know it's kind of weird that I called. How much do you know about the layout of the second floor?"

"Uh, not that much? I've been up there, but I don't have a blueprint or anything. There are, what, six bedrooms?" And what would have been a nursery off one of those, I thought sadly, but I didn't say that out loud. Seeing Bethany again, I remembered her kindness, and the ordinary, human interactions we'd had in our first meetings. Some of my uncertainty melted away. I dashed off a quick text to Josh in the carriage house and decided to let Bethany show me whatever it was she had thought was so important. After all, it was nice to spend time with people who got excited about Victorian architecture the way I did.

"Did Henry and Mary have separate bedrooms?" I asked. I unlocked the front door as we talked, and Bethany walked in ahead of me and began climbing the grand staircase. I followed, wondering where this conversation could be going.

"I think so. That was more of a thing back then. You can tell which is which by the décor. But maybe your research person can confirm that. Definitely not my specialty."

When we reached the second floor, I paused to admire the light coming in through the window and highlighting the old William Morris wallpaper. No expense spared,

even in the nonpublic spaces. "So, you started working at
the top of the house?"

"Yes and no. I checked out the main lines in the basement and made some educated guesses about where they
led. There aren't many on this floor. People didn't have
stuff like hair dryers to plug in back then."

"What about irons, in the days before permanent press?"

"Oh yeah, lots of ironing. But not like how we do it
now. You had to heat an iron on a small stove that had
a flange around the exterior to hold the irons while they
heated. They cooled pretty quickly, so you needed to keep
a lot of irons going, and switch them out every couple of
minutes."

"Oh, like 'too many irons in the fire'?"

"Right, I guess so."

I could see Bethany was now itching to show me whatever she had found, but this talk of historical ironing had
piqued my interest, so I pressed on, following a thread of
thought.

"Can I ask you something?"

"Sure, go ahead." Her eyes darted back and forth as if
making sure no one else was present, but to her credit, she
stayed engaged in the conversation.

"There are several different ways we can go with this
house. Would you rather see this place as a shining example of the ultimate in luxury in its day, or should it
demonstrate how day-to-day life actually worked for regular people—servants included? Like your clothes irons, for

example. I'll bet most people have never seen that setup. I definitely haven't."

"This place'll be open to the public?" Bethany asked. I nodded. "And when you go on with the town renovation, will there be other examples in the town about how ordinary people lived?"

"I haven't gotten that far. Up until now, we've been focusing on this house, and the factory in town, which Henry Barton also built. But eventually, yes. We'll have shops and craftspeople demonstrating different facets of public life a hundred-plus years ago."

"That sounds cool. I definitely think it's important to show how people without a lot of money lived—servants, even slaves. Were there ever any enslaved people here?"

"I don't think so, no. But Carroll can look at that in her research."

Bethany's eyes swept around the space we stood in, with its high ceilings and gilt finishes. "I'd say, exhibit this place as the best of the best. It's rare to see a house as fancy as this, old or new. You definitely want to give a sense of real life for real people—who were mostly *not* millionaire factory owners—but this rich stuff is really compelling to visitors, you know? It's a total time capsule in here. And it's cool to look at it from a design perspective, for sure. As long as you find a balance—like, don't pretend servants didn't live here at all. But I think it makes sense to show off the house, let it be impressive. And you want to have great big parties for donors here, right?" Bethany grinned.

"Exactly. Good wine, canapés—the whole deal." I smiled back at her. "And I want to do other programming here too. Kids' stuff, activities, camps. Maybe your nieces could come join in sometime?"

"That'd be nice," Bethany said.

"So . . . what was it you wanted to show me up here?"

"Oh, right." She cast a glance down the grand staircase before turning and leading me down the hall. Surely no one was within a mile of us, except for Josh out in the carriage house, but she obviously wanted to make sure our talk would not be overheard. "This way. It's in Mary's bedroom."

Bethany led me past the main bedroom, a large room filled with ornate mahogany furniture and lots of velvet. I'd been in these rooms before, but had never really stopped to sit and think about the lives that took place in them. The kitchen and all its attendant problems had been my sole focus thus far. The room Bethany brought me to was lighter and airier than Henry's bedroom. It wasn't pink, in the contemporary style designating feminine things, but rather a warm ivory, with small dashes of color here and there—subtle floral motifs woven into the fabrics, a butterfly mounted under glass—and a good deal of lace. It was delicate and airy, the kind of space that makes one take a calming deep breath. Large windows at one end let in the afternoon sun; they were festooned with lace curtains, only slightly dusty now. A crystal pendant hung from a ribbon in the center window, refracting shards of rainbow light when I set it gently swinging. I looked around the room and realized the only light fixtures I could see were a pair of sconces mounted high on the wall over the bed.

"So, not much electricity in here," I said to Bethany. She too seemed to be momentarily entranced by the slow motion of the pendant, and snapped back to attention as I spoke.

"Nah, they didn't need much," she said.

"So what am I looking for here?" I asked.

"Help me pull the bed out from the wall." She hiked up the legs of her work pants slightly and squatted to lift the heavy wood frame, moving it carefully so as not to damage the floor. I gave her a puzzled look but followed suit to the best of my ability. It took the two of us to budge the sturdy bed more than a couple of inches away from the wall. When we had moved it far enough to see behind it, Bethany spoke again.

"I was looking to see how they fed the wires into this room for the reading lights over the bed here. There was a place where they joined the incoming wires, where someone had cut a box into the floor by removing part of a floorboard—but when I saw that, I stopped." She was pointing down at a hole in the floor, with a piece of floorboard that functioned as a lid lying beside it. I didn't immediately know what I was supposed to learn from this. A fine detail of wiring she wanted me to understand? A potential problem in our work plan? She crouched down on one side of the bed, beckoning me to do the same on the other. "Take a look."

On my hands and knees, I stretched my head as far as I could into the narrow space behind the bed and peered into the void in the floor, which looked about eight inches deep and over a foot wide—the width of a single old-style wooden floorboard. I could see a couple of wires feeding into the space, but they disappeared under a row of . . . books? I stared for a moment, and then I realized what they could be. "Diaries?" I whispered to Bethany. She nodded at me from the other side of the bed frame.

"Yeah. I pulled one out to check, but I put it back right away—it's not my business, and I thought you'd want to see them first. Of course, they could just be a description of the weather every day, for all I know."

Please, no. I need some proof of life in this place! Judging by the size of the pile, it appeared Mary might have written in these small leather-bound books for many years. She'd taken care to hide them out of sight, although who she might have been hiding them from, I couldn't say. Maybe she simply valued her privacy. I reached out, almost afraid to touch them. Would they crumble in my hand? "I think I need a box," I said.

"Coming right up," Bethany said, rising from her crouch. She went out into the hall and returned with a sturdy cardboard box that might once have held a pair of boots. We slid the bed out a bit farther from the wall so that I could get a better angle, and then we formed a short line: I gently retrieved each book—luckily not crumbling—and handed it to Bethany, who laid it carefully in the box. By the time we were done, twenty volumes were neatly lined up to-gether. From what little I'd seen, the pages were anything but blank—Mary had apparently been an avid writer.

I crawled out of my narrow space and stood up. Beth-any placed the box of books in the center of the ivory bed-spread, and we both gazed reverently at the contents of the old shoebox. I noticed Bethany was shifting her weight from foot to foot, glancing out the window now and then. It occurred to me now that she hadn't been acting shifty—she was nervous. But why?

"Are you okay?" I asked.

"Yeah, fine. Just . . . I don't know. Since the whole thing with Steve, I just don't feel great. Kinda scared, you know? And then the guy even died, which is terrible, but still—you'd think I wouldn't feel like somebody was coming to get me if that person actually *died*, right? But I don't really feel safe."

"I'm so sorry. Maybe you could talk to a professional about this? Of course I want you to stay on the team, but it's hard to work—heck, it's hard just to live—if you keep feeling this way."

"That's probably a good idea. I'm on my wife's insurance—I'll see if I can find someone."

We were silent again, both looking at the slowly spin-ning crystal in the window and the golden light on the hills beyond it.

"Thank you," I said.

"For what?"

"For finding these. For telling me about them. This house has been feeling kind of haunted—even before Steve died—and this might put a little light back into the space. I hope so anyway. And Carroll will be thrilled! These might be Mary's firsthand accounts of life in the manor house, maybe even before Henry decided to improve on it. Original sources are always important. I can't wait to take a look at them."

"Good," Bethany said. "If they're anyone's, they're yours. You totally have first rights."

"Look, can I ask you not to mention these to anyone else? Maybe it's selfish of me, but I think they're kind of personal—private, you know? I want to look through them before I make them public knowledge. There might even be a book about it—maybe one that complements a similar book on Henry's work in Asheboro. I know I'm getting way ahead of myself, and of course I'm not a writer, but I'd kind of like to be alone with Mary, if that makes sense."

"Sure, no problem. That's why I was trying to keep it on the down low too, asking you to meet me before Morgan came back. I hope that doesn't seem wrong—I definitely trust Morgan, but I thought this might be just for you, for now."

"I appreciate your discretion. But I will share them with Carroll, and maybe Josh, although I'm not sure he'd have the right touch for a woman's story."

"I can't wait to hear what you find out. I don't usually get such an interesting story with the jobs I do."

"I hope the final result will make us all proud," I said, looking around the sunlit room and thinking of all the work we had to do before that result would be a reality. *One step at a time, Kate.* I picked up the box of diaries and left, but I couldn't erase the grin on my face. And now I knew how I'd spend the rest of my day: hunkered down at the bed-and-breakfast reading Mary's diaries! I descended the stairs, with Bethany following behind. If Carroll had the time today, we could start reading together—and not let anyone interrupt us. My eyes glazed over with pleasure just thinking about it. I turned to face Bethany when we had both stepped out onto the front porch.

"I'll get in touch with Morgan about starting up work again. But . . . will you look into finding someone to talk to?"

"Sure, I'll try."

"Let me know if you have any trouble. Lisbeth used to be a social worker before she had the kids, and she might have some local connections. I know you're a contractor, and we didn't offer you any benefits, but we can figure something out. I want you to be okay and feel good working in this house."

"Thanks, Kate. I'll let you know. And I do want to get back on the job." She looked up at the pale blue paint of the porch ceiling and seemed to say something quietly to herself. Then she turned on her heel and descended the stairs, climbed into her truck, and drove off.

23

The streets were quiet, everything hushed as if the whole town were sharing my anticipation of reading Mary's diaries. I had stopped just short of buckling them into the passenger seat as I would a child. It took me about fifteen minutes to get back to town and park in front of the B&B. When I let myself in, Carroll was in the kitchen, staring silently into an open cupboard where boxes of cereal might have been, if we had bought any cereal. She turned her head to me as I walked in.

"What's that?" She nodded at the cardboard box I was holding carefully in front of my chest. I could barely contain my excitement.

"A treat! A treasure! Serendipity! You won't believe it. I just got back from talking with Bethany. It turns out she was following electrical wires through the house and she found a stack of Mary's diaries hidden under a floorboard in her bedroom."

Carroll's eyes widened. She let go of the cabinet she had been holding open, turned to face me, and spread her hands wide on the kitchen island between us. "So no one has seen them? Have you looked at them? Are they for real?"

I grinned at her. "Yes to all of those—and they're in good condition. I'd guess she never shared them with anyone— maybe not even Henry, considering how well hidden they were. I've only read a few lines so far, but it's definitely more than a shopping list." I stopped for a moment, playing coy. I put the box down on the island between us and slowly pushed it toward Carroll. "Want to read them?"

Carroll looked briefly like a terrier who's cornered a juicy rat. "Are you kidding? Of course I do! When can we start? I'm free now. I was looking for a snack, but that is *so* not important right now." Her slight hands fluttered in front of her, not daring to touch the box without permission, but clearly aching to get her mitts on those primary sources.

"Well, I don't have anything else planned for the afternoon, so I figured we could lock the doors, pull the curtains, turn off our phones, and settle in to read them cover to cover. We probably won't finish before bedtime, but we can get a good start and keep going tomorrow. Deal?"

"Deal." Carroll turned and retreated to the sink, washing her hands thoroughly—she knew to be careful with old paper. I respected that. I followed suit when she was done, looking back hungrily at the box of diaries as I dried my hands on one of Cordelia's monogrammed shell-pink kitchen towels. Forget the cereal, which we didn't have anyway—if Carroll and I came up for air long enough to consider dinner, we could order takeout.

I carried the precious box of diaries as though its contents were made of glass. "Where do you think we'd be most comfortable?" I asked Carroll.

"The office? There are two nice leather chairs in there, and good lighting."

"Got it. How fast do you read?" I picked up the box, and we walked into the office as we spoke, setting the volumes down on the coffee table and canvassing the room to shut off any outside sight lines or interior distractions. I even unplugged the landline. I had never felt so serious about reading before.

"For research, mostly I skim," she answered, "unless I stumble on something that might be important. This will probably be more personal, so I could go slower. But I'll follow your lead. I suppose it's a good thing that there weren't many relatives—not too many names to confuse. Remember, no food or drink in there—I'd be heartbroken if we damaged anything."

"Okay, okay, I get it. Shall we don our cotton gloves?" I gestured daintily with my newly cleaned hands, and Carroll shot me a smirk. "And how will we do this? Both crowd around one volume and read it together, or should one of us read the books out of order to keep things moving?"

"I think asynchronous, sequential study may be best in this case," Carroll demurred, pulling out a few of her best ten-dollar librarian words. "Which is to say: Why don't you start with the first volume on your own, and when you've finished, you can hand it to me and start on the second? It might be important to keep events in proper order in our minds. I'll take notes, of course."

"Are you sure you can wait that long? Old handwriting can be hard to read—for me anyway, since I don't do it much. You may have to wait awhile."

Carroll bit her lip, genuinely considering the delay she'd have to endure before diving into Mary's writing. She made a brave face and met my eyes with a sober seriousness, which I found more than a little funny. Then she nodded. "I'll be okay. Make a note of anything you don't understand—are the pages numbered? We'll have to see—and we can correspond at a stopping point whenever we get too tired." I had to give it to her: the girl had solid research methods.

"Aye, aye, Cap'n," I said, tipping an imaginary hat in her direction. I straightened one final curtain, joining its two sides at the center so the golden sunlight of late afternoon wouldn't creep through the window and distract us or allow prying eyes from the outside to interrupt our time with the books.

I sat down in one of the room's two well-worn leather chairs, moved a lamp a little closer, and carefully opened the first diary. Written in the upper-left corner of the pastedown inside the front cover was the year: 1865. Mary had written her name atop the first page—she didn't waste paper creating an otherwise-blank cover page, but inked her name on top of the first viable space and filled the rest of it entirely with dense, looping text. I was rapt immediately.

The first thing I noticed was the name given: Mary Gawther. I realized I hadn't come across her maiden name before. The first volume contained terse summaries of her days in the farmhouse: the war had just ended, Henry was a presence but only dimly described in a few places, and the sadness and chaos of the postwar town were evident. Mary and her mother were scraping by, nursing Henry and a handful of other straggling soldiers back to health, collecting money from the government and the grateful families of recovered soldiers wherever they could. I found myself wondering how she and Henry had gotten together. Was there a negotiation? Had it been a love match, or a practical decision, made more by the mother than Mary herself? I realized I'd begun staring into space, rather than at the page in front of me, when Carroll cleared her throat suggestively. She had obviously been waiting for me to finish the volume, glaring at me from the armchair a few feet away.

I chuckled and returned to the writing. Mary's diary pages were no larger than four by six inches. The binding was leather, smooth and soft in my hands; the paper was of nice quality and had survived well. Mary wrote with an ink pen, although I couldn't begin to guess what kind—maybe Carroll would know. Just as I began to wonder how this fine volume had come into the possession of someone so impoverished as Mary had been at this time, there it was, a detail offhandedly offered: Henry had given it to her. It seemed he had brought it along to the war to record his own experiences, but had been unable to find the words, and so had passed it on to his nurse—and future wife. How lovely.

When I reached the end of the first volume, I handed it to Carroll, who pounced on it with glee, having in the meantime retrieved a small magnifying glass from her bag, in case she should come upon details in need of close inspection. And so we passed the hours of the afternoon and into the evening, reading one volume and then the next, getting almost halfway through the stack. I jolted awake at around 9:00 p.m., not aware of having fallen asleep at my post. And there it was, on the page in front of me: a new detail. I whooped aloud.

"Florence!"

"What?" Carroll raised her head slowly to look at me, evidently feeling the heavy pull of sleep as well. "Who's that?"

"I'm in this volume from, er"—I flipped the pages carefully back to the front cover to check—"1873. Mary has just had a second child, and though they're still in the old farmhouse, she and Henry clearly need help. They're getting to have a bit of money at this point, so they go ahead and hire someone. Florence!"

"Oh, Florence the maid!" Carroll's face regained its usual animation. "I'm so glad to have a name to put in that attic room up there. Anything else about her?"

"She's young—just turned eighteen, it says here. Not much else about her, but Mary seems to like her. She's glad to have another woman in the house."

"Is that all she said?" Carroll asked.

"For now, yes. At least we have a name and a date for her."

We resumed our silent reading, but I didn't last long. Just after 10:00, another sudden jolt awake informed me that my body had decided to go to sleep for the evening, whether my brain consented or not. I tried to soldier on, but my vision was getting bleary, and my mind was working like a car with a flat tire—I kept losing the thread of what I was looking at. I decided I'd better call it a night.

"Carroll? I think I have to go to bed. Can we start again where we left off tomorrow?"

She lifted her heavy head, nodded, and closed the volume she was holding, carefully sliding a slip of thick paper between the pages to keep her place.

"How far did you get?" she asked sleepily.

"It's 1875, Henry and Mary have two kids, the factory is going gangbusters . . . It's all good for them right now, but I know what happens. Or, I don't know, actually—but I know it's sad, whatever it is. Those kids don't stay in the story forever. I almost don't want to know."

"I see what you mean." She stood from her seat and briefly wavered, as if even remaining upright long enough to head upstairs and fall into bed was too much to ask of her remaining energies. "That's the thing, though: when you start reading history, you learn a lot about child mortality. It wasn't all pretty, living in those times. Very sad."

Carroll waved vaguely and turned to ascend the stairs. I remained in my seat a few minutes longer, then climbed the stairs myself and flopped onto the big, eyelet-covered bed, still in my clothes, teeth unbrushed. I drifted toward sleep, remembering something from my distant past: an aunt who'd once sat me down in my teen years for a talk that was both jarring and revelatory. She had been a pediatric nurse, by then retired, as well as an amateur historian, and she was the first person who ever clued me in as to just how good I had it, living in the modern era. Call it a supplement to my high school history studies. Even a hundred years ago, she told me, many things I considered normal were not customary or widely available: running water, antibiotics, ultrasound machines. Even in the most heightened and precarious moments—surgery, childbirth—consistent handwashing wasn't a guarantee. I shuddered at the thought.

It all flashed through my mind, real and imagined: the myriad small mistakes of flesh that could take a child, or a whole string of them, before the interventions of modern medicine. And there on the back lawn of the mansion, right in front of me in the grass and brambles, had been direct evidence of three such casualties, though what had taken them—genetic problem? accident? infection?—I still didn't know. My eyelids fell shut like heavy blinds, and I drifted into silent sleep. Poor Henry, poor Mary. Did they ever get what they wanted?

24

I slept deeply, dreaming of a vortex in deep space, into which all matter—even thoughts, ideas—was being sucked, then vaporized, never to be seen again. The vortex looked oddly familiar, emitting a faint gray dust as it circled endlessly in the void. As soon as I woke, I realized I had been picturing the hole in the Barton kitchen wall. Would Mary's diaries elucidate anything about that strange chapter in the house's history? Did she know the identity of the man who had fallen face-first through time, waiting a hundred years to meet us on the other side of a hobbyist's spy camera? Would she even have known about him? It was still possible that Henry had done something nefarious and kept it from her. I didn't want to think this was true, but I couldn't rule out anything, given how little information we had.

I dressed and walked downstairs to find Carroll seated in the kitchen, applying peanut butter to a banana and staring dreamily at the sunlight coming through the house's front windows. As soon as we had both eaten and washed up, a glance between us confirmed the next move: back to the diaries. We resumed our positions in the sitting room, the blinds drawn.

Mary Barton was a good writer: not showy or terribly descriptive when it came to physical detail, but basically competent at recording the events of her time. And there were many events to recount. From the end of the war, her life had radically transformed; she had married Henry, given birth to three children, seen her husband's business grow until she was wealthier than she could ever have imagined as a child. Her mother died from what sounded like some type of abdominal cancer, though Mary's language about it was veiled and allusive, a sign of the time. At last, it seemed like the renovation of the old farmhouse was imminent. Carroll, who had abandoned her insistence on chronological reading and leapfrogged to the diary ahead of the one I was on, let out a sorrowful moue from the chair beside me.

"What?" I asked.

"The children," she said, suddenly near tears. I stood and perched myself on the arm of the large leather chair she was sitting in and read over her shoulder. Mary had written, in a shaky hand:

The children woke today with a ghastly expression: eyes gray and sunken, red cheeks, and begging for water. I have been bringing it all day, pitchers by the bedside, and applying cool cloths to their heads, but nothing will comfort them. They will not eat and have only expelled that which was taken in.

We read silently, in horror, as the children suffered under this mysterious illness. By the third day, they had all died. Carroll carefully placed her bookmark and shut the diary, and we both sat silent for a long time.

"Poor Mary," she said at last. "There was nothing she could do."

"And things were going so well!" I added. "They had such a beautiful life together—all the money they could want, and a big piece of land to develop. They were expanding the garden and beginning plans to renovate the house. I just read this interesting part about a scheme Mary came up with to irrigate their garden crops. They'd just dug a well by the edge of the property, and she had the workers dig a trench—"

"A new well?" Carroll broke in. "I was wondering about that. This illness sounds a lot like cholera. People got it from contaminated water sources, and it killed them in days—sometimes even hours. Terrible. Just be glad you're alive today, when we've figured all this out, and not back then."

"Oh, I am," I said softly, thinking again of that talk with my aunt all those years ago. We returned, somewhat more somberly, to our separate reading. A hush fell over the whole house as Carroll and I hunted for clues of the past. An hour later, I was startled back to the present by a knock on the front door. When I opened it, Josh walked right in.

"I'm taking a break from writing. Too quiet over there. Where have you been? You aren't picking up your phone. What's this—Barton book club?" He stood in the parlor doorway and looked at Carroll, still engrossed in the tiny volume in her hands. I hadn't told Josh—or anyone else, for that matter—about the existence of the diaries. Of course, this sort of personal writing wasn't exactly in Josh's academic wheelhouse, but I figured he should know sooner or later.

"It's sort of a secret at the moment," I told him. "Bethany found these under a floorboard at the mansion, in what must have been Mary's bedroom. Diaries. They go through many years of her life in the house."

He stood up straighter, his body at attention looking something like an exclamation point. "Personal accounts? That's huge!" To my relief, he didn't seem annoyed to have been left out at first, but genuinely excited to hear about the find. This pleased me, as I wanted us all to work together. "I hope you'll let me get my eyes on them some-day," he said.

"We'll think about it, Professor," Carroll shot back with a smirk. When she returned her eyes to the page in front of her, she startled. "Gotcha!"

"Gotcha what?" I asked.

"Bill. They just hired a new guy to work at the house. His name is Bill. There's our second servant."

"Aha! So what was he hired to do?"

"It sounds like they brought him on as a sort of all-purpose handyman: keeping the horses, tending the grounds, fixing up the gardens."

"Wasn't Mary into overseeing the gardens?" I asked.

"It seems like she never quite recovered after the children died. She might've had a milder case of cholera—she made it through alive, but she was changed after that. The way she writes about her days, she sounds . . . tired. Like that sadness just kept following her. So she's not doing much gardening at this point in the account—she doesn't appear to be going outside at all, actually."

"Poor Mary. Is there anything else about Bill? Was he working there long?"

Carroll flipped through the pages in the volume, scanning for further mentions of the mysterious groundskeeper's name. There didn't seem to be much. She stopped on a page near the end, reading silently.

"Well," I asked, eager for news. "What are you seeing?"

"He doesn't come up much, honestly. There's a long period where it's just brief accounts of the weather that day, sometimes what Henry's up to at the factory. Her friendship with Florence. It sounds like Florence and Mary could talk to each other—that's nice. But—oh, there's this little note here: Mary seems to be annoyed with Bill. I can't tell if they had a confrontation, but she implies that he's been poaching fruit from their little garden orchard. She sees him from her bedroom window, collecting it into bushels—but also pocketing a bunch of it."

My mind turned its gears at the mention of fruit.

"Wait, Carroll—when the body was removed from the staircase, we found those fruit pits in the space. Probably cherrystones. The medical examiner told me there were also some in the dead man's pocket."

"You don't think . . . ?" She looked up from the volume, and I could see her own mind at work.

"I think old Bill might have been the man behind the wall."

We sat in stunned silence for a moment, until Josh came back into the room, having wandered off to the kitchen to make himself a cup of tea.

"What'd I miss?" he asked, blowing steam off the hot beverage.

"Good timing, Professor." I filled him in on the clue of the fruit pits, and our guess as to what it meant.

"That can't be the whole story, though," he said. "Why was he killed? If we think he was killed. Stealing some fruit from your employer's gardens is not usually cause enough for murder."

"Certainly not," said Carroll, "but we may not know the whole story yet. There are more diaries left to read." We looked at each other gravely, deciding without words to forgo lunch in favor of finding out what had happened, if we could. There was no guarantee this was a full account.

People often tired of diary writing, or grew too ill to keep up, or simply forgot. Samuel Pepys, the famed English diarist Carroll had told me about, had stopped writing after ten years, when his eyesight began to fail him. We could only hope Mary had been a diligent recorder.

But did she even know what happened to Bill, such that he ended up inside the kitchen wall? There was still the possibility that Henry had done it and kept it from his wife. This was especially possible if she had stopped leaving her room by that point. I picked up the next volume in the chronology, and Carroll took a place by my side to read along. We wanted to be on the same page now, literally and figuratively. Josh sat across the room, sipping his ginger tea—he was forbidden to get too close to our primary sources with anything that might spill—and awaiting any news.

After a few uneventful entries on weather and banal news of the town, I turned another page, and stopped. The next entry, dated from late 1879, was clearly longer than the ones that had come before, and more detailed. It looked as though Mary had decided to record one particular episode, and she wanted to get it right. As if intentionally leaving a record of the event. I didn't say anything to Carroll, but we both started reading carefully, almost holding our breaths. It began abruptly:

Florence is with child. The baby will be Henry's. He has not told me, but I have only to look at Florence and it is

*clear. She will give him what I cannot, now, and I bear
no ill will against her. She has been a good friend. The
child will be born in the new year, though I may not
be here to see it. If I am still living then, I will claim the
child as my own, and Henry will be glad. The house
may thrill again with laughter and small footsteps.*

She went on, remembering what she missed about having her children in the house. I wanted to cry—what an
unexpected arrangement. Had it been Mary's idea? She
had so loved their children, had wanted to give them the
beautiful life she didn't have growing up—and she had lost
them all. But apparently she'd given her blessing to Florence in her place.

But what had happened to Florence and Henry's child?
Had it been born? Had it lived? Was there any public record? I leafed through the following pages of that diary, and
then jumped ahead. And I found . . . something. Not an
answer, exactly, but another piece of our growing Barton
puzzle. It was one more overlong page, on which Mary's
handwriting appeared increasingly small and shaky. It read:

*An awful thing has happened. The stable hand Bill
has attempted to do Florence harm, to violate her body,
thinking her a loose woman, for her condition has become clear. He seized Florence in the bedroom last
night and tried to force himself upon her, believing me
asleep in my room. But I heard her shriek and came*

out to confront them, to protect Florence, and Henry's child. The man was strong, accustomed to heavy work, but I brought down a pewter vase upon his head and wrested Florence from his grasp, and he fell down the old kitchen stairs. His neck was turned, and we knew he was dead. Florence and I returned to my room and held each other close until Henry returned from the factory. We told him all that had happened, and he has resolved to take care of this in silence.

There was a gap of several pages after this entry, and then Mary had added one more brief statement:

Henry has sent Florence away to her family several towns away, to have his child. Florence was frightened badly by Bill, but we pray the child will be healthy, even if the baby will not live with us. Henry will furnish them with whatever they need to make a happy life. Now we are two again in this airy house. Henry promised that he would conceal what happened to Bill, and the man was never seen again in Asheboro. I suspect that he lies in Eternity somewhere on the grounds of our home, but I prefer not to ask. No one will know. As I have feared, I much doubt that I will survive long enough to greet Henry's child, if ever Florence should return to our home. It is just as well. The child will not bear Henry's name, to preserve his reputation in the town, but will take that of

Florence's family, Simmons. Henry is a good man,
and he has helped us through this great difficulty. I
miss our children terribly, remembering at the close
of each day their faces as they played in the garden,
weaving among the trees. Would that our lives had
been different, would that they had stayed.

That was essentially the end of Mary's writing. It was
clear that she was failing rapidly, and that her last act had
been for Henry's sake—and for the safety of Florence, her
friend. Henry had never told, nor left a record, of what had
happened with the maid and the baby. Nor had anyone
ever mentioned Florence's child—though apparently Henry
had given her family money to raise it in a level of comfort
not guaranteed to the average farmer of that time. I flipped
through the rest of the volume, and it was mostly empty.
There was one more diary in the box, which Carroll then
picked up and paged through. It was entirely blank, which
I had somehow failed to notice before. And thus we came
to the end of Mary's story, as she told it. I closed the book in
front of me and pushed it away on the little table it rested on.
Carroll and I stood and headed silently toward the kitchen,
beckoning Josh to come along. We found a bag of mixed
nuts deep in the pantry, and stood around the kitchen island,
snacking while silently mulling over all that we'd read.

And then I remembered something. I took out my
phone and began to dial.

25

H ello, Kate?" Frances's mannered voice crackled over a dubious connection on my cell phone. "What can I do for you?"

"Hello, Frances. Carroll and I have been doing some reading at the B&B, and a name came up. I thought it sounded familiar. Didn't you mention someone with the surname Simmons to me the other day at lunch?"

"Yes, I think I did. It was in connection with the old town feud going back many years in Asheboro's history. I can't say as to whether it's still an active concern, but as recently as my youth, there was property destruction in the mix. Some people were killed, if you look back further, though it appeared to be accidental. But I have my suspicions, based on the parties involved."

My forehead felt clammy. There was one more thing I needed to know.

"And didn't you say that name was connected to some family still living in the area today?"

"Why, yes. Your foreman, or what have you—Morgan? It's his mother's side, if I'm not mistaken. They've never been from Asheboro proper, though. A few towns off, some- where near Sharpsburg. But this is all ancient history. Why do you ask?"

"No reason, Frances," I hedged. "I'm sorry to have both- ered you—I'll tell you later. Thanks for your help." She hung up first, and I stood with the phone still up against my ear, thinking. Could Morgan be a direct descendant of Florence, the Barton family maid—and thus, clandes- tinely, of Henry Barton? If so, was he aware of this? An- other thought nagged at the back of my mind. I returned to Carroll and Josh in the kitchen.

"Carroll, did you ever find anything about Steve's fam- ily history in Asheboro? Everyone seems to know they go way back, but did you find hard evidence to support that?"

She grabbed her laptop and opened it up. "Well, I did some digging, like you asked. And Frances was right; the Abernathy roots in Asheboro go deep. I found independent contractors in carpentry and plumbing going back several generations. And then I saw here . . ." She clicked through a few tabs, looking for the relevant document. "This guy. Interesting life. William Abernathy Jr. Our former plumber Steve's great-great-uncle, if I counted right. Sounds like he was something of a roustabout. Served in the Union army, briefly went AWOL right after a battle, somehow avoided court-martial proceedings, came home to Asheboro, lived with his mother and brother while performing odd jobs around town, and then got a job . . ." Her eyes brightened as she trailed off. She paged back to another tab she had open.

"Wait just a minute. This manifest of workers in Henry's household. That squiggle I saw a few days ago . . ." She squinted once again at the image on the screen that had flummoxed us both with its illegibility. "That's it! It says 'Bill.' Bill . . . Abernathy." I stood behind her and looked into the screen. She was right.

"Oh no," I said, my mouth agape.

"Oh yes. Looks like it's a direct line of Abernathys in Asheboro, from our friend Bill in the staircase down to Steve . . . in the other staircase. That's a little creepy. Do you think Steve knew?"

"That his historic forebear was none other than the desiccated body in the wall of his new work site? So he came back to avenge his fallen great-great-whatever? I doubt it. Unless the guy was a genealogy buff like you."

"Hey, it's not impossible!" she protested.

"I honestly doubt that Steve knew about Bill in the wall. The way Mary told it, Bill's death didn't sound like part of an ongoing argument—more like a direct result of his attempted assault on Florence. And it appears that Henry Barton covered up the death—literally and figuratively.

Mary wrote that Henry told anyone who asked about his missing servant that the man had skipped town."

"And depending on how much they knew of Bill's character, they might not have had any reason to doubt that story," Carroll added, finishing my thought. "The guy was a real cad. And when he disappeared, maybe people even thought he had run away with Florence when she left Asheboro around the same time."

"That's right—they might have thought her child was Bill's! That's convenient—and also kind of awful, considering he's the one who tried to assault her. But remember how Frances said memories in the country are long? Maybe there was some piece of family lore—half a story, a fragment, a hunch—passed down through the generations, and when Steve took the job at the mansion, he thought he could finally confirm it?"

We both stopped talking, the implications of all this whirring through our minds. Of course, Steve was dead, so we would probably never know what he'd had in mind when he took the job working on Henry Barton's house. And Morgan had seemed strictly uninterested in the subject of the feud when we'd spoken at the house. But wouldn't he want to throw me off the scent if it were true?

The heavy revelations of the morning were yielding diminishing returns in my overloaded brain. I suggested to Carroll and Josh that we make a stop at the mansion and stretch our legs on the grounds for a while, and they agreed. We locked up and piled into my car, our minds buzzing with new details.

When we arrived at the Barton property, Carroll and Josh took to the back field, discussing the potential plotting of fruit trees, flowers, and decorative hedges around the gazebo that might be in the house's future as a public attraction. I was touched that they were so keen to collaborate, as I'd been worried about their bickering over rights to historical sources only a few days ago. I said I'd join them in a few minutes, and let myself in through the front door of the mansion. I had been meaning to open up the library door again for airflow, now that the police had cleared the scene.

I unlocked the room's door and swung it open. I inhaled the deep, leathery scent of old books and wondered if anyone had ever made a perfume to mimic this enchanting aroma. I remembered that I needed to reshelve the volume Morgan had returned to me after Steve pocketed it. Just then, my phone buzzed in my pocket, and I picked it up, lost in thoughts of what I needed to do to get this house in order.

"Kate." The gruff voice of Brady Reynolds came through without a formal salutation. "We got a partial print off the button on Steve's overalls. Ran it through the system, and it was a match to an old petty theft case, ten years ago. I thought you should know, since he's on your crew. The print belonged to Lars Abernathy."

"So what? Maybe he folded his brother's laundry last week?"

"The garment in question had not been recently laundered, and the print was fresh. This may point to the brother's involvement in Steve's fatal injury."

I stared at my reflection in the large mirror set into the library wall: a stunned woman standing stock-still in an antique room. I took the phone from my ear and blinked at it.

"Lars? But . . . he wasn't even in town when Steve died. So you think—"

"I can't say anything conclusive right now. But he's a person of interest. Have you heard from him?"

"No, I haven't. Morgan said he spoke with him a few days ago, but they didn't talk much." A *thunk* from down the hall turned my head. "Can I call you back?"

"Of course. And contact me immediately if you hear from Lars Abernathy."

"I will." I hung up and stepped from the library into the hall, peering around the handrail of the grand staircase toward the kitchen. I could see the back door, and it was ajar, a crack of sunlight slipping through it like a knife. Another *thunk*. I drew back from sight just as someone emerged from the kitchen and turned to face the door to the basement steps. I heard a struggle with the door, which didn't budge—the detective and his crew must've locked it after they cleared the scene. A stumbling sound alerted me that whoever this was might not be operating with their full faculties. And then came a pitiful yelp, like the cry of an injured animal. Moving very slowly, I stepped back across the library threshold into the hallway, moving step by step toward the basement door. When I got close enough, I saw the intruder sitting on the floor with his back against the locked door. It was Lars. He appeared to be crying. He didn't see me immediately, so I backed up a few steps and took out my phone. I didn't dare make a phone call right now, but I dashed off a text to Brady Reynolds: "Lars at mansion. Get here now."

A banging sound came from the basement door. Lars was now beating his fists against it, having failed to get it open. Then a clinking sound, as of metal objects. When I approached the door once again, Lars was on his knees, trying to pick the lock with the same kind of pocket tools I had seen Morgan use in the attic some days ago. He wasn't doing it very well. This time, he saw me.

"Kate. I . . ." His speech was slow, careful, and a bit slurred. "I had to see, uh . . . where my brother . . . where he died."

"Lars, how did you get in here? You can't be in here now."

"I know how to get in." Was he drunk? His body wavered a bit as he kneeled, still holding the tools and jiggling them in the lock, leaning one shoulder against the door and squinting. "I grew up here . . . Anybody can get into this place."

"Lars, I thought you were in the city."

"Nah. Thas' just what I told my brother to get him off my back. I don't even have a girlfriend. I jus' have to get away from him sometimes . . . He took my wallet off me, you know. Thinks he's so funny. I had to walk back from the station an' get it back from him the other night . . ." He gave up on the lock-picking tools, slumping forward with his forehead against the heavy wood door.

"I see. I'm so sorry about your brother, Lars." I glanced again at the back door. No sign of Josh and Carroll, and Reynolds would probably take ten minutes to get here, even at top speed with his sirens on. I'd have to deal with Lars until then. Was he really feeling sentimental about the brother he clearly hadn't liked, or had he broken into the house today for some other reason? I decided to call his bluff. "Lars, do you want me to open the door for you? I have a key."

He turned his head slightly in my direction and seemed to size me up for the first time. He acted a lot more like his brother when he was drunk—meaner, sloppier, and potentially hiding something.

"Yeah . . . okay. You open it." He stood with considerable effort, coming to rest with his back against the kitchen doorway. He leaned there, staring at me, chewing the inside of his cheek thoughtfully. I didn't dare turn my back on him, so I made an awkward half circle and stood facing him, in front of the door, as I searched for the right key on my ring. I figured a little chatter might distract him.

"So, Lars, were you and your brother close?"

"I would not say that," he said, picking out his words carefully and plunking them out like stones between us.

"He was older. Had his own friends. Not much room for me . . . But I wasn't into his stuff anyway."

"But you'd been apprenticing under him? Learning plumbing?"

A cloud descended over Lars's expression. I had narrowed my search down to two keys, and now began trying each in the lock, moving as slowly and evenly as I could so as not to look frantic. Which, for the record, I was.

"He let me learn his trade. He 'let' me—he always said that, like it was a big favor. Like I was nobody and he had this great thing going. But when I lost my job in the city last year, I figured . . . maybe it could be good for me."

I turned the final key in the lock. *Click.* Thank heaven. I had one more thing to ask Lars.

"But when you came back to the house on Thursday night, he was mean to you, wasn't he?"

"He was! Said my 'girlie' probably told me not to come, he said she probably dumped me over the phone . . . Ha. Shows what he knows. Didn't even have a girlfriend. Stupid."

"And he was drunk, which probably made him meaner. So when he went too far, you just . . . gave him a push?"

"He wouldn't stop shoving me. He said I ruined his chances with Bethany, said I was hitting on her and it made her hate him. That doesn't even make sense. So I jus' pushed him to get him off me. But he went . . . down."

Lars's gaze drifted to the basement door as he remembered that moment. I swung the door open with a loud creak. "That sounds awful, Lars. But I completely respect your need for closure. Take your time." I stepped aside and gestured for him to go ahead. He took a few shambling steps to the doorway, and then stood swaying at the top of the basement stairs, a hand on each side of the frame.

"Hey, how'd you know about that?"

I pointed down the dark stairs. "There's a light switch at the bottom there, Lars. Can you get it? I'm a little afraid of the dark. I'll just follow you. You're braver than I am." I smiled as girlishly as I could, and Lars's face melted into a lusty smirk—unnervingly like his big brother's.

"Sure, yeah." He seemed to forget his question, and started down the steps, his hand gripping the rail for all it was worth. I watched him long enough to be certain he wasn't going to take a header down to the basement floor—I wasn't hoping for another one of those—and then I closed the door silently behind him and locked it with the key still gripped in my shaking fist.

"Hey! Kate? Is there—ow! Where's the switch?"

I turned my back to the door, took a deep breath, and let it out. But how long did I have until Lars, clumsy as he was right now, remembered there was another exit onto the back lawn?

26

I moved swiftly through the kitchen, ignoring the shouts now coming from Lars in the basement, and opened the back door. Carroll and Josh were in sight, about a hundred feet from the house, examining something in the grass.

"Hey, you two! Get over here!" I waved my arms over my head in what I hoped was a universal signal of distress, and they started running toward me. From the corner of my eye, I saw another figure approaching—Morgan, in his stained coveralls and old green cap, was just turning the back corner of the house and heading my way. He met my gaze, looking surprised.

"Miz Kate, are you all right?"

"Morgan, what are you doing here? I didn't give you permission to start working again."

"I know—I hope I haven't overstepped. But things have been stressful, what with Steve's death. And this place . . .

it calms me. I thought I'd just walk the fields for a bit. But what's going on? I heard you yelling. Do you need help?"

"As a matter of fact, I do. Lars is trapped in the basement. He just admitted to pushing Steve down the stairs." Morgan's weathered face blanched at this. "The police are on their way, but I need to keep him in there until they arrive. So—you'll have to sit here." I indicated the slanting double door that opened from the cellar onto the back lawn. In my panicked state, the thought drifted into my mind that this door was like the tornado cellar from which Dorothy Gale emerges in *The Wizard of Oz*, into a new and confusing world. Except right now, the tornado was inside the cellar. And we had to keep it there. Carroll and Josh arrived from the other side of the lawn. "You two—I need you to get on top of that door. Keep your weight there, don't let it open."

They all did as I asked, climbing onto the rough wood and balancing there uncertainly. Carroll sat balled up with her knees against her chest, while Morgan and Josh braced against the surface, preparing for impact. I climbed up too. An eerie silence hung over the scene as the honey-colored sun began sinking over the hill in the distance ahead of us.

And then the banging started. Lars was a slight man but strong, and was clearly demented enough in his inebriated state to throw his full weight against the doors. But he was coming at the task from below, and we had gravity on our side; we could hold on to our position by merely sitting in place. Still, we all held our breaths as the repeated thuds shook the doors beneath us. In another minute, the peal of sirens broke into our strange scene, and I faintly heard Detective Reynolds enter through the house's front door.

"We're back here!" I called out, and soon the detective and his crew were upon us.

✤

Half an hour later, the fields behind the Barton mansion were quiet again, the day beginning to turn blue and darken. Reynolds had extracted Lars from the basement, and I'd relayed to the detective what Lars had told me inside. As he was led away in handcuffs, Lars had seemed sorrowful but also angry—betrayed by me in his casual confession, and perhaps also by himself. I wished he had found a way to just leave the house when his brother harangued him, instead of fighting back. But that couldn't be changed now.

Carroll, feeling shaken, had gone back to the B&B with Josh. They had taken my car, but Morgan said he'd give me a ride back to town when the scene was clear. Now that everything was quiet again, we looked at each other, baffled but relieved. I realized there was something I needed to tell him.

I gestured for Morgan to follow me, and he did. We walked together over the bumpy ground that was once a household orchard, up the swell of hill toward the carriage house and past it, beyond the gazebo, all the way over to the busted-up old wood fence and chain-link remnants that marked the property line. I stopped just short of the tangle of greenery where Henry and Mary were interred. The spot didn't look like much if you didn't know it was there. Morgan looked at me quizzically. *Now or never.* I dug my heels into the soft turf beneath us and started to speak.

"The first time Carroll and I came out here to walk the grounds of the estate together, we just sort of wandered. And we ended up here. But I'll get back to that in a minute. It's been hard to come by much personal information on Henry Barton, but we knew that he died without heirs. That's how the town came to own this place. Henry and his wife were both very private people, it seems—they didn't socialize, throw parties, or have many friends. What they did have, after the first few years living here, was a maid and a general handyman to tend the grounds and the horses. Two people to take care of everything. We were curious about that. We didn't know anything about them at first, but—"

"The maid's name was Florence," Morgan said quietly.

"What? How do you know that?" Morgan was watching my reaction with a faintly amused expression.

"Florence was my great-great-grandmother. She died before I came around, obviously, so I never knew her. But my grandmother remembered her telling some wonderful stories about the great Barton house."

"So you knew you had a personal connection to this place? Why didn't you mention it to me?"

"I didn't want you to think I was asking for special treatment, honestly. If I was the right man for the job, it shouldn't have mattered where I came from, who my people were. And it's not much of a connection. I'd never been here before you called me up to get a quote—it was only an old family story. I had heard that Florence worked there, but it never dawned on me there were only two house servants for the whole place. As far as I knew, Florence was one among many. And as I said, I never knew the woman myself. Though I would've liked to."

"So, Florence had a child," I said, proceeding cautiously. I still didn't know how much of the story Morgan knew. "Do you know who the father was?"

"I don't. I've never taken a hard look at the family tree, beyond what my relatives said. But no husband was ever mentioned. My great-grandfather was raised by Florence along with other family members. It was one of those stories that children hear and remember but don't quite understand. We've had a long line of unusual family structures through the generations—widows going it alone, sisters who lived together and raised their children that way. But why are you asking about this?"

"Well . . . Let me back up. There are a few things I want you to know. First of all, Mary Barton kept diaries. Bethany found them concealed in the floor of her bedroom. And they contained a lot. Like, the fact that Bill—the dead man in the wall, who had been the handyman here—didn't just fall. He was pushed."

"Oh my," Morgan said softly. "Pushed by whom?"

"Mary. Or possibly Mary and . . . Florence. It sounds like Bill had tried to rape Florence. Mary came out of her room to see what the commotion was, and there was a struggle. And Bill . . . went down the stairs."

"Oh . . . my," Morgan said again. "History repeats itself."

"Endlessly," I said. "But here's the other thing: Florence was pregnant, with the child who would become your great-grandfather."

"She was? Already? I thought she gave birth to that child at home, at her mother's place?"

"She did. She left the Barton house after that incident, and Henry boarded up Bill's body in the wall—possibly with the help of his brother, who visited the house around that time. I'm not sure about that part—but maybe that's why the brother never came back again, and didn't want to take ownership of the house after Henry passed. Carroll's still working on the details of the time line. But there's one more thing you need to know. The baby Florence was pregnant with—it was Henry's."

"Excuse me?" Morgan sputtered, looking stunned. "Henry Barton?"

"Yes. Henry and Mary had three children—a fact the town lore seems to have lost track of—but they all died quite young, possibly of cholera. So Mary, who was sick after that and never quite recovered, gave her blessing to

Henry and Florence, whom she quite liked, to conceive a child together. And they did. An unconventional setup, to say the least. It sounds like Mary would have publicly raised the baby as her own, but she died not long after the incident with Bill. So Florence went home, rather than stay in the Barton house—as a worker or otherwise."

"That sounds like a difficult choice."

"I'm sure it was. Henry probably could have gotten away with marrying the maid, given how rich and powerful he was in the town. But it seems he respected Florence's choice to go home and live with her family. And he provided money for her and the baby to live on."

"That's good of him. And it must have been enough for them to buy the small farm they lived on," Morgan said quietly. "I always wondered about that—there's never been much money in my family, but somehow they acquired that piece of land. Made a big difference in their lives. My brother-in-law and I still work that land today, and plan to pass it on to his daughter and son when we're gone."

"There's something else to discuss here, Morgan." I wanted to tread carefully, as I was uncertain what Morgan would make of this—or how it would affect the nonprofit and all our plans for the mansion going forward. "Henry died without an heir, officially, since all his children with Mary were gone, and he never remarried. But now, with this new information, it looks like there *was* an heir to the fortune, and the bloodline continued into the present day. To put it bluntly: it's you. You might have a claim on this property, Morgan, if you want to pursue it. I don't know what you'll think of that idea—heck, I don't know what *I* think about it yet—but I wanted you to know. It could derail my whole plan, honestly, if our working group no longer owns the building we're working on, but I couldn't hide this from you, ethically or legally. You would've figured it out when the diaries were made public, even if I'd tried to keep it from you. And you deserve to know."

"I see, Kate. That's . . . a lot to take in, you know." He stared off at the horizon beyond us, and then his eyes came to rest on the tangle of vines and small trees behind me. "Say, why did you bring me here? Is there something you wanted me to see?"

I had almost forgotten. The graves. I nodded to Morgan and waved for him to follow me. We approached the copse, and I parted the greenery as best I could, in the spot where Carroll and I had first entered only a week ago—though it felt like a century. Morgan stepped through the opening, and I dropped the vines back into place and stood outside the circle, looking off toward the soft swells of land beyond the mansion's grounds. Time seemed to stand still as Morgan regarded the graves silently in the waning afternoon light. Perhaps ten minutes passed, and then he came back out, a pale figure emerging from a tangle of green and woody stems.

"Thank you, Kate," he said to me. "It was good to meet them, if I can call it that. And as far as what you said—about making me king of the castle around here—thank you, but no. It's news to me that I have any relation to this place other than being descended from 'the help,' but even so, I don't feel an urge to possess this property. I'm happy to work on it. That's what I do—I love these houses, and I want to see them respected. And I see that you have a vision for what this place can be. I want to honor that too. So if you'd like to make some kind of gesture, in light of the past and what we know now, perhaps you could put me on the board. I know you'll be doing more work on the buildings in town once this place is up and running, and I think I could be of help with that too. Anyway, if you need to draw up some paperwork with that lawyer fellow, I can officially abdicate my familial claim, or what have you. But if you're asking what's important to me, here and now, it's not money or a grand estate all to myself—it's the work. And I'd like to keep doing it."

A wave of relief washed over me. The words I'd heard up in that dim attic room came back to me: *Here am I, send me.* Here was a man who saw the project laid out before him, and said yes. And I remembered something I had taken from the house to give Morgan. I withdrew from an envelope inside my bag the dog-eared old Bible from Florence's room and handed it to him.

"I think you should have this. I'm sure Florence meant to take it with her when she left, but it sounds like things were intense in that moment, and she just had to get out. But it belongs with your family—with you."

"Thank you, Kate," he said, cradling the book's flaking

leather cover in his hands. "Now, is that all? Because the wife is expecting me back home, unless you've got any more stunning revelations for today."

"Yes, Morgan," I said with a smile. "Let's get going. We can talk more tomorrow morning about the next steps. I want to get back to work too."

"I appreciate it," he said, tipping his cap. "Now, let's ske-daddle." He turned and began walking back toward his truck, over the gently sloping grounds of the Barton estate, Florence's Bible tucked under one arm.

I felt an unusual lightness in my step. Had I been getting more exercise lately than I did in my usual city life, going from condo to car to office and back again? Probably. I'd been climbing the steep Victorian stairs of the Barton mansion, striding across these fields as I imag-ined what they might be in the coming months, taking walks through the old town I used to call my home, once upon a time. My legs felt strong beneath me.

I picked a few grapes off the vines on the rear side of the carriage house, and as I rounded its corner, popping the sweet fruits into my mouth, the mansion came into view in the honeyed light of late afternoon. It really was a handsome thing, even with its peeling paint, its shingles missing here and there. We'd fix that, in time.

Morgan and I were silent as he drove, and only when he dropped me in front of the B&B and I stepped out into the evening did the weight of the day's events hit me. I walked into the house feeling shell-shocked, and found

Carroll sitting alone in the front parlor. Josh was evidently upstairs taking a nap. When Carroll turned to look at me, her eyes were red.

"Kate, I'm so glad you're back. I found something. Can I read it to you?"

"Sure, you can read it to me. What is it?"

In her hand was a volume from Mary's diaries. It was the blank one we'd come to at the end of the stack. She cradled it gingerly between her hands.

"I was wondering if this blank diary could be of some use to a historian—maybe Josh knows somebody who studies antiquarian book materials at Johns Hopkins? But then I noticed something. It's not blank. Or, it's not *completely* blank. There's one little entry toward the end—on a random page, it seems like."

"So Mary wrote one last entry in an empty diary?"

"No, not Mary. Henry."

"What?" My breath quickened. We had found box upon box of Henry Barton's business correspondence, financial records, patents for light bulbs he experimented with—but never something so personal as a diary. He and Mary didn't even write love letters. I hardly had a clue as to what the man was like on a human level, beyond being a shrewd businessman and something of a recluse. "Read it to me."

I put away my keys and sat down across from Carroll as she began to read. The entry said:

Mary—You have been gone some three months now. I sit on the west lawn of our home, and in the setting sun, your face sinks beyond the hill, and in the next day's sunshine, your visage beams back to me, a daily blessing. Every morning at my prayers, you are with me, and every evening. In the bright light of day, I recall your freckled nose, your dove-gray eyes, the chestnut hair loosing at your temples. It pains me to walk the halls of this house each day without you, but I know too that you are with our Maker, and you are reunited with Winifred, Elizabeth Ann, and David, whom you so faithfully carried, and then lost. You are in His eternal light now and I must find solace in the end of your earthly pain. Your troubles are ended, the frailty of your body no longer a weight upon you. I remain yours for the rest of my lonely days, here in our valley. Each day at dusk I visit you in the small grove we planted for the children, where you now lie with them in Eternity. I will join you when my time arrives. My life's work—the war, the tools, and the instruments of light—now seems a distant memory. How shall I continue? I love you, and I will forever. Your Henry.

Carroll finished reading and fell silent, but I heard a little sniffle as she turned her head from me. So I had been right, in my freewheeling and hopeful guessing about

Henry and Mary—it *had* been a love match, a joyful union cut short by Mary's early death. I pictured Henry walking the grounds of his estate, his head bowed, hands clasped behind his back, alone, pacing the rows of fruit trees just to pass the empty hours. Poor Henry, poor Mary. They hadn't had enough time. We now knew another little piece of who they had been, though it meant something to only a few of us. How would we show the broader world the private and enduring love we had discovered between the inhabitants of this place, along with the majestic structure they had built to live in as a family?

I walked upstairs, knocked on the bedroom door, and waited for the handsome face of Josh Wainwright to appear. I would fill him in on our latest news with Carroll, over dinner.

27

The first days of December had brought a fine coating of snow to Asheboro this year, and now, two weeks before Christmas, it had started up again, the wind casting a fleet of big, fluffy flakes all over the silent grounds of the Barton estate. I stood on the back stoop of the mansion and watched, absentmindedly rubbing my chilly hands together. Josh was making his way across the broad lawn as I looked on; he wore a blue down jacket and carried in front of him the last bushel basket of chestnuts gathered from the tree behind the carriage house. We had stored them in a spare room for the past month, away from the prying eyes of squirrels and other visitors, and this was their big day.

It was late afternoon, with the light over the hillside beginning to fade, the hills beyond the house turning a soft and shadowy blue. Inside, Bethany's teenage niece, Rekia, along with her baby sister, Eve—who had just started walking—sat near the kitchen fire as Morgan stoked it, setting the scene for an epic round of chestnut roasting. Bethany had asked her sister's permission to bring the kids over to the mansion one day, and they had never wanted to leave. The place must've seemed like a castle to them. For the past six weeks, Rekia had joined in with Lisbeth's son and daughter, a few other local kids, and two grad students in agricultural studies to gather the chestnuts falling from the tree in the autumn months, all of them wearing thick leather gloves to shield their soft fingers from the burs. I'd checked in with Ryan to make sure this didn't somehow constitute child labor, and he said we were all clear as long as we kept the kids supplied with juice boxes, called it a learning experience, and didn't sell anything to anyone. It was sort of a practice run for children's programming at the Barton house; we could think about summer camps and school tours later, but I wanted to get a taste of what it could be like having groups of kids there, showing them around the place, studying the tasks and customs of another time. And it had worked marvelously. All the kids loved being outdoors as the seasons changed, the thick heat in the after-school hours when they visited giving way to soft breezes, and then infusions of colder air. When the day's gathering was done, they all ran wild circles over the Barton lawns, inventing new games every day.

The grad students had even taught me a few things. They suggested that the relative remoteness of Henry Barton's lone chestnut, its distance from town and from other

stands of trees, might have been what saved it from the fun-
gal blight that had taken out most members of its species
in the past century. There were perhaps some benefits,
they opined, to being reclusive.

To my left, on another patch of lawn, the hardy members of the Asheboro Gardening Society had set up two
folding tables and were putting the finishing touches on
a dozen wreaths to decorate the outside of the mansion,
swirls of holly animating wire frames that had been bare
just hours ago, their red berries standing bright against the
backdrop of white lawn.

Josh reached the stoop and gave me a peck on the cheek
as he went past, hoisting the heavy basket up against his
chest as he passed through the door to the kitchen, to the
delighted squeals of the girls inside. Morgan had consulted
the town gardeners, the grad students, and even a few food
historians to get just the right technique for roasting the
chestnuts, which none of us had ever tasted before.

Meanwhile, a small army of decorators was roaming
the upper floors of the mansion, steaming any imperfec-
tions out of the old fabrics (and a few modern replace-
ments where necessary), then ferociously dehumidifying
the rooms to ensure against mold. The place wasn't quite
ready for the public, but it was looking good—good enough,
the board had decided, to woo some potential donors,
who were expected to arrive within the hour for a wine-
and-chestnut reception, a lecture on Henry Barton's life
and work from the eminent industrial historian Joshua

Wainwright, and a tour of the rooms that were present-able enough to show them, with commentary from Mor-gan as the renovation lead. Little sharp pings of pain in my fingertips told me that I'd been standing outside long enough, and I turned and joined the crowd in the kitchen.

As Josh set to scoring the shiny shells of the chestnuts with a small knife, explaining to the girls that these small fruits had once been a staple food to many poor farmers in this part of the country, I locked eyes with Morgan, who rose from his station and followed me down the house's main hall into the library at the front of the house. We stopped and looked silently out the large windows for any approaching cars; the other board members were on their way, to schmooze with our would-be donors and observe the roasting experiment. So far, no one. The room, in its shell of Victorian lime plaster, held a deep silence. Henry Barton's books had been replaced where they belonged on the shelf. The furniture, all recently cleaned of its decades of dust, shone as it must have in Henry's day. Morgan turned to me, and I saw that he had brought along two tiny flutes of sparkling wine from the kitchen. He handed one to me.

"Don't worry," he said with a twinkle in his eye. "It's just fizzy apple juice. I didn't want to break open the real stuff until the crowd got here."

"How considerate of you, Mr. Wheeler. Although I think the board bought enough champagne to satisfy the whole town if they showed up. I guess it'll keep for the next event, right?"

"I suppose it will, Miz Kate." He stopped speaking, the both of us regarding the heavy drapes, their deep red velvet swags absorbing some of the chill seeping through the old warped glass windows. Peals of children's laughter from the kitchen broke the silence every few seconds. "You know," Morgan said, after a long contemplation, "I like what you've done with the place." He reached out and clinked my glass with his.

"I rather like what you've done with it too, Morgan. I think Henry would be proud of you. And Florence too."

"Why, thanks." We stood silently, drinking our bubbly juice as the scent of the first roasting chestnuts drifted toward us down the long hall.

Acknowledgments

D ear readers, the year is 2021 and I am writing this note to you on behalf of my mother. As you may have heard, Sheila Connolly died in the spring of 2020 at her cottage in Ireland, following a diagnosis of cancer she kept very close to the vest.

My mother didn't want to talk about her health; she wanted to talk about books, writing, and her next subject of research, at all times. She wanted to drink coffee and eat pastries, go to conferences in different cities, discover new relatives, and chat endlessly with her friends, both Irish and American, about all these things as they happened.

She came to writing after the age of fifty, following a series of careers in different fields, and being a full-time mystery writer was absolutely her favorite thing, a source of delight that animated her every conversation. She wrote the first draft of this book, and by the time the manuscript came back with requested edits, she was too ill to finish the work. I am grateful to have had this opportunity to collaborate with her, even under such unfortunate circumstances.

I wish to thank my mother's longtime agent, Jessica Faust at BookEnds, and her editor, Hannah O'Grady at St. Martin's, both of whom have been nothing but patient and kind as I navigated the stages of the editorial process for the first time. The past few years would have been immeasurably more difficult without various kinds of advice and assistance from friends, neighbors, and capable professionals on both sides of the Atlantic, including Katherine Jhumann, Avril O'Brien, Diarmuid and Mary Lucey, Joan Browne and Lisa Whelton, Koreen Santos, Valerie Williams, Eileen and Ray Houin, Jenny Magnus, and my dear friend Beau O'Reilly.

Immense thanks go also to my mother's many comrades in mystery writing, especially Edith Maxwell and Krista Davis, who tracked down Sheila's whereabouts when she went missing from her usual online hangouts, and then rallied the troops to write a few dozen kind letters. Real-life sleuths of the cozy scene, I salute you. I send my gratitude to Cheryl Cantrell and Marcia Armstrong, from my mother's Wellesley College cohort, both of whom braved the small and rural roads of West Cork to visit, cook meals, and laugh with their old friend, just before the world shut down. In a year severely lacking in comfort and good cheer, I know you all made a difference.

And most importantly: Thank you for reading.

—Julie Williams